FATAL QUEST

Recent Titles by Sally Spencer from Severn House

THE BUTCHER BEYOND
DANGEROUS GAMES
THE DARK LADY
DEAD ON CUE
DEATH OF A CAVE DWELLER
DEATH OF AN INNOCENT
A DEATH LEFT HANGING
DEATH WATCH
DYING IN THE DARK
A DYING FALL
THE ENEMY WITHIN
FATAL QUEST
GOLDEN MILE TO MURDER
A LONG TIME DEAD
MURDER AT SWANN'S LAKE
THE PARADISE JOB
THE RED HERRING
THE SALTON KILLINGS
SINS OF THE FATHERS
STONE KILLER
THE WITCH MAKER

FATAL QUEST

Woodend's First Case

A Chief Inspector Woodend Mystery

Sally Spencer

This first world edition published 2008
in Great Britain and the USA by
SEVERN HOUSE PUBLISHERS LTD of
9–15 High Street, Sutton, Surrey, England, SM1 1DF.

British Library Cataloguing in Publication Data

Spencer, Sally
  Fatal Quest
  1. Woodend, Charlie (Fictitious character) - Fiction
  2. Police - England - Fiction 3. Detective and mystery
  stories
  I. Title
  823.9'14[F]

  ISBN-13: 978-0-7278-6682-0   (cased)
  ISBN-13: 978-1-84751-084-6   (trade paper)

I am indebted to Martin Chambers for several
valuable suggestions he made at the earlier
stages of this book. Many thanks, Martin!

All Severn House titles are printed on acid-free paper.

Printed and bound in Great Britain by
MPG Books Ltd., Bodmin, Cornwall.

10 November 1950

The girl looked around her in total panic. But she could not see far, because the smog – that swirling layer of yellow filth which sought out the weak-chested and mercilessly clamped itself around their throats – had all but isolated her from the rest of the world.

'Get in the car,' the man said, his voice harsh and commanding.

'I . . . I don't want . . .' she protested.

'Get in the car!' the man repeated.

And she did.

Even though her every instinct screamed that she shouldn't.

Even though she already knew it was a mistake, perhaps the biggest – and last – mistake she would ever make.

Because she was too afraid to do anything else.

It was a dead city through which they drove. The buses had stopped running hours earlier, and now the few cars still in evidence moved at a crawl, like wounded animals desperate to return to their lairs.

The girl grasped her right arm with her left hand, and her left arm with her right, and hugged herself tightly. She felt all alone – and so she was.

From somewhere deep inside herself, she found the courage to speak.

'Where are we going?'

The man said nothing. She wasn't even sure that he knew the answer himself, because most of the time he wasn't looking at the road ahead of them at all, but at the pavement.

The car slowed, then came to a halt.

The man opened his door. 'Stay there!' he said.

She stayed. She had no choice. Her legs felt like lead. Her head was pounding. There were so many things she needed to say, but she couldn't find the words.

The man walked around the front of the car and opened the passenger door.

'Get out!'

'I . . . I don't think I can.'

The man grabbed her arm and yanked her out of the car.

'You're hurting me!'

He didn't reply, and she realized that he didn't *care* if he was hurting her – didn't care about her *at all*.

He dragged her round the car, across the pavement and onto a piece of waste land. The ground was rough, and several times she stumbled. But the man kept his tight grip on her, and wouldn't let her fall.

When they had gone perhaps a dozen yards – and looking over her shoulder, she could no longer see the pavement – they came to a stop.

The man swung her around, so that she was facing him.

'What were you doing, back there?' he demanded.

Back there!

He meant the place in which she'd first caught sight of him, and then – with a look of horror quickly coming to his face – *he'd* first caught sight of *her*!

'I . . . I . . .' she began.

'Tell the truth, because if you're lying to me, I'll know,' he said menacingly.

And she believed him – believed he could see right through her.

'I . . . I was looking for you,' she confessed.

The man nodded sombrely. 'That's what I thought,' he said

And then he put his free hand into his overcoat pocket, and when it emerged again, she saw it was holding a razor.

'Please, no!' she gasped. 'I didn't mean to . . . I only wanted to . . .'

But even as she spoke, she understood that she was wasting her breath – that the emptiness and yearning which had been eating away at her for years would soon be gone.

Because *she* would soon be gone.

6 June 1973

The barman in the buffet of Whitebridge railway station had been studying the racing form, but now he laid the paper down on the counter and turned his attention to his sole customer – a big bugger in a hairy sports jacket – who seemed engrossed in a tattered paperback.

The man had an interesting face, the barman thought. Like the rest of him, its features were writ large – long nose, wide mouth, square jaw. It was not an unattractive face, but it did somehow manage to give the impression of having been hastily carved by a sculptor using a blunt chisel.

The barman knew who this customer was, of course. Anyone in Whitebridge who had an interest in crime – or even someone who'd simply picked up a local newspaper in the last decade or so – would have known.

'Another pint, Chief Inspector?' he called across the empty room.

Woodend looked up from his book – which was Charles Dickens' *Bleak House*. 'What's the latest news on the delay?' he asked.

'No news at all. But if you want my opinion, it'll be at least another couple of hours before normal service is resumed. It always takes that long when a train comes off the track.'

Woodend nodded. 'In that case, another pint would be in order,' he agreed. 'An' by the way, it's not *chief inspector* any more. As of yesterday, I'm retired.'

'Good for you!' the barman said, trying not to sound as if he envied the other man his retirement – and *almost* making it.

The door swung open, and a blonde woman walked in. She was probably in her mid to late thirties, the barman thought, assessing her with a professional eye, but she had a cracking figure which – by rights – should belong to a much younger woman.

The blonde walked over to the table, and sat down without waiting for an invitation.

'What are you doin' here, Monika?' Woodend asked. 'You should be at my farewell bash.'

'So should *you*,' Monika Paniatowski pointed out.

Woodend shrugged awkwardly. 'Aye, well, I've never been much of a one for makin' myself the centre of attention when I didn't have to. An' as long as there's plenty of booze flowin' – which there should be, because it's cost me a packet – the lads won't even notice that the guest of honour isn't there.'

'You never *did* quite appreciate how popular you were, did you, Charlie?' Paniatowski asked.

'I've never really given a bugger about whether I was popular or not,' Woodend said, in what was almost a growl.

Paniatowski smiled. 'I know you haven't. That's one of the reasons why people like you so much.' She paused, to light up a cigarette. 'Well, are you going to buy me a drink, or what?'

Woodend grinned. 'You want me to buy you a *drink*?' he asked, feigning astonishment. 'I'd have thought you sank enough last night in the Drum an' Monkey to have lasted you a lifetime.'

Paniatowski returned the grin. 'I wasn't alone in that,' she said. 'You and Beresford more than matched me.'

'Aye, I will say that for Sergeant Beresford – he's turned into no mean boozer.'

'And no mean detective,' Paniatowski said, in defence of the man who would soon be her second-in-command.

'An' no mean detective,' Woodend agreed. He signalled to the barman. 'A vodka for Chief Inspector Paniatowski, please. On second thoughts, make it a double.'

'I'm not a chief inspector yet, Charlie,' Paniatowski hissed, as if she was embarrassed to hear him use the title.

'That's true,' Woodend agreed genially. 'But you will be tomorrow.'

'And where will *you* be tomorrow?' Paniatowski asked, more sharply than she'd intended.

'I'll be in London, with Joan an' our Annie,' Woodend said.

'And next week, you and Joan will be in your castle in Spain,' Paniatowski said – and now there was a definite hint of bitterness to her tone.

'Scarcely a *castle*,' Woodend said. 'But it *is* a pleasant little villa, with a view of the sea.' He paused. 'I had to go *sometime*, you know,' he continued gently. 'It's the way of the world. I move on, an' you move up.'

I don't *want* to move up, Paniatowski thought. Not without you there to watch me – not without you there to *approve* of me!

But all she said was, 'No regrets?'

'Some – but not a lot,' Woodend told her. 'There are a few things I'll miss, like best bitter an' mushy peas. A few people, too – an' you're right up at the top of that particular list.' He chuckled. 'It's a real turn up for the books, isn't it, Monika?'

'Isn't what?'

'My leavin' the Force of my own free will – exitin' with an engraved clock rather than a notice of dismissal.'

'It *is* a bit of a miracle,' Paniatowski agreed.

And so it was, she thought, because in order to count the number of times that Woodend had nearly been kicked out – and her along with him – she would need the fingers of both hands.

They fell silent, and in that silence Paniatowski found herself wishing that she could bring herself to tell her boss how much he had meant to her over the years. But from early on in their relationship, the exact nature of it had been too deep to put into words, perhaps even – on occasion – too *dangerous* to put into words.

The silence continued, until Paniatowski felt it would choke her. She needed to say something, she told herself. Something superficial. Something that could pass as banter.

'Of course, the real miracle isn't that you stayed a DCI for so long – it's that you ever got to be one in the first place,' she said.

'Now that hurts,' said Woodend, seeming as grateful to be playing the game as she was. 'That cuts me to the quick. You're surely not suggestin' – are you, Sergeant Paniatowski – that I was never chief inspector material?'

Sergeant Paniatowski, Monika noted. As if they were back in the old days, when he was her guide and her teacher and would *always* be there for her.

'What I'm suggesting, Charlie, is that you're awkward and unorthodox, that you play by nobody's rules but your own – and that if there's any way to get right up a superior's nose, you'll find it in record time.'

Woodend smiled as if she'd paid him a compliment – which, in fact, she had.

'You're right, of course,' he agreed.

'So how did you get to be a DCI, Charlie?' Paniatowski asked, realizing to her own surprise that she really *did* want to know.

Woodend gave the matter some thought. 'I suppose the short answer is that I earned my promotion by arrangin' to have somebody killed,' he said finally.

'Is that meant to be a joke?' Paniatowski asked, slightly shocked.

Woodend shook his head – seriously.

'No,' he said. 'It may be an over-simplification, but it's certainly not a joke.'

'Then tell me more.'

Woodend shook his head again. 'I've already said too much. I've already told you somethin' that only three men knew for sure – an' two of them are already dead.'

'You can't leave it there,' Paniatowski insisted. 'You just can't. It wouldn't be *fair*.'

'Life rarely *is* fair,' Woodend told her. Then his face softened and he turned to the barman and said, 'Any news on that train yet, lad?'

'Not a dickybird,' the barman replied. 'Like I said, you could be here for another two hours.'

'Which leaves you plenty of time to tell your story,' Paniatowski said firmly.

'Which leaves me plenty of time,' Woodend agreed. 'Well, it happened like this . . .'

One

S itting at his desk on the third floor of New Scotland Yard, Detective Sergeant Charlie Woodend watched as the smog tightened its grip on the city. Ten minutes earlier, he had been able to see the mighty River Thames – albeit hazily. Now the extent of his vision stretched no further than halfway across the Victoria Embankment, and though he had no doubt the river was still there, he had no way of proving it.

The phone rang, and he picked it up.

'DS Woodend.'

'A girl's been killed!' a woman's voice shrieked at him down the line.

But though it undoubtedly *had* been a shriek, it had been a shriek delivered in a *whisper* – as if, despite her emotional state, she still didn't want others to hear it.

And there *were* others around. Woodend could detect both a background hum of conversation and – even further away – some sort of music blasting out.

'Are you still there?' the woman demanded, as if hours, rather than seconds, had passed since he'd last spoken.

'I'm still here,' he said reassuringly, as he reached across for a pencil. 'Keep calm, madam.'

'Keep calm? How *can* I keep calm? The girl is dead!'

From her accent, she sounded well educated, Woodend thought. And though, given the near hysteria in her voice, it was difficult to pin her age down, he would guess she was in her mid-thirties.

'I'll need your name,' he said.

'I'm not telling you that!'

'I'm afraid you have to. It's standard procedure.'

'I don't care. I *won't* give you my name.'

It seemed pointless to try and push her any further. 'In that case, if you could just give me some details . . .'

'Mitre Road! She's on a bomb site in Mitre Road!'

'And you're sure she's dead?'

'He *said* she was dead. And he doesn't lie. Not about things like that. He's not that kind of man.'

'He?' Woodend repeated. 'Who are we talkin' about here, madam?'

But by then, the woman had already hung up.

The smog turned the short walk to Mitre Street into a journey of almost epic difficulty. Woodend got lost twice, ending up back at the river the first time, and in front of Waterloo Station the second. He met only a handful of other pedestrians, and even these few – with their heads down, moving with the heavy reluctance of men wading through water – seemed more like phantoms of the night than real people.

Finally, nearly an hour after receiving the phone call, he arrived at his destination, the bomb site on Mitre Road. Even then, he might have walked straight past, had it not been for several thin beams of light which were dancing around erratically in the soupy air.

He was reaching into his inside pocket for his warrant card when one of the beams moved towards him, and a uniformed constable in his mid-forties stepped out of the murk.

'Just keep on walkin', son,' the constable said gruffly. 'No point in trying to rubber-neck, 'cos there's nuffink for yer to see 'ere.'

'I'm from the Yard,' Woodend told him, holding up the warrant card. 'It was me who called you out.'

The constable ignored the card, and instead shone his torch up and down Woodend's body.

'Yer don't *look* much like a detective,' he sniffed, noting that instead of the expected suit, Woodend was wearing a hairy sports jacket and cavalry-twill trousers. 'Don't sound much like one, eiver.'

Meaning I don't sound like I was born within the sound of Bow Bells, Woodend translated mentally.

Meaning, in addition, that since I don't have a Southern lilt to my voice, I must be some kind of yokel.

'From the Norf, are yer?' the constable asked.

'From the North, are you, *Sergeant*!' Woodend snapped back, in much the same tone as he would have used when he'd been another kind of sergeant – one who wore battle-dress.

'No need to take the hump,' the constable said. Then, after a while, he came to something like attention, and added a reluctant, 'Sorry, Sarge.'

'Where's the body?' Woodend asked.

'This way. Mind 'ow yer step.'

Woodend followed the constable over the heaps of rubble which must once – before a Luftwaffe bomb paid it an unwelcome visit – have been part of a substantial building.

There were thousands of sites like this all around London, because even though the War had been over for five years – and even though there was a desperate housing shortage – the capital city (like Britain as a whole) was teetering on the edge of bankruptcy, and simply could not *afford* to rebuild.

Four men were gathered around the corpse on the ground – three uniformed officers and a civilian whose stethoscope and black bag conveniently identified him as the police doctor. Despite the gagging smog, they were all smoking cigarettes, and Woodend felt his own hand reach automatically in his jacket pocket for his packet of Capstan Full Strength.

'DS Woodend,' he told the doctor, as he lit up. 'What's the story?'

'She's a girl, and she's dead,' the doctor replied curtly.

'And?'

'I'll save the details till your guv'nor gets here, because there's no point in me saying everything twice, now is there?'

'My guv'nor won't be comin',' Woodend told him.

'A bit too damp for him, is it?' the doctor asked.

'Somethin' like that,' Woodend agreed.

Although what DCI Bentley had actually *said*, when Woodend had phoned him at home, was, 'I've spent years arsing round this city, cleaning up other people's shit, Sergeant – and now it's your turn.'

'I'll have a look at the body now, if you don't mind,' Woodend said.

'Be my guest,' the doctor replied indifferently.

Woodend knelt down and shone his torch on the girl's face.

'Bloody hell!' he said.

'Didn't I mention the fact that she was a nigger?' asked the doctor innocently, though his tone suggested that Woodend's obvious surprise was a source of some amusement.

'No, you didn't,' the sergeant replied coldly.

He objected to the use of the word 'nigger' on principle and, in fact, though she had black curly hair and a broad nose, this girl was not particularly dark at all.

'I don't expect you've got many niggers up Norf, Sarge,' one of the constables said.

'I'd like you to refer to her as "coloured", if you don't mind,' Woodend told him.

'Oh, come on, Sarge, what's the harm?' the constable asked. 'It's not as if she can hear me, is it?'

'An', in case I didn't make myself clear, I'd like you to refer to her as "coloured" even if you *do* mind,' Woodend said, with an edge to his voice.

'Fair enough,' the constable replied sulkily.

He'd been right about one thing, though, Woodend thought – there *were* no coloured people in Lancashire, and the first time he'd ever seen a black face, it was in London.

'Cause of death is a slit throat,' the doctor said.

'I'm no medical man, but I think I might have been able to work that out for myself, even if you hadn't been here,' Woodend replied, shining his torch on the violent gash beneath the girl's delicate chin.

'Do you think she was on the game?' the doctor wondered.

'It's possible,' Woodend said cautiously.

'Wouldn't be the first time a prostitute's met a sticky end in London, would it, though?' the doctor asked jovially. 'Shades of Jack the Ripper, eh?'

'Not you as well!' Woodend growled.

'I beg your pardon?'

'Can't you show a little respect for the dead, for Christ's sake!'

The doctor shrugged. 'You see a lot of death in my business, and I suppose you just get used to it,' he said, in what might – or might not – have been a vague apology.

I've seen a lot of death myself, too, Woodend thought. *I've* seen mountains of bodies piled up inside a German concentration camp. But that doesn't make this particular death any less tragic.

'When was she killed?' he asked.

'Three hours ago at the earliest, two at the latest.'

From the near distance came the sound of a bell chiming midnight.

'Big Ben,' said one of the constables, as if he thought that the yokel sergeant with the Northern accent would need the information.

Woodend stood up and looked back towards the pavement. There was no way the woman who'd called him could have seen the girl's body from the road, he thought.

But then she'd never *claimed* to have seen the body, had she?

What had her actual words been?

'He said she was dead. And he doesn't lie. Not about things like that. He's not that kind of man.'

She not only knew there'd been a murder, but she knew the murderer's name. So why wouldn't she tell him that name? Why wouldn't she even give him her *own* name?

Both those questions would be answered if he could find her – but how the hell was he supposed to do *that*?

Two

It was a long walk through the smog from the scene of the crime to the dingy one-and-a-half-bedroom flat which Woodend was still reluctant to call 'home', and it was a quarter past two in the morning before he finally opened the front door and saw that his wife, Joan, was sitting in the living room, half asleep.

'I wish you wouldn't do that, lass,' he said.

'Do what?' Joan asked innocently.

'Wait up for me.'

Joan yawned. 'Who *says* I was waitin' up?'

He grinned. 'I'm a detective, love. It's printed on my warrant card. An' usin' my detectin' skills, I've deduced that you were waitin' up because you're still here.'

'The reason I'm still here is because I wasn't *tired* enough to go to bed,' Joan lied. 'Anyway, you'll be wantin' somethin' to eat.'

'I don't want to put you to any trouble,' Woodend told her.

'An' I've got just the thing,' Joan continued, with the showmanship of a magician who was just about to pull a rabbit out of his top hat. 'What would you say to some nice lamb chops?'

Woodend's stomach turned over. 'I'm really not hungry,' he said.

He felt guilty about disappointing her, but the simple truth was that, after seeing the girl with her throat cut, he no longer had any appetite.

'I had to queue in the butcher's for over an hour to get them,' Joan said, disapprovingly.

'I'm sure you did, but—'

'I got the very last ones he had. You should have seen the way the women behind me in the queue glared at me. If looks could kill . . .'

'I'm sorry, love, I really am,' Woodend said.

Joan nodded, as if she'd suddenly understood. 'Another murder?' she asked.

'Yes.'

'A nasty one?'

'Very.'

'You take it all too personally, Charlie.'

'I know,' Woodend said. 'But that's the way I am.'

'Yes, that *is* the way you are,' Joan agreed. 'Still, I suppose I shouldn't complain, because if you *hadn't* been the way you are, I'd never have married you in the first place.' She paused. 'Are you *sure* you wouldn't fancy the chops?'

'Maybe I'll have them tomorrow,' Woodend said.

'An' maybe you won't,' Joan replied, as if she had already foreseen what the next twenty-odd years of their married life held – her buying the food, and Charlie being too wrapped up in his work to eat it.

'You get yourself off to bed,' Woodend said.

'An' what about you?'

'I'll just have a last fag, an' then I'll join you,' Woodend promised.

'Make sure you do,' Joan warned, as she headed for the bedroom.

Woodend slouched back in his chair, lit up the cigarette he'd promised himself and traced in his mind the events that had led him, a Northern lad who had always considered Southerners a breed apart – and who had never even *been* to London before the War – to be actually *living* there now.

'How did *you end up in London, Charlie?' Paniatowski asked.*

Woodend smiled. 'A few minutes ago you were clamourin' to hear how I got a man killed, an' now you're askin' for my life story. Which is it you want?'

'Both,' Paniatowski said.

And she meant it. By asking about Woodend's first case, she had inadvertently found the key to a part of her boss's life she had known nothing about – had stumbled on the opportunity to build up a more complete picture of the man she was already missing, even as she sat there opposite him.

'I suppose the decision was taken in Berlin, back in 1945,' Woodend said. 'You should have seen the place at the time.'

Then he noticed Paniatowski shudder, and added, ruefully,
'I'm sorry, lass, you did see it, didn't you?'

'Yes,' Monika agreed. 'I did.'

But though she had managed to keep her voice flat and
emotionless, her heart was beating faster and there was a
pounding in her head.

It was all over half a lifetime ago! she thought. More than
half a lifetime! So why does it feel like it only happened
yesterday?

After six years of wandering Europe as refugees, she and
her mother, hoping to make contact with the victorious Allies,
had reached Berlin just after it had fallen. And what they had
found was a city devastated by RAF bombs and Russian shells.

A wasteland.

A true vision of hell.

They had looked on as German civilians, clad in little more
than rags, sifted desperately through the rubble, looking for
something they could use or something they could sell. Or
perhaps even just something – anything – that would remind
them of their old lives, before the inferno.

They had looked on, and they'd felt something they'd thought
they'd never feel for the enemy – pity.

'Anyway,' Woodend said hurriedly – as if he could see the
pictures in Monika's head himself, and felt a strong urge to
distract her – 'anyway, I was sittin' in this jeep with Major
Cathcart, who I was servin' under at the time, when the major
turns to me an' says, "So what are your plans once you're
demobbed, Charlie?" An' I told him the first thing I was goin'
to do was to get married.'

'To Joan?' Paniatowski asked, as a little of the colour
returned to her cheeks.

'Of course to Joan. There was never anybody else but Joan.
So then the major says, "Good idea. We could all do with a
little of the peace and stability that marriage brings." An' that
was when I made the mistake of askin' him if he was married
himself.'

'Why was that a mistake?' Paniatowski wondered.

'Firstly because it's not an NCO's place to go askin' officers intimate questions. But secondly – an' more importantly
– because of the effect it had on him.'

'What effect was that?'

'He was older than me by a good ten years, but suddenly he seemed much younger an' much more vulnerable. "No," he said. "No, I . . . er . . . never quite seemed to get around to it." Well, I apologized for pryin', an' he told me it didn't matter – though it clearly did. Then he shifted ground – which is what people do when they find themselves in sticky situations – an' he said, "Tell me, Charlie, have you given much thought to how you'll support a wife and – soon enough, I would imagine – a family?"'

'And you said, "Well, I've always had this burning ambition to work for the Metropolitan Police Force"?' Paniatowski suggested.

'No, I didn't,' Woodend replied. 'The fact was that even though I wouldn't admit it – even to myself – there was a part of me which believed that if you had any plan for a future, you wouldn't get one, whereas if you expect to be killed, you just might survive. Still, the major was clearly expectin' an answer to his question, so I said, "I'll probably get a job as a tackler in one of the mills. It's what I did before the War." '

'And how did he react to that?'

'Didn't like it at all. He was back in control of himself by this point – very much the officer again – an' he clicked his tongue disapprovingly an' said, "You disappoint me, Sergeant. There's no future for you as a . . . as a tackler, was it?" '

'Cheeky bastard!' Paniatowski said. 'He had no idea what a tackler does, did he?'

'No, he didn't,' Woodend agreed. 'But he meant well. "The mills are finished," he said. "Everybody knows that." Not in Lancashire, they don't, I thought. But aloud, all I said was, "Is that right, sir?" "Yes, it certainly is," he told me. "In ten or fifteen years' time, all the cloth we buy in England will be made in India or China. And even if the mills weren't finished, that's not the kind of job to really stretch a man of your obvious abilities, now is it?'

'A man of your obvious abilities!' Paniatowski repeated, teasingly. 'Do you think he fancied you or something?'

'No, I don't,' Woodend said firmly. 'There was nothin' even vaguely homosexual about Major Cathcart – as you'll find out for yourself if you stop interruptin' an' just listen to the story.'

'Sorry, Charlie,' Monika said, with mock humility.

'Anyway, I asked him what he thought I should do,' Woodend continued, 'and he suggested I should think about becomin' a bobby. "I was a policeman before the War," he told me. "In the Met. And when I'm demobbed, that's what I shall be again." I said it was certainly worth thinkin' about once I was back in Lancashire, an' that's when he started clickin' his tongue disapprovingly again.'

'Why did he do that?'

'He said, an' I think I'm quotin' exactly here, "If you're going to paint a picture, set out to produce a masterpiece. If you're going to write a book, aim at it being the best one ever written. And if you intend to become a policeman, join the best police force in the world – which is the Met." I pointed out that would mean livin' in London, an' he laughed an' said, "Well, of course it would – so there's another advantage for you." '

'That's the problem with Londoners,' Paniatowski said. 'They believe there are only two kinds of people – those who live in London and those who want to live in London.'

'Those were exactly my thoughts at the time,' Woodend agreed. 'An' there were other considerations to be taken into account. "I'm not sure my fiancée would fancy the idea of movin' down South, sir," I told him. "For God's sake, Charlie," he said, "you're going to be the head of a family – so you'd better start thinking like one, even before you're married. The Met's desperately short of good men at the moment, and for anyone who's even halfway competent – and you're much more than that – it's a golden opportunity. If your wife has anything about her, she'll see that, and want you to do whatever's necessary to get on in life. And if she doesn't like it, well, as I said, you will be the head of family, so she'll just have to lump it, won't she?" '

A smile played on Paniatowski's lips. 'And did Joan "just have to lump it"?' she asked.

'As a matter of fact, she raised no objection at all,' Woodend told her. 'What she actually said was, "I've got faith in your judgement, Charlie. After all, you showed enough of it to be pretty desperate to marry me, now didn't you?" '

Paniatowski laughed. 'That sounds like Joan,' she said. 'But tell me, Charlie, did you ever regret taking the decision?'

'Now an' again,' Woodend admitted. 'On nights like the one

I've just been talkin' about, when the smog was so thick it settled in your lungs an' didn't seem like it would ever go away, I did get a bout of the blues an' start to yearn for home, where even the industrial filth seemed to taste better. But when that happened, there was always somethin' – one thing – I could do to lift my spirits.'

'And what was that?'

'Go an' look at our Annie, sleepin' peacefully in her little bed.'

Woodend stood in the doorway of his daughter's bedroom. From the illumination provided by her nightlight he could see that she was deeply asleep, but still he held his breath for fear of waking her.

She was a wondrous child, he told himself. A precious gift that – most of time – he felt unworthy of.

She had been born just before the move to London, and, after much thought, he and Joan had christened her Pauline Anne. Woodend was still not sure which of the two names he preferred. And neither, it appeared, was his daughter, since for weeks on end she would insist on being called Annie, and then – completely out of the blue – would recognize no other name but Pauline.

He realized suddenly that the War – or at least *his* War – had been for her. That before she'd even been conceived, it was for her future – for the future of children everywhere – that he'd been fighting.

But there was one child who would *have* no future, he thought with rising anger – one child whose future had been drained out of her, as if she were no more than a stuck pig, on a sordid bomb site.

The sudden and unexpected ringing of the telephone in the living room filled the silent flat with a noise which sounded loud enough to waken the dead. Woodend glanced anxiously down at his small, precious daughter, saw that she was still sleeping peacefully and retreated from her bedroom as quietly as he could.

Once in the hallway, he clicked his daughter's door gently closed and turned to face the instrument which had dared to shatter the peace.

He was sure the call must be a mistake – who the bloody

hell would be ringing *him* at half-past two in the morning? – but since the only way to silence the infernal racket seemed to be pick up the receiver, that was what he did.

'Detective Sergeant Woodend?' asked a man's voice.

Not a mistake, he told himself.

And not the Yard, either – because the first thing someone from the Yard would do would be to identify himself.

'Yes, I'm Woodend,' he said.

'Well, yer 'ave been a busy boy, ain't yer?' the caller replied.

'Who is this?' Woodend demanded.

'Fing is, yer don't want ter go takin' this case too seriously,' the other man continued.

'What are you talkin' about?'

'The girl, you wally.'

'The murdered girl?'

'Unless yer can fink of any uvver.'

'If you've got any information on the murder, it's your duty to report it.'

'I ain't got any information, *as such*, but what I 'ave got is a bit of advice for yer.'

'Go on,' Woodend said.

'Yer want to tread carefully.'

'An' what does that mean, exactly?'

'It means that nobody expects yer *not* to investigate the case wot's been assigned to yer. That's yer job, after all. That's 'ow yer earn yer crust and keep a roof over yer 'ead.'

'Get to the point!'

'All I *am* saying is, if yer know what's good for yer, yer won't do that job *too* thoroughly.'

'That sounds like a threat,' Woodend growled.

'Now yer catching on, Charlie boy,' the other man agreed. 'It's a threat. Start making too many waves, and somefink very nasty could 'appen to yer.'

'An' who'll be makin' this "very nasty" thing happen to me?' Woodend wondered. 'You?'

'Could be.'

'I hope it *is* you. I hope we get a chance to meet face to face. Because if we do, I'll rip your heart out.'

The other man sighed. 'Well, don't say I didn't warn yer,' he said.

And then he hung up.

Three

By morning, a favourable wind had blown away the smog, and with its departure the events of the previous evening had assumed an almost dreamlike quality.

Except that they hadn't been a dream at all, Woodend said to himself, as he marched along the Victoria Embankment, towards the imposing red-brick building that was New Scotland Yard.

Because even though the visible signs of the smog had gone, its sulphurous fumes still hung heavily in the air as a reminder.

And even though the poor coloured girl would, by now, be housed in much less sordid surroundings than the ones in which she'd initially been discovered, she was still dead!

He reached the main entrance to the Yard, and nodded to the two constables on duty there.

'How are you, Sarge?' one of them called out to him.

'Fine,' he answered.

But he wasn't – he bloody well *wasn't*!

DCI Bentley's office space was divided into two unequal sections by a wooden partition wall. The larger of the sections – the outer office – contained five desks, and was inhabited by Woodend and four detective constables. The smaller section, known unofficially as the Wolf's Lair – a name it shared, only partly ironically, with Hitler's mountain retreat – was reserved for the exclusive use of Bentley himself.

Somewhere in the dim and distant past the chief inspector may well have lived up to his lupine nickname, Woodend thought, as he stood in the doorway of his guv'nor's office, studying the man himself. The photograph hanging on the wall behind him – in which he was shaking hands with a minor royal – certainly seemed to suggest there had been a time when he had been lean and hungry, capable of single-mindedly stalking his prey for days on end. But the man that he had become – the man with his feet up on the desk, flicking through the newspapers – had none of these qualities.

Bentley had put on a lot of weight in the years since the photograph had been taken, weight he had either not noticed or decided to ignore. His hair had thinned dramatically, but he continued to plaster it with as much hair cream as he had done when he'd had a full thatch, so that now the pink skin on his scalp glowed with a sheen of grease. And as his cheeks and jowls had expanded, his features had retreated, leaving him with piggy eyes and a tight, disapproving mouth.

The chief inspector lowered his newspaper and glanced across at the clock on the wall.

'A quarter to eight,' he grunted. 'So this is how you carry on when I'm not here, is it, Sergeant – not bothering to put in an appearance until it's practically time to take a tea break?'

That was rich, coming from a man who rarely turned up himself before ten o'clock, Woodend thought, but he contented himself with saying, 'I had a late night, sir. There was a murder I had to investigate.'

Bentley sighed, theatrically. 'So there was,' he said. 'Well, I suppose you'd better tell me about it.'

Woodend gave him a concise summary, and when he'd finished, Bentley said, 'Was there anything on her to identify her?'

He'd only been half-listening, Woodend thought – half-listening at best.

'No, sir, as I've already explained, she didn't have a handbag, or even a purse,' he said.

'Still, even without formal identification, putting a name to her shouldn't be much problem, should it?' Bentley asked.

'Shouldn't it?'

'Of course not. After all, there can't be that many niggers in London who match her description, now can there?'

'There can't be that many *coloured* girls, no,' Woodend agreed. 'I read somewhere that the entire *coloured* population of the British Isles doesn't come to much more than eleven thousand.'

It was a mild rebuke, and he knew it, but it was as far as he dared go with the man who held his future in his hands, and he could only hope that Bentley would take the hint.

'And most of the niggers who aren't too bone idle to earn

an honest day's pay have jobs on the docks, don't they?' Bentley said, with complete disregard. 'So the chances are that this particular girl will have *lived* near the docks.'

'That's probably true,' Woodend agreed, resignedly.

'Then all you have to do is go around the dockland police stations with her photograph and find a local copper who knows her. And once you've done that, I expect the same local copper will be able to tell you who killed her.'

'How would he know?' Woodend wondered.

'He'll know because he knows *these people*,' Bentley said, speaking more slowly now that he'd realized he was dealing with an idiot. 'And because he knows them, he'll also know which of them it was that this girl managed to rub up the wrong way.'

'So you're assumin' she was killed by a coloured man, are you?' Woodend asked.

'Of course I am,' Bentley said. 'It's the only *logical* assumption to make, and I don't see why you're not making it, too.'

'I don't think that the woman who reported the murder was coloured,' Woodend said.

'What does that prove?' Bentley asked dismissively. 'She doesn't have to have been coloured to have seen the murder and then report it, now does she? Where's your problem with that?'

'She didn't *see* it at all, sir. She was *told* about it.'

'So?'

'So why would a *coloured* man tell a *white* woman that he'd just committed a murder?'

'To impress her,' Bentley said easily.

'To *impress* her!'

'He was probably trying to get into her knickers, and thought that he'd have more of a chance if he gave himself a dangerous edge.'

'Do you really believe that's possible, sir?' Woodend asked, incredulously.

Bentley shrugged. 'Well, I admit it's not something you or I would have done if we were trying to get our ends away,' he said, 'but then these jungle bunnies don't think like us, do they?'

An' I don't think like you, Woodend thought – but if I ever start to, I promise I'll shoot myself.

'Mitre Road's a fair way from the docks,' he pointed out. 'What was the victim doin' there at all, unless it had something to do with white people?'

Bentley sighed again. 'Do you know what the trouble with you keen young coppers is?' he asked.

'No, sir.'

'It's that you're always trying to make things seem far more complicated than they actually are.'

For a moment Woodend considered telling Bentley about his second phone call, the one in which the caller – again, obviously white – had warned him not to investigate the girl's death too enthusiastically. But he'd just be wasting his breath, he decided – because the chances were that the chief inspector would either tell him it was of no importance or – worse – would suspect him of inventing the whole thing in an effort to advance his own theories.

'I don't suppose there's any *real* harm in you indulging in your flights of fancy for a while – as long as, ultimately, they don't get in the way of good police work,' Bentley said magnanimously. 'So you just go ahead. Come up with as many ridiculous theories about white men being involved as you like. But I think you'll find, when you've completed your investigation, that I was right all along – and it was a nigger wot done it.'

'Did you say *my* investigation, sir?' Woodend asked, almost sure he must have misheard.

'That's exactly what I said,' Bentley confirmed. 'I'm putting you in sole charge.'

'But it's a *murder* case, sir!'

'No doubt about that. She certainly didn't cut her *own* throat.'

'An' I'm only a sergeant.'

'Exactly,' Bentley agreed. 'And there are plenty of DCIs in this place who wouldn't trust their sergeants to do a job like this. But I'm not one of them, you see. I realize that if you're ever going to develop your skills as a detective, you'll need the experience of handling a case on your own. So I'm giving you the chance now.'

Or to put it another way, since the victim in this case was only a 'nigger', he couldn't be bothered to get off his fat arse and investigate the case himself, Woodend thought.

'Thank you, sir, I appreciate the confidence you're showin' in me,' he said.

'Think nothing of it,' Bentley told him. 'But bear in mind, I shall expect an arrest by lunchtime.'

'By lunchtime!' Woodend repeated.

Bentley chuckled throatily. 'Just my little joke, Sergeant,' he said. 'Some time tomorrow will be early enough.'

The doctor who had carried out the post-mortem on the dead girl was fresher, younger – and seemed altogether less callous – than the one who had examined the body at the scene of the crime.

'I expect you're surprised that we've managed to get the whole business of the PM over and done with so quickly,' he said to Woodend, as he led him through the morgue.

'Yes, I am rather, sir,' the sergeant admitted.

Sir! he repeated silently, with just a hint of self-disgust.

What he'd *wanted* to call the other man was not 'sir' at all, but 'Doc', as a more seasoned detective would have done. But somehow, despite the fact that they were more or less the same age, he simply hadn't been able to force the word out.

'Because of the smog, things have been pretty quiet around here, you see,' the doctor continued. 'But we know from experience that that's just the lull before the storm. By this afternoon, we'll be swamped with bods whose respiratory systems have packed up. So, bearing that in mind, I thought I'd get your girl out of the way while I had the chance.' He slid open a refrigerated drawer. 'There she is. Want to take a closer look at her?'

'If you wouldn't mind, si— Doc,' Woodend said.

The doctor pulled back the sheet, and the sergeant looked down at the victim.

The girl's face was frozen in a death mask which seemed to combine horror with panic, but even that could not entirely disguise the fact that she must have been quite pretty in life.

'What can you tell me about her?' Woodend asked.

'She was probably sixteen or seventeen,' the doctor said. 'Whoever killed her did a professional job – her throat was cut with a single slash, rather than being hacked at. And if you asked me what the killer used, I'd put my money on it being a cut-throat razor.'

Shades of Jack the Ripper, Woodend thought, remembering what the other doctor had said the night before.

'Yes, my guess would be a razor,' the doctor repeated. 'Which is a rather old-fashioned sort of weapon to employ, don't you think?'

It was, Woodend agreed. Modern criminals preferred to use flick knives, or – when they could get their hands on them – guns.

'The girl was healthy and well nourished,' the doctor continued. 'It's true there's evidence of contusions on her legs, but I don't think that's something you should be particularly concerned about.'

'Why not?'

'Because it's not the kind of bruising you'd expect from a deliberate beating. My guess would be that it's evidence of some kind of sporting injury – most probably hockey.'

Hockey! The more he learned about this girl, the more of an enigma she became, Woodend thought.

'Was she a virgin?' he asked.

'Yes, she was.'

Not a prostitute, then.

But despite some of the evidence pointing that way, Woodend had never really thought that she was.

'Was she sexually interfered with in any way, before – or after – she died?' he asked.

The doctor shook his head. 'Absolutely not. There's not a trace of bruising around her private parts.'

The knowledge that she'd at least been spared that humiliation should have made her death a little easier to take, Woodend told himself – but it didn't.

'I'd like to look at her things, now, if that's all right with you,' he said.

'No problem at all,' the doctor replied. 'I'll get one of the porters to take you to where they're stored.'

The porter was an old man with a pronounced limp, and as he led Woodend slowly down the corridor, he chatted away about the experience of working in the morgue during the War.

'At the height of the Blitz, with all them bombs dropping on London every night, we had so many bodies in this place you could hardly move for them,' he said. 'If I'd have been of a mind to, I could have done in the missus and got clean away with it, because the doctors were so run off their feet that they'd never even have noticed it wasn't natural causes wot had laid her out.'

Woodend grinned. 'But I take it that you *weren't* of a mind to?' he said.

'No, I wasn't,' the porter agreed, shaking his head seriously. 'With all that was going on, you see, I was far too busy. An' besides,' he added, almost as an afterthought, 'I'd have missed her cooking.'

The room in which the dead girl's effects had been stored was at the end of the corridor. There was only one piece of furniture in it – a metal table close to the door – and around the walls there were cardboard boxes stacked to waist height.

'Some of these boxes have been here for years,' the porter said. 'We all know nobody's ever going to claim them, but we have to keep them anyway, just in case anybody does.'

'What about the personal effects that I'm interested in?' Woodend asked.

'They're over there,' the porter said, pointing at the table. 'All neatly laid out for you.'

Neatly, but almost heartbreakingly, Woodend thought.

There was a red dress (covered in dark brown stains which could only be blood), a brassiere, a pair of knickers, a suspender belt, a pair of nylon stockings (heavily laddered), and the girl's shoes.

Woodend picked up the stockings, and – though he knew it was hardly appropriate – found his mind drifting back to what would turn out to be his last home leave before the end of the War.

He had arranged to take Joan out dancing, and had arrived at her back door at seven o'clock with a bunch of freshly cut daffodils in his hands.

'They're lovely, Charlie!' Joan had said.

'An' so are you!' he'd exclaimed.

And so she was. Not lovely like the glamorous models in the pin-up magazines – legs all the way up to their arses, and breasts which threatened to break out of their confinement any second – but lovely in a quieter, fresher way, lovely enough for him to want to spend the rest of his life with her.

And then he'd noticed that she was wearing stockings –
nylon or silk, he was not sure which – and he'd felt his stomach
knot up. Because there was one way – and one way only –
that she could have got her hands on them.

'You haven't been gettin' too friendly with any of the Yankee
soldiers, have you?' he'd asked, though he'd been dreading
her answer.

'Of course not, Charlie,' Joan had replied.

'Then where did you get them stockings from?'

'I'm not wearin' stockings,' Joan had told him, with laughter
dancing in her eyes.

'I'm not blind, you know,' Woodend had said, feeling a
helpless anger growing inside him.

'No, but you're not very observant, either,' Joan had countered. 'I said I'm not wearing stockings, and I'm not. I've
dyed my legs.'

'What with?'

'With tea.'

He hadn't been convinced, even though the twinkle had
still been there in her eye – even though he couldn't see the
point of her telling a lie which it would be so easy to expose.

'Where did you get an idea like that from?' he'd asked
suspiciously. 'Is it somethin' all the other girls do, an' all?'

'No, all the other girls *don't* do it,' Joan had said.

'Well, then, I don't see how you could have come up
with—'

'Some of them don't like usin' tea, so they use gravy
brownin' mixture instead.'

'Turn around,' he'd said, perhaps a little gruffly.

And Joan had given him a dainty twirl.

'That "tea's" got a seam runnin' up the back of it, just like
it was a stockin',' he'd pointed out.

Joan had laughed. 'That's drawn on.'

'*Drawn* on?'

'With my eyebrow pencil,' Joan had explained. Then she'd
stood on tiptoe and kissed Woodend on the forehead. 'You
don't know much about women, do you, Charlie?'

'No,' Woodend had admitted. 'Apparently I don't.'

Laying the victim's stockings to one side, Woodend picked
up the dress. He had already seen it on the murdered girl,

but only when she was sprawled out in a pathetic heap on a piece of rough ground. Now, holding it at arms' length, he tried to picture how she would have looked in it when she was alive.

It was one of those dresses designed to show off the kind of hourglass figure that most women could achieve only through elastic assistance. It had a V-neck which plunged a little more than most of those Woodend had seen on the street, but still avoided crossing the line which divided daring from risqué. The bottom half of the dress had clearly been tight-fitting – he recalled Joan saying something about a 'pencil' style, though that had never made much sense to him – but the hemline would have been at least an inch or two below the girl's knees. It was, in other words, the kind of dress that would be chosen by someone flirting with the idea of being a bad girl – but only half-heartedly.

Woodend replaced the dress on the table, took an edge of it between his finger and thumb, and rubbed.

'Does that tell you anything?' asked the porter, who was hovering at his side like an aging trainee detective.

'It tells me it's wool,' Woodend said.

'In that case,' the porter said gravely, 'it must have been bought sometime after May of last year.' He paused, then continued, 'Go on, ask me how I managed to work that out.'

'I don't need to, because I already *know* how you did it,' Woodend told him.

'Then explain it to me,' the porter challenged.

'You know because until last May, clothin' was rationed. An' as long as it was on the ration, the manufacturers weren't allowed to use wool.'

The porter looked somewhat deflated. 'Well, at least you seem to know your job,' he said, as if to console himself.

Woodend turned his attention to the dead girl's knickers. They were plain – almost, in fact, frumpy – a childlike garment which would have been hidden from view by the semi-vampish red dress.

But what did that prove?

That, essentially, the girl had only been acting a part, and that her true self was reflected more in her undergarments than in her outward appearance?

Or merely that having spent all her money on an expensive

dress, she simply could not afford the kind of knickers that should have accompanied it?

And how was it possible to reconcile the sophisticated aspirations that the dress implied with the bruising which – according to the doctor – was most likely the result of a vigorously healthy game of hockey?

'It's funny, isn't it?' the porter asked.

'Isn't what?' Woodend wondered.

'Well, when you think about it, you just wouldn't expect a half-caste girl to be dressed up like a much older white woman, now would you?'

'No,' Woodend agreed. 'You wouldn't.'

Four

Woodend was in the middle of Canning Town. A cold wind was blowing in from the river, and though he was walking at a brisk pace, it chilled him to the bone.

A few years earlier, a river wind would never have reached this far inland, he thought, because there had been countless buildings – docks and factories and rows of crumbling terraced houses – to block it. But the War had changed all that – as it had changed so many other things.

The whole of London had suffered from the Blitz to some extent, but nowhere had taken more punishment than Canning Town, where eighty-five per cent of the housing had been destroyed in just a few short months in 1941. And the evidence of that destruction was still there for all to see in what had once been a normal street – with houses and shops running alongside it – but was now no more than a path through the rubble.

Some of the buildings he passed still bore signs of what they had formerly been – a pub with its top storey missing, a garage with only three walls and no roof, a small factory, outside which a rusting sign proclaimed 'Quality products at reasonable prices' – but more often than not there was just a pile of rubble.

Perhaps, someday, the place would rise again, phoenix-like, from the ashes, Woodend told himself – but, for the moment, it was mostly the ashes you noticed.

The desk sergeant at Canning Town Police Station was Scottish, had red hair, and said his name was McBride. His welcome was warmer than the mere professional courtesy to a fellow sergeant which protocol dictated, and Woodend suspected that in him McBride recognized a kindred spirit – another bobby who hailed from an area of the country that

the average Londoner considered to be well beyond the edge
of civilization.

Once the pleasantries were over, Woodend showed McBride
a photograph of the dead girl.

'I don't recognize her myself, but if she's from round here,
I guarantee that one o' my wee laddies will know her,' McBride
said confidently.

His confidence proved to be well placed, for though Woodend
drew a blank with the first constable he showed the picture to,
the second – a fresh-faced young officer of twenty-two or
twenty-three – gulped and said, 'Oh shit, that's Pearl Jones.'

'You're sure of that?' Woodend asked.

'I'm sure. She's a nice girl.' The constable gulped again,
and corrected himself. 'I mean, she *was* a nice girl.'

'What can you tell me about her?'

'I don't know,' the constable said helplessly. 'I can't think.'

'Take your time, lad.'

'I . . . I was only talking to her the other day, and, to tell
you the truth, it's a bit of a shock to be told she's dead.'

'Of course it is. That's only natural,' Woodend agreed,
soothingly.

The lad had gone into a complete panic, he thought. If he
was to learn *anything* useful from him, it might be best to
start with a few easy questions first.

'Where did this Pearl Jones live?' he asked.

'On Balaclava Street. With her mum.'

'Just her mum? No dad?'

'She hasn't got a dad as far as *I* know. At least, I've never
heard anybody mention him.'

'Did she have any brothers or sisters?'

'No, there's just the two of them – Pearl and her mum.'

'Do you happen to know where Pearl worked?'

'Worked? She didn't work anywhere. She was still at
school.'

Then she must have been younger than she looked – much
younger than the medical examiner had estimated her to be.

'How old was she?' Woodend said.

'Sixteen, I think.'

'Then she *can't* still have been at school, can she?' Woodend
asked gently. 'By my calculations, her school days must have
been over two years ago.'

'I suppose they would have been, if she'd gone to the secondary mod.,' the constable agreed.

'But she didn't?'

'No. Pearl went to a private school.'

Private school! Hockey injuries!

'Tell me about Balaclava Street,' Woodend suggested. 'Is it in the posh part of Canning Town?'

The constable laughed, then – given the circumstances – looked guilty about it.

'There *isn't* a posh part of Canning Town, Sarge,' he said.

'Then how could her mother afford to send her to a private school? Does she have a good job? An' *if* she does, why is she livin' in Balaclava Street?'

'Mrs Jones doesn't have any sort of job at all, as far as I know,' the constable said. 'But I have heard it said that Pearl was quite bright, so maybe she was on some kind of scholarship.'

'Maybe that *is* the answer,' Woodend agreed. 'I'll need you to give me the mother's address.'

The constable pursed his brow as he counted out the street numbers in his head.

'It must be Number 36,' he said. 'Will you be going to see Mrs Jones?'

'Yes, I think I better had.'

'And would you . . . er . . . would you like me come with you, Sarge?'

'Do you *want* to come with me?' Woodend asked.

'Well . . . er . . . I think I should, since I know the family,' the constable said unconvincingly.

He looked about ready to throw up right there in the police station, Woodend thought. God alone knew how he'd feel when he had to break the news to Mrs Jones that her only daughter had had her throat slit.

'I think I can handle it on my own,' he said.

'Thanks, Sarge,' the constable replied – and sounded as though he meant it.

The north end of Balaclava Street had taken a terrific battering during the Blitz, and was now in ruins. The south end had miraculously escaped the bombs, though looking at the row of ramshackle terraced houses of which it was made up,

Woodend thought it might have been best if the Luftwaffe had got rid of it, too.

The street was dirty, not just from the industrial filth which the foul smog had carried with it, but through lack of care. Rusting tin cans littered the pavement, old prams and discarded stoves lay rotting in the street.

There were a few women lurking in their doorways, but none was making any attempt to donkey-stone their doorsteps or clean their filthy front windows, and though soap rationing had ended two months earlier, the news had plainly not reached Balaclava Street yet.

He had reached Number 36, and he knocked on the door. His knock was answered by a woman – a handsome black woman, who he guessed was around thirty-five years old.

'Mrs Jones?' Woodend asked, showing her his warrant card.

'Dat's me,' the woman said, in a voice which betrayed just the slightest lilt of a West Indian accent. 'What do you want?'

'I'm afraid that I may have some bad news for you,' Woodend told her.

The woman's jaw wobbled. 'Pearl?' she gasped. 'Is it about my Pearl?'

'Would you mind if I came inside?' Woodend asked gently.

'Yes, I . . . I mean, no . . .' Mrs Jones said.

Then she turned, and gestured to Woodend to follow her.

The inside of the house came as something of a surprise. Woodend found none of the flaking plaster and signs of dampness which he might have expected. Instead, it was solid and substantial, the kind of interior which belonged in a well-built semi-detached house, rather than in a crumbling terrace.

The living room brought more surprises. The Woodends' dingy flat had been furnished by the landlord with Utility Furniture, plain but serviceable articles, built – because of the shortage of raw materials – to strict government specifications. And while it was true that furniture had been off the ration since June 1948, non-Utility was still difficult to find, and very expensive. But neither shortages nor expense seemed to have bothered Mrs Jones. The floor was covered in thick-pile carpet, the three-piece suite was leather, and in the corner of the room was a sideboard – displaying photographs in silver frames – which seemed to be made of real rosewood.

'You asked me if I'd come about Pearl,' Woodend said. 'How long has she been missin'?'

'Who said she was missin' at all?' Mrs Jones demanded.

'Please, madam, let's try to make this as easy as possible,' Woodend suggested.

Mrs Jones looked down at the floor. 'She didn't come home last night,' she admitted.

'Does she often stay out all night?' Woodend asked.

'Never!' Mrs Jones said, suddenly angry. 'My Pearl don't do dat. My Pearl is a *good* girl.'

'I've got something to show you,' Woodend said. 'But before I do, I think it would be best if you sat down.'

'Don't want to sit down,' Mrs Jones told him.

But when Woodend put his hands on her shoulders and gently eased her into the leather armchair, she did not resist.

Woodend took the photograph out of his pocket and held it out to the woman. 'Is this your daughter?' he asked.

Mrs Jones's eyes widened, and tears began to cascade from them. 'Oh, my God!' she moaned. 'Oh, sweet Jesus!'

'I'm most terribly sorry to be the bearer of such terrible news, Mrs Jones,' Woodend said.

And then, something quite remarkable happened. The woman took a deep breath, and – by a sheer effort of will – forced her tears to stop.

'Dat is not my daughter,' she said, in a voice which fell somewhere between hysterical and eerily calm.

'I know you might find it quite hard to accept . . .' Woodend began.

'I feel sorry for de poor girl, but she is *not* my daughter,' Mrs Jones said firmly.

Woodend walked over to the sideboard on which the silver photograph frames rested. All the pictures were of the same girl, and charted her development from infant to young woman.

Little Pearl, smiling broadly at the camera, as she took her first few tentative steps towards whoever was holding it.

Pearl at four or five, sitting under the Christmas tree and proudly clutching a doll which was almost as big as she was.

Pearl at nine or ten, all her attention focused on the picture she was drawing, her tongue licking the corner of her mouth as she strove to get it just right.

In the last photograph, Pearl was dressed in gym clothes.

She had a hockey stick in one hand, and her free arm was draped over the shoulder of a blonde white girl, who had her own free arm draped over Pearl's shoulder.

Both girls were smiling. They looked so happy. So innocent!

Woodend shook his head sadly, and turned to face Mrs Jones again. The woman had not moved from where he'd sat her, and though her shoulders shook, she was still managing to hold in most of her sorrow.

'I'm sorry, Mrs Jones, but the girl in the photograph I showed you *is* your daughter,' he told her. 'There's no doubt about it.'

Mrs Jones struggled to her feet.

'It's not her!' she screamed, waving her arms wildly in the air. 'I done told you, it's not her.'

'I know it's hard, but the sooner you accept the fact that she's dead, the sooner you'll be able to start coming to terms with it,' Woodend said softly.

'Get out o' my house!' Mrs Jones demanded. 'Get out o' my house right now!'

'Mrs Jones—'

'I tell you – get out!'

There was nothing he could do – no way he could refuse to go.

Woodend walked down the corridor to the front door, with Mrs Jones at his heel.

'And don't come back!' the woman told him, when he was back on the street. 'Don't you *ever* come back.'

When he turned, as if to walk away, she slammed the door violently on him. But he did *not* walk away immediately. Instead, he simply stood there, looking back at the house from which he'd just been ejected.

And from the other side of the door, he thought he could hear Mrs Jones sobbing uncontrollably.

Five

The bus carried Woodend across the river, and when it finally deposited him on the corner of Buckton Road, he found himself in a completely different world from the one he'd left behind him in Canning Town.

It was true that this part of London – being far enough away from the docks for the German bombers to have largely ignored it – had not suffered from the Blitz as Canning Town had, he admitted in fairness. But even if both areas had taken the same battering from the Luftwaffe – even if they'd been equally reduced to ashes – the two would never have been confused, because, as any passer-by would immediately have seen, the ashes of Buckton Road would have been of a far better *class* than those from Balaclava Street.

Woodend wondered how Pearl Jones had managed the difficult transition – how she had felt, every single school day, about leaving the mean streets of Canning Town behind her for this leafy suburb, but then returning to those same mean streets when the final bell rang.

Had she ever thought of running away?

Had the red dress, perhaps, been a part of the *process* of running away?

Just ahead of him lay his destination – a large Georgian building which might once, long ago, have been a duke's summer palace, but was now the Newton High School for Young Ladies.

'So how did *you* feel about bein' a "young lady", Pearl?' he said softly to himself. 'Did you ever really *believe* that that was what you were?'

The headmistress introduced herself to Woodend as Dr Jenkins, with an emphasis on the 'Dr'. Her hair was tied back in a severe bun, and a pair of half-moon spectacles rested on the bridge of her long, thin nose. She wore a single row of cultured pearls around her neck, and was dressed in a tweed jacket which had been cut on almost masculine lines. And though he could not see her feet because of the desk, he was almost certain they were clad in heavy 'sensible' shoes.

'I must admit to having experienced a certain amount of surprise, and perhaps even a little concern, when my secretary informed me that you wished to see me, *Detective Sergeant*,' she said.

Detective Sergeant! Woodend noted. Not *Mr* Woodend, or even *Sergeant* Woodend, but just his rank. It was all titles with this woman!

'I can assure you, I never *meant* to concern you,' he said, giving nothing away.

'I'm sure you did not,' Dr Jenkins agreed. 'But you must understand that it is a very rare occurrence indeed for the forces of law and order to enter this temple of learning.'

'Aye, an' you're probably not used to havin' the Old Bill visitin' your school, either,' Woodend said – though he knew he shouldn't have done.

Dr Jenkins frowned, perhaps not quite sure whether he was poking fun at her or was merely stupid.

'So how may I assist you?' she asked, apparently settling on the 'stupid' explanation.

'I wanted to ask you a few questions about one of your pupils,' Woodend said.

'One of my *pupils*?'

'That's right.'

'And *which* pupil might that be?'

'Pearl Jones.'

A look of distaste flickered briefly across Dr Jenkins' face – but not briefly enough for Woodend to have missed it.

'And why would you wish to know anything about Pearl?' the headmistress asked.

Because she's *dead*! Woodend thought.

But he couldn't say that.

Not when he couldn't actually *prove* it.

Not when her *own mother* refused to admit the truth.

'I'm afraid that, given the confidential nature of my inquiries, I'm not in a position to go into any details,' he said.

'And yet you still expect *me* to speak freely about the girl?'

Dr Jenkins asked, haughtily. 'You still expect me to betray *my* confidences?'

She was anticipating him being crushed by the remark, Woodend though – a mere *detective sergeant* put in his rightful place by a *doctor of philosophy*.

But he wasn't. He'd got the woman sized up by now – and he knew just which buttons to push.

'I can see your problem,' he admitted humbly. 'I myself wouldn't like to be put in to the position that I've put you in.'

'Well, then, there's really no more to be said, is there?' the headmistress asked triumphantly,

'But, you see, I'm just a simple copper,' Woodend continued. 'When I'm treadin' the line between what's confidential an' what isn't, I'm never quite sure whether I've stepped over it or not. That's where you're different, Dr Jenkins. You have a subtlety of mind that's quite lackin' in me.' He paused, and frowned. 'Or maybe I'm wrong. Maybe we're two of a kind, an' it *would* be just as difficult for you as it would be for me.'

The idea of them being 'two of a kind' seemed to truly appall Dr Jenkins.

'I am, of course, willing to help in any way I can,' she said, somewhat hastily, 'though you must be willing to accept that certain areas of Pearl's life within this school cannot be explored.'

'Of course,' Woodend agreed.

'Very well, then. Pearl is an exceptional pupil, both in terms of her sporting prowess and her academic excellence. We expect her to do very well indeed. In fact, a place at either Oxford or Cambridge is certainly not out of the question.'

But the look of distaste was definitely back on the head-mistress's face, Woodend thought, and whatever she might *say*, Dr Jenkins clearly didn't like the fact that a black girl from the slums was doing better than many of her white middle-class pupils.

So if she didn't like it, why did she tolerate it? Why was Pearl even *in* the school?

There was a sudden loud mechanical roar from below, and looking out of the window, Woodend saw that a digger was attacking the tarmac in the corner of the playground.

'Trouble with your drains?' he asked.

Dr Jenkins shot him a disdainful look, as if it was bad taste on his part to even mention drains at all – as if he was expected to believe that the pupils and staff at this fine school didn't have the ordinary, nasty, bodily functions which *required* drains.

'We are in the process of laying the foundations for our new science block,' she said. 'It will be an unpleasant disruption to the scholarly life we are used to here, but there is no choice in the matter, for though we excel in the classics, we must also move with the times.'

Woodend wondered if he should applaud the carefully balanced statement, but decided that even someone as self-absorbed as Dr Jenkins might see it for the sarcasm it was.

'Is Pearl good at science?' he asked.

'As I've already indicated to you, Pearl is good at everything,' the headmistress said.

And the distaste was back on her face again.

'You mentioned sport, earlier. Does she play hockey?'

'Yes, she is a very strong player indeed,' Dr Jenkins said, forcing the words through her teeth.

And one who was not afraid to get hurt playing the game, Woodend thought.

'How strong?' he asked. 'Is she the best player you've got?'

'All things are relative, but I suppose, in a way, she is.'

'So she'll be captain of the team, then?'

'No, not the captain,' Dr Jenkins admitted. 'There is another girl who is more suited to that particular role.'

So that was at least one small triumph that the bigoted Dr Jenkins had been able to deny her.

The sound of the digger outside stopped as abruptly as it had begun, and Dr Jenkins breathed a sigh of relief.

'I don't see why they couldn't just use men with pickaxes, instead of all that noisy machinery,' she said. 'But I suppose they simply can't get the labour any more. Working men don't seem to want to do any actual *work*, these days, do they?'

There speaks a woman who's never wielded a pickaxe in her life, Woodend thought.

He took out his cigarettes, then, seeing the glare in Dr Jenkins's eyes, slipped them back in his pocket again.

'What I find quite surprisin', given her humble background, is that Pearl's a pupil at this school at all,' he said.

'In educational matters, it is talent, not background, which should always prevail,' Dr Jenkins said, though with perhaps not as much conviction as she would have liked.

'Yes, I'm sure talent is very important,' Woodend agreed 'But, when all's said an' done, the education still has to be *paid for*, doesn't it? An' I don't see how Pearl's mother could possibly afford the fees that you must have to charge. That's why I was wonderin' if you'd given her some kind of scholarship.'

'I'm afraid I couldn't possibly comment on that,' Dr Jenkins said stonily.

'Why not?' Woodend wondered. 'If she *is* on a scholarship, it's to both your credit an' hers. Besides,' he added, his voice hardening for the first time in the interview, 'I'm a policeman.'

'I am aware of your position,' Dr Jenkins said, bemused by his sudden change of tone.

'An' *bein'* a policeman, how long do you think it will take me to find out whether or not Pearl's on a scholarship, even if you *don't* choose to tell me?' Woodend continued.

'This school does provide a *number* of scholarships for deserving cases,' Dr Jenkins said, picking her words carefully. 'Pearl is not currently the recipient of one of those scholarships, but were she to apply for one, we would certainly look favourably on that application.'

Oh, absolutely! Woodend thought. I bet you'd be fallin' over yourself to give it to her, you snobby bitch.

'In other words, what you're sayin' is that she never *has* applied for a scholarship?' he asked.

'I did not say that at all,' Dr Jenkins replied, though the expression on her face clearly revealed that she now realized she'd *implied* it.

'So she got her scholarship to this school from some other source,' Woodend mused. 'Was it from some kind of charitable foundation, perhaps?'

'I am not all happy with the direction in which this conversation is now moving,' Dr Jenkins said sternly.

'Now that is strange,' Woodend said. 'Why is it such a secret? I would have thought that philanthropists would like it to be generally known that they're bein' philanthropic. I would have thought anybody who'd given money to a coloured girl from Cannin' Town would have been shoutin' it from the rooftops.'

There was no answer to that, and Dr Jenkins seemed to know it.

She reached out her hand, and stabbed at a large black button at the edge of her desk. Woodend heard a buzzer ring, somewhere beyond the office, and the headmistress's secretary appeared almost immediately.

'Please show this gentleman to the door, Miss Stapleton,' Dr Jenkins said coldly.

Well, at least she's callin' me a gentleman, even if her tone suggests I'm anythin' but, Woodend thought.

He rose to his feet and stretched out his hand. 'Thank you for your time, Dr Jenkins,' he said.

But the headmistress, who was making a great show of reading a document which lay on her desk in front of her, acknowledged neither the hand nor the words.

'If you'd like to follow me,' the secretary said.

'Of course,' Woodend agreed.

As he was leaving the room, the digger started up again. He knew it *shouldn't* have pleased him that the sound would distress the headmistress – but it did.

Six

DC Ted Cotteral was sitting at his desk, his fingers peri-
odically striking one of the keys of his battered typewriter.
Woodend had decided long ago that Cotteral wasn't much of
a detective, but now, watching him from the doorway as he
slowly and agonizingly tip-tapped out his report, it was
becoming apparent that he wasn't much of a typist, either.

There were no other detective constables in the outer office,
and looking across the room, through the open door of the
Wolf's Lair, Woodend noted that DCI Bentley was absent,
too.

Well, there nothing surprising in that, he told himself.
Bentley was famous for sloping off home early, so the fact
that the fat idle bastard was not there now shouldn't bother
him at all.

But it *did* bother him. Or rather it bothered his gut, which
suddenly seemed to be encircled by a tight iron band.

He turned to face Cotteral.

'Any idea where the guv'nor is, Ted?' he asked.

'Shit!' the constable said, looking first at where his index
finger had landed on the keyboard, and then at the key that
it had impelled to strike the page. 'You've just made me
mistype, Sarge.'

'I asked you if you had any idea where the guv'nor is?'
Woodend repeated.

Cotteral reached for his eraser, and began to rub gingerly
at the surface of his report.

'He's in one of the interview rooms, Sarge,' he said, almost
absently.

When he'd been a sergeant in the army, Woodend thought,
he'd never have tolerated this casual attitude from the other
ranks. But then, the army had been different. The officers he'd
served under had had confidence in him, and would have

backed to the hilt whatever action he'd decided to take, whereas
Bentley . . .

'What's the guv'nor *doin'* in the interview room, DC
Cotteral?' he asked. 'Talkin' to a suspect?'

'Not a suspect *as such*,' Cotteral replied. 'He's having a bit
of a chat with a coloured woman.'

The iron band tightened another notch. In later years, when
he had learned to respect his gut more, Woodend would take
it as a certain sign that something had gone seriously wrong.
But for the moment – even though what he'd just heard was
disturbing – he wasn't entirely convinced it was any more
than just acid indigestion.

'A coloured woman?' he repeated. 'Do you happen to know
her name?'

'As a matter of fact, I do.' Cotteral consulted his report.
'She's called Victoria Jones, and she lives at 36 Balaclava
Road, Canning Town.'

'Since you're the one writin' the report, I'm assumin' you're
the one who brought her in.'

'That's right. I was.'

'Are you bein' deliberately bloody minded, DC Cotteral?'
Woodend demanded.

'No, Sarge,' Cotteral said, looking innocent.

'Then tell me who *told you* to bring her in. Did you do it
on the guv'nor's specific instructions?'

Cotteral chuckled. 'Oh, they were certainly his instructions
– and they were definitely *specific* enough.'

Woodend sighed heavily. 'Life is full of choices, Cotteral,
an' I'm about to offer you one,' he said. 'You can either give
me a complete run down on exactly what happened . . .'

'I'm not sure the guv'nor would be happy about me doing
that, Sarge.'

'. . .or you can run the risk of breakin' your bloody neck
when I haul you out of the chair an' throw you across the
room.'

Cotteral blanched. 'Fair enough, Sarge,' he said, after a few
seconds had passed. 'At around half past two, the guv'nor got
a phone call in his office – and that's when things started
happening.'

'Who was this phone call from?'

'I don't know,' Cotteral said. Then, as Woodend started to

move towards him, he shrank back into his chair and continued, 'I swear to you, I don't know. But whoever it was, it had an effect on him, because five seconds after he'd rung off he came tearing out of the Lair like he'd got a red-hot poker up his arse, and said he wanted the woman picking up.'

'Did he tell you *why* he wanted her pickin' up?'

'No, he didn't.'

'But he must have told you what to say to her if she asked why she was bein' brought in.'

'He didn't do that, either,' Cotteral said evasively.

'The choice is still yours,' Woodend growled. 'Tell me what I want to know or find out what it feels like to fly through the air. It's really up to you.'

'He wrote her a note, put it in an envelope, and told me to give it to her,' Cotteral replied sulkily. 'He said once she'd read it, she'd come quietly.'

'What was in the note?'

'I don't know! Bentley had *sealed* the envelope before he gave it to me, and I wasn't going to open it, was I?'

'So what happened once you got to Mrs Jones's house?'

'She didn't want to come with me at first. In fact, she started screaming at me to go away and leave her alone. Then I gave her the guv'nor's note, and it worked just like he'd said it would. She was as meek as a lamb after that.'

'She was as meek as a lamb,' Woodend repeated silently.

Remembering the way she had thrown him out of her house just a few hours earlier, it was hard to imagine her acting *meekly*.

So what had Bentley's note said?

And just *what* game was the chief inspector playing?

Did he think he could solve the murder himself – without even leaving the Yard?

That didn't seem likely – but if it did turn out to be the case that he could, it would certainly be a personal humiliation for his sergeant, who had spent the whole day pounding the streets, and still come up with practically nothing.

Bentley returned an hour later.

'My office,' he barked at Woodend, as he headed for the Wolf's Lair himself.

The sergeant followed him in. Bentley sank back gratefully

into his comfortable chair, but did not invite Woodend to take a seat.

'I've just spent the last two hours talking to a darkie woman by the name of Victoria Jones,' he said.

'Is that right, sir?'

'Yes, it is. And do you know what the first thing she told me was?'

'No, sir.'

'She told me that you'd *already* talked to her.'

'May I ask you where you got her name and address from, sir?' Woodend said. 'Did she phone you herself?'

'Let me ask *you* a question, first,' Bentley countered. 'All right?'

'All right,' Woodend agreed.

'Who's in charge here?'

'You are, sir.'

'So who gets to do the talking, and who gets to do the listening?'

'You get to talk, and I get to listen.'

'And if there are any questions to be asked, who asks them?'

'You do, sir.'

But how *had* Bentley got her address? Woodend wondered.

And what had been in the chief inspector's note which made Victoria Jones agree to come *meekly* to the Yard?

'Are you still with me, Sergeant?' Bentley asked.

'Yes, sir.'

'Good, well, since we seem to have got the question of who's in charge out of the way, let's get back to the matter in hand, shall we? Now, where was I? Oh, yes. You went to see this darkie woman, and blandly informed her that her daughter was dead. And even though she told you, *several times*, that the girl in the picture which you showed her *wasn't* her daughter, you kept insisting that she was. Why was that?'

'Because Mrs Jones wasn't tellin' the truth.'

'And you know that for a fact, do you?'

'Yes, sir.'

'How can you be so sure?'

'Mrs Jones had several photographs of her daughter on the sideboard, and I could see it was the same girl.'

'Oh, for God's sake, is that all you've got to say in your defence?' Bentley exploded.

'Isn't it enough?'

'No, it bloody isn't enough. The girl in the photographs may well have *looked* like the girl in the morgue, but then all darkies look alike *anyway*, don't they?'

'No, sir. Not to me.'

'Of course! I should have known that, shouldn't I?' Bentley said. 'After all, you're so much more sensitive – so much more *intelligent* – than the rest of us. And how would you feel, Sergeant Genius, if I told you that ten minutes after you'd accused Victoria Jones of lying, her daughter rang up to say she was all right.'

'I'd be surprised, sir,' Woodend said.

'Why? Because you think you're so bloody clever that you can never be wrong?'

'Because Mrs Jones doesn't have a phone in her house. Nobody on Balaclava Street does. That was one of the first things I noticed when I was down there.'

There was short pause – perhaps no more than two or three beats – before Bentley said, 'Did I actually tell you that the daughter rang Victoria Jones *at home*?'

'Not in so many words, but—'

'Good. Because, as a matter of fact, that *isn't* where she rang her.'

'No?'

'No. Victoria Jones has a weakness for the drink, you see, Sergeant, and her daughter knows that better than most. So she *also* knows that if she needs to contact her mother during opening hours, all she has to do is ring the local boozer.'

The chief inspector was good, Woodend conceded. Very good!

Most other men would have been quite lost after having being caught out in the first lie, but it had taken only moments for Bentley had come back at him with a story which explained the inconsistency away. But as skilful as the manoeuvre had been, it still didn't make him any *less* of a liar.

'What I've really been doing for the last two hours, Sergeant, is saving your bacon,' Bentley said.

'Savin' my bacon, sir?'

'That's what I said. The woman wanted to lodge a complaint against you. Either that, or take her story to the newspapers. A few years ago, I'd have told her that if she didn't like the

way the police treated her in this country, she could piss off
back to the jungle, where she bloody belongs. But we can't
do that kind of thing these days, because the old order's gone,
and our new masters are all bleeding-heart liberals. So what
did I have to do instead? I had to demean myself by sitting
there and listening to her darkie whining. And when she'd
finished, I had to cajole her into not taking the matter any
further. It stuck in my craw, I can tell you. But I did it. And
not because I like you personally – make no mistake about
it, I don't! – but because, as a point of principle, I stick by
my men, right or wrong.'

Having made his little speech, Bentley sat back in his chair,
no doubt waiting for the effusive thanks that his sergeant was
about to shower on him.

'She'd never have taken it to the police complaints authority
or the newspapers,' Woodend said. 'She couldn't – because
she doesn't have a leg to stand on. Whatever she says, sir, the
girl is *dead*.'

Bentley sighed, almost despairingly. 'I shouldn't expect grat-
itude, should I? Not from a cocky bastard like you. But listen
very carefully to what I have to say next, Sergeant. I don't
care whether or not you still think the girl is dead – you are
not to approach Victoria Jones again *under any circumstances*.'

'But I don't see how I can continue my investigation if I'm
not allowed to—'

'It isn't *your* investigation any more, Sergeant. I'm reas-
signing you – as of right now – to the Waterman's Arms
murder.'

'The Waterman's Arms murder?' Woodend repeated, mystified.

'Yes, it's a pub – in case you haven't managed to work that
out for yourself,' Bentley said, with heavy sarcasm.

'I know it's a pub,' Woodend replied. 'It's just off Tooley
Street.'

And a very rough pub it was, he thought.

'What I *don't* know,' he continued, 'is anythin' about a
murder.'

'Then let me enlighten you,' Bentley said. 'This afternoon,
just before closing time, a man was murdered in the
Waterman's Arms. That makes it a case for the police, don't
you think?'

'Yes, sir.'

'And since *you* claim to be a policeman, I thought you might be willing – if it's not *too* much trouble – to look into it yourself. DC Cotteral already has all the details, and if you ask him nicely, I'm sure he'll show them to you.'

'But if I'm involved in this new case, who's going to be investigatin' the Pearl Jones's murder?'

'Not that that's really any of your business, but I'll tell you anyway,' Bentley said. 'I'll be taking personal charge of the Pearl Jo— of the dead black girl's murder, myself.'

'Then perhaps I should brief you on what I've—' Woodend began.

'In my experience, when you're taking over a case that some other bugger has already made a serious hash of, the best thing you can do is start again from scratch,' Bentley interrupted him.

'I just think—'

'I know you bloody do! You think *far too much* for my liking. And now, DS Woodend, you can get out – because I'm sick of the sight of you.'

Woodend sat at his desk, studying the newly opened file on the murder in the Waterman's Arms. It was a typical docklands killing, and it made depressing – if all too familiar reading.

Twice, in the previous few minutes, he had contemplated handing in his resignation. The second time, he'd even taken a sheet of notepaper from his drawer on which to draft it.

'But I can't just resign,' he argued silently. 'I have responsibilities. I have a wife and child to support.'

Yet even as he was making the argument, there was a part of his brain which acknowledged that he wasn't being honest with himself.

Yes, he did have responsibilities, but he was well regarded back in Whitebridge, and it would not be long before he landed some kind of job there.

And true, he would probably not be earning as much back home as he did in London, but then it didn't cost nearly as much to live in the North. Even on a much lower wage, he'd be able to provide better accommodation for his family in Whitebridge than he could ever hope to provide in London.

And to top it all, he genuinely did *miss* the North, and was itching to get back there.

So what was really stopping him from writing that letter of resignation, he admitted, was Pearl Jones.

As a coloured girl attending a posh, all-white school, Pearl must have had things tough. Woodend didn't know how the other girls at the school had treated her – though he did know she'd had one good friend, at least, the blonde girl in the photograph – but if the headmistress had resented her getting on, the chances were that other people had followed her lead, and resented it too.

Yet Pearl had persevered. More than *persevered* – she had *triumphed*.

In another year or so, she could well have found herself studying at Oxford or Cambridge. And who was to say what she might have achieved after that? She could have become a famous writer or a brilliant scientist. She might have found a cure for a deadly disease, or spent her life fighting for the rights of the other coloured people she had left behind her.

And because of all the effort she had made – the struggles she had endured and the courage with which she'd faced them – she deserved better treatment than she'd been getting, even in death.

If *he* didn't try to get justice for Pearl, then who would, he asked himself.

And what chance did he have of getting that justice for her if he handed in his warrant card now?

Seven

The man who sat facing Woodend across the interview-room table went by the name of Jed Horrocks. He was forty-five years old, and had a square, muscular build. His nose had been broken at some time in the past, and there was a long, vivid scar over his right eye, which was probably the result of a knife or bottle fight. He was clearly a hard man, which, Woodend thought, was a very necessary job qualification for anyone wishing to run a pub like the Waterman's Arms.

For perhaps a minute after he'd entered the room, Horrocks simply glared at the newly arrived sergeant, then he said, 'You ain't got no right to keep me here.'

'As a matter of fact, we have,' Woodend told him, sitting down. 'You're what we call a "material witness".' He turned to the uniformed constable who was standing by the door. 'Isn't that right, Constable?'

'Definitely, Sarge,' the constable agreed.

''Ow can I be *any* kind o' witness when I don't know nuffink at all?' Horrocks grumbled.

'You'll excuse me if I say that I think you're talkin' complete bollocks, won't you?' Woodend asked.

'Fink wot yer want.'

'Let's just consider what happened this afternoon,' Woodend suggested. 'There was in a fight in your pub. Correct?'

'I suppose there must 'ave been.'

'You *suppose* there must have been? Are you sayin' that you somehow managed to avoid seein' it?'

'Yeah, that's right. When whatever 'appened, 'appened, I was in the cellar, bringing up a crate of bottles.'

'So, in this fight which you *didn't* see, a man called Wally Booth was punched in the face, an' knocked to the ground. Now the beatin' he'd received wouldn't normally have killed him. But when he fell, he banged his head on the brass foot-rail running along the front of the bar – and that did for him. Correct?'

'Can't say, 'cos I wasn't there and I ain't no doctor. All I *do* know is that when I come up from the cellar, he was lying on the floor.'

'And apart from the dead man, the bar was empty?'

'Yeah.'

'So you called the police?'

Horrocks smirked. 'Of course I did. It was my duty as a law-abiding citizen.'

'And when the local Old Bill arrived, you were unable to give them the names of any of the customers who'd been drinkin' in the bar just prior to Wally Booth's death?'

'That's right. They were all complete strangers to me. I didn't know any of 'em from Adam.'

'In fact, not only didn't you know them, but you couldn't even *describe* a single one of them to the officers?'

Horrocks shrugged – though scarcely apologetically. 'I've never been very good wiv faces.'

Woodend slammed his fist down – hard – on the table. The action would have made most men jump, but Horrocks didn't even blink.

'You're pissin' me about!' Woodend said. 'If there's one thing that every pub landlord has to have, it's a good memory for faces. It's part of the job, for God's sake.'

Horrocks grinned. 'Maybe they do, and maybe it is,' he said. 'All I can tell yer is that I'm the exception wot proves the rule.'

'An' anyway, the place can't have been filled with strangers,' Woodend continued. 'Pubs like yours don't depend on passin' trade for their business – what they rely on is a hard core of regular boozers. Which is why I'm willin' to bet that you knew every single feller who was in your place this afternoon.'

'You're wrong,' Horrocks said flatly.

'I could charge you with bein' an accessory after the fact, you know, Horrocks,' Woodend threatened.

'Then charge me, if that's what yer want to do,' the landlord said indifferently. 'But yer'll never make it stick.'

Woodend sighed. 'Do you think a few more hours in the cells might serve to jog Jed's memory?' he asked the constable stationed at the door.

'Could do, Sarge,' the constable said.

'Then you'd better take him back there, hadn't you?'

Horrocks stood up. 'Once my brief gets on the case, he'll have me out of here in no time at all,' he said confidently.

And he was probably dead right about that, Woodend thought, as he watched the constable escort Horrocks out into the corridor – because while it was as clear as daylight that he was lying, it would be almost *impossible* to prove it.

So how should he go about conducting this investigation, the sergeant asked himself, as he lit up a Capstan Full Strength.

Questioning the landlord again would be a complete waste of time. Horrocks would never crack, and though he'd just gone through the motions of interrogating the bloody man, he'd realized that the moment he'd seen him across the interview room.

So what *would* it take to get a result?

One thing, and one thing only! It would take one of the customers who had been there at the time of Booth's death to come forward and start naming names – and that was simply never going to happen!

But then, Woodend suspected, this sudden reassignment of his didn't actually have much to do with the Waterman's Arms murder anyway. Instead, it had been a convenient way of removing from the Pearl Jones case the one man who seemed interested in finding her killer!

The Crown and Anchor pub was on the corner, at the southern end of Balaclava Street. From the outside it reeked of neglect, and Woodend guessed that the brewery was only holding on to it until the government was once again rich enough – whenever *that* might be! – to buy it with a compulsory purchase order, and pull it down.

The inside of the pub matched its exterior perfectly. The paint was cracked, the wallpaper was peeling, and the ceiling was browned with generations of nicotine stains. There was a battered piano up against one of the walls, but no one was playing it, and Woodend doubted if it was even still playable.

Yet despite all this, the landlord was a cheery, amenable soul – the sort of landlord who prevented fights not by being a hard man himself, but by somehow managing to remind those customers intent on violence of their favourite uncle, who would be disappointed in them if they behaved badly.

Woodend ordered a pint of best bitter, then showed the landlord his warrant card, and said, 'I'd like to ask you a few questions about one of your regular customers.'

'Oh yes? And which particular customer might that be?'

'Mrs Victoria Jones.'

The landlord smiled ruefully. 'She's no customer of mine.'

'Really? I was told she was.'

'Victoria Jones is a strict Methodist,' the landlord said. 'As far as she's concerned, what I sell is the devil's potion.'

'So she's never been in here?'

'She wouldn't even *think* of setting foot in the temple of the arch-fiend.'

Woodend grinned. 'Is that what this place is? The temple of the arch-fiend? I didn't know that.'

'Neither did I – till I read it in one of the pamphlets she's forever sliding under my front door.'

'*Victoria Jones has a weakness for the drink, you see,*' DCI Bentley had said.

Bloody liar!

'So if I want to learn more about Mrs Jones, I'm talkin' to the wrong person, am I?' Woodend asked the landlord.

'Couldn't be talking to a much wronger one,' the other man agreed. 'But if you want to talk to the *right* person, she's over there.'

He was pointing at a woman sitting in the corner of the bar. She was old, and so small she could have been mistaken for a child, but for her heavily wrinkled face. She was wearing a purple beret and was wrapped up in a heavy, old-fashioned coat which could just as easily have been a carpet as an article of clothing. There was a glass of milk stout in front of her, and occasionally she would lift it to her mouth and take a bird-like sip.

'I have to tell you, she doesn't *look* like she'd be much help to me,' Woodend said doubtfully.

'Don't be fooled by appearances,' the landlord told him. 'Round here, everybody calls her Lene.'

'Lene?'

'After Windowlene – you know, the stuff that you use to make your panes of glass sparkle.'

'So she spends a lot of time sittin' at her front window, does she?' Woodend asked, getting the point.

'When she's not in this pub, she's at that window of hers. She don't miss much that's going on. And, you may be interested to learn, she just happens to live directly opposite Victoria Jones's house.'

'I'm *very* interested to learn that,' Woodend agreed.

With a pint of bitter in one hand, and a glass of milk stout in the other, Woodend made his way across to the old woman's table.

'Do you mind if I asked you a few questions?' he said, placing the milk stout in front of her.

'Wot about?' the old woman replied.

'About Victoria Jones,' Woodend said.

'She's a darkie,' Lene told him, in a tone which suggested there was nothing more to be said on the subject.

'An' you don't like darkies?'

'Nuffink against them – as long as they stay in their own country.' Lene took a sip of her drink. 'I will say this, though – that girl of hers is all right. Always willing to lend me a 'elping hand when I need it.'

'Do you see much of what goes on with the family?' Woodend wondered.

'Are you accusing me of being a nosey parker?' Lene demanded.

'No, of course I'm not,' Woodend said hastily. 'It's just that, living opposite them as you do, there'll have been times when you'll have been bound to see things, whether you intended to or not.'

'What kind of fings?'

What kind, indeed? Woodend wondered.

'Anythin' unusual,' he said.

Lene thought about it for some time. 'Well, o' course, there is the motor car,' she said finally.

'What about it?'

'Big black shiny thing, it is. Don't belong to nobody wot lives round here. Much too expensive.'

Woodend waited for her to say more on the subject, but it soon became plain that she wasn't going to.

'So what's special about this car?' he asked. 'Does it sometimes pick the Joneses up from their home?'

'Now why would it want to do that?' Lene wondered.

'Then what *does* it do?'

'It just sits there.'

'Where?'

'On the street.'

Woodend suppressed a sigh. 'So what has this car got to do with the Jones family?' he asked.

'Well, it's only there in the early morning and late afternoon, ain't it?'

'You've lost me again,' Woodend confessed.

Lene looked at him pityingly.

'It's only there when the girl is eiver going to school or coming back from it,' she said.

Woodend felt a tiny shock of excitement run through his body, making his fingertips tingle.

'How many people are usually in the car?'

'Just the one. A man.'

'An' could you describe him to me?'

'He wears a big 'at.'

'Is that all?'

'It's all I can see from my *winder*. Like I said, it's a very *big* 'at.'

'How often does this car turn up? Every day?'

'No, nuffink like that. Sometimes I don't see it for weeks on end.'

For weeks on end! Woodend repeated to himself.

So whoever had been watching Pearl Jones hadn't just started doing it recently.

'How long has this been goin' on?' he asked. 'Months?'

Lene gave him a look which was even more pitying than the last one. 'Months?' she said. 'Yer must be joking!'

'Then how long has he been comin'?'

'Bloody hell, it must 'ave been *years*!'

The Conway Club had no sign over its entrance to announce its existence, since the management had long ago decided that if you didn't already know it was there, then it probably wasn't for you anyway. Its customers were mostly journalists who plied their trade in nearby Fleet Street – hard-drinking men who lived under the constant pressure of deadlines. Ladies – of *any* sort – were generally discouraged.

It was at the bar of the Conway Club that Tom Townshend was sitting, a ten-year-old malt whisky in one hand and a Craven A cigarette in the other. He was aware that other hacks kept glancing at him, some with looks of pure admiration on their faces, some with expressions which burned with deep envy – and he didn't give a damn about any of it.

Townshend had started out his career as a cub reporter on his local newspaper, and, but for the War, would probably have been perfectly content to carry on covering christenings, weddings, and jam-making competitions at the local Women's Institute, until the day he retired. The Normandy landings had changed all that. He had seen his comrades die in ways it was too horrendous even to describe. He had killed men he didn't even know, but who, he suspected, were just as decent and ordinary as he was himself. And he had faced death himself on numerous occasions, and had come to understand that if a certain bullet had been two inches further to the left, or if a certain German soldier had swung his bayonet just a little quicker, he would have ceased to be.

And so it had been a new Tom Townshend who had walked though the gates of the army camp in his demob suit – a Tom Townshend who had learned to value life, and was determined to make his mark on it.

It had taken him just four years to go from junior reporter on the *Daily Globe* to its crime editor, he reflected, as he sipped at his whisky. And that did not have to be the end of it. Many of those who knew him saw even this as just one small step in his inevitable rise – and who was he to disagree?

He felt a light tap on his shoulder, and turned to see the big man in the hairy sports coat who was standing next to him.

'A pint of your best bitter, Horace,' he called to the barman. 'And since it's for one of our friends from the North, you'd be well advised to make sure it's got a good head on it.'

'Good to see you, Tom,' Woodend said, holding out his hand.

'Good to see you, Charlie,' Townshend replied, taking it. 'But I assume you're not here by chance.'

'No, I'm not,' Woodend agreed.

'So to what *do* we owe the honour of your presence amongst us? It can't be to re-fight old battles, since we've already clearly established that it's only because of the efforts of Sergeant Charlie Woodend and Corporal Tom Townshend that Adolf Hitler isn't living in Buckingham Palace today.'

Woodend grinned. 'You always did exaggerate the part we played in the War,' he said. 'Me, I'm more realistic. I believe that even without us, the Allies could probably still have won.'

Townshend returned the grin. 'Why don't you tell me what it is you want, Charlie?' he suggested.

Woodend took the picture of the dead girl out of his pocket, and laid it on the bar. 'She was killed last night,' he said. 'No one's claimed the body yet.'

Townshend shook his head. 'Poor little bugger,' he said sadly. 'I take it that you'd like me to print her picture in the paper?'

'That's right.'

'And what sort of headline would you like? Something on the lines of "Do you know this girl?" '

'Yes.'

'Well, if it'll help you to put a name to the face, I'd be glad to do it,' Townshend told him.

'Actually, I already know who she is,' Woodend confessed.

'Then why . . .?'

'Because other people know, too – only they won't admit it. But once her picture's been printed – an' once you get a couple of dozen calls identifyin' her – they won't have any choice but to acknowledge the truth, now will they?'

Eight

There were three detective constables already at their desks when Woodend arrived at the office the next morning, but two of them were busily pretending to be absorbed in their work, and it was only DC Cotteral, with an unpleasant smirk on his face, who seemed willing to even acknowledge the sergeant's presence in the room.

'Did you happen to glance at the morning papers on your way to work, Sarge?' Cotteral asked.

'No,' Woodend replied. 'I didn't.'

'Not even the *Globe*?'

'Not even the *Globe*.'

'Well, the guv'nor's seen it,' Cotteral said, as his smirk widened. 'Oh yes, he's seen it, all right. And now he wants to see *you*!'

The chief inspector was sitting at his desk, with a copy of the *Globe* spread in front of him. When Woodend entered his office, he picked up the paper with his left hand, and pointed to the picture of Pearl Jones, prominently displayed on the front page, with his right index finger.

'That's the dead darkie,' he said, unnecessarily. 'Do you happen to know, Sergeant Woodend, how this hack — ' he glanced at the by-line – 'how this hack, Townshend, managed to get hold of the picture?'

'No, sir,' Woodend said, forcing himself to do his best to sound convincing – but not giving a damn that he was failing.

'Yes, I'd be very interested indeed to know how he got his hands on it,' Bentley mused. 'Come to think of it, you had a copy of the photo yourself, didn't you, Sergeant?'

'I did, sir,' Woodend agreed. 'But then so did the morgue. In fact, I'd imagine that the morgue had *more than* one copy.'

'Suppose I was to ask to see your copy right now,' Bentley said. 'Could you show it to me?'

'I'm not sure I could, sir,' Woodend admitted. 'In fact, now I think about it, I'm almost sure I threw it away when you took me off the case.'

'How convenient,' Bentley said. 'Well, I suppose you must be feeling like a real smart-arse this morning, mustn't you, Sergeant?'

'I beg your pardon, sir?'

'Don't try playing the innocent with me,' Bentley growled. 'Ever since the paper hit the streets, the switchboard's been jammed with callers identifying the darkie in the picture as Pearl Jones. Which means, doesn't it, that you were right all along?'

'Yes, sir, I suppose it does.'

'But much more important than any petty feeling of triumph you might have, it means that the mother *lied* to me. To *me*!'

'She does seem to have done,' Woodend agreed.

'But she's not the *only one* who's made a fool of me,' Bentley continued. 'By handing that picture over to the *Globe* – and there's no point in denying it was you, because I won't believe it – *you've* made a fool of me, too.'

There was no logic to that argument, Woodend thought, but then logic had never been one of Bentley's strong points.

'Does it really matter *who* gave the picture to the newspaper, sir?' he asked. 'Isn't the important thing that it's clearly established, once an' for all, who the dead girl is?'

'Of course that's the important thing,' Bentley agreed gracelessly, and without a great deal of conviction. 'But the authorization to print it should have come from me, not from some young copper who was still in shitty nappies when I first started collaring villains.'

But you *didn't* authorize it, Woodend thought. And I don't think you ever *would have* authorized it.

'Victoria Jones has made me look bollock-brained,' Bentley said. 'A *nigger* has made me look bollock-brained. Well, it won't be long before she starts to feel sorry she ever did *that*. Because the kid gloves are off, as far as I'm concerned – and within an hour or so, I'll have her spilling the beans.'

'Spilling *what* beans?' Woodend asked, before he could stop himself.

'What beans do you think I mean, you moron?' Bentley asked. 'She's been up to her sweaty armpits in something very bent, and it's more than likely that her daughter was involved in it, too.'

'I don't think it *is* likely at all, sir,' Woodend said. 'According to Pearl's headmistress, she was a—'

'Did I ask for a comment from you, Sergeant?' Bentley interrupted.

'No, sir.'

'Then keep your trap zipped until I tell you that you can speak. As I was saying, the kid was probably involved in some shady business or other, which was why she was killed. And look at *how* she was killed! With a razor! That's a typical underworld weapon!' Bentley paused. 'You should have told me the murder weapon was a razor, Sergeant. If I'd known about the criminal connection earlier, I'd probably have had this case sewn up by now.'

'I *did* tell you,' Woodend protested. 'When I briefed you yesterday morning, one of the first things I said was that—'

'Don't you dare contradict me, Sergeant!'

'No, sir.'

'And I will *not* be lectured to about how to conduct a complex case by a man who seems completely incapable of conducting even a simple one,' Bentley said. 'Or am I wrong about that? Have you already arrested Booth's murderer?'

'You know I haven't.'

'Do I?' Bentley asked. 'You didn't tell me about the razor, so why should I assume that you'd tell me about making an arrest? After all, why I should I need to know? I'm only your *guv'nor!*'

Woodend said nothing.

'Are you, in any way, shape or form, on top of the case I've assigned you, Sergeant?' Bentley wondered. 'Did you even know that the landlord of the Waterman's Arms has been released?'

'I imagined he would have been by now.'

'That's not what I asked. Did you actually *know?*'

'No, sir, I didn't.'

Bentley shook his head, despairingly. 'Do you know what the real trouble with you smart-arses is?' he asked. 'It's not that you're cocky and self-righteous, although that's bad enough – the real trouble is that you're not *half* as smart as you think you are.'

Wally Booth had a long criminal record. But there were no surprises there, Woodend thought, as he skimmed through the file at his desk. In fact, since it was highly probable that he'd been a regular patron of the Waterman's Arms, it would only have been surprising if he *hadn't* had any form.

Booth's criminal career had begun in the 1930s. He'd been a cat burglar at the outset of it, but – like many young men with the ambition to get on in their chosen profession – he'd soon graduated to smash-and-grab raids.

It was during one of these raids – on a jeweller's premises on Bond Street – that he'd first come seriously unstuck. The car which the gang had been using for their getaway had stalled not thirty yards from the shop, and Booth had been arrested and given a two-year stretch for his part in the raid.

When he'd been released, in May 1942, he found that the reception committee waiting for him at the gates took the form of two military policemen, who immediately handed him his call-up papers and informed him he was in the army now.

Booth's military career had been neither long nor glorious. After only two days in an army camp near Bradford, he'd done a runner, and headed straight back to London, which – according to an old lag called Ozzie Phelps, who Woodend had once been handcuffed to in the anteroom of the Bow Street Magistrates' Court – had been a thieves' paradise during the War years.

'He did a good job for us, did ole Adolf Hitler,' Phelps had said. 'It was 'cos of his bombing raids that we 'ad the blackout in London, yer see, which is the finest fing that ever 'appened to a burglar. Yer didn't 'ave to worry about the street lights any more, 'cos there *wasn't* no street lights. And making yer getaway was a lot easier in the dark.'

'It must have been,' Woodend agreed.

'And then, o' course, there was the police themselves. Before the War, they could be shit hot – when they put their minds to it. But see, all the younger coppers were called up, and the only ones left were the ones wot was too old for military service. Well, us young lads could run rings round ole blokes like that, couldn't we?'

'It must have seemed as if all your birthdays had come at once.'

'Exac'ly. But that wasn't even the best part. The best part was the *black market*. See, by 1942, almost everyfink was rationed, and stuff wot 'adn't even been worf nicking before was suddenly like gold. I knew blokes wot would 'ave considered it beneaf their dignity, *before* the War, to steal anyfink uvver than jewels. But it didn't take them long to realize that there was good money to be made from 'aving it away with chests of tea, 'cos there was always a market for them. Then again, faces 'oo'd only dealt in fur coats before, found they could sell any coats – even cheap ones – for top dollar. I tell yer, they was real good times.'

'An' didn't it bother you, even for a minute, that there was a war goin' on at the time?' Woodend wondered.

'Look, we should all do wot we're best at,' Phelps reasoned. 'We'd never 'ad made good soldiers, 'cos we wouldn't take orders, but we was very good at nicking fings. In a way, we was like Robin Hood and his Merry Men.'

'Stealing from the rich an' *sellin'* to the poor?' Woodend asked.

'That's right,' Ozzie agreed, completely failing to see the irony.

'An' you never got caught?'

'Not once. O' course, there was always the *risk* of getting nabbed – the Flyin' Squad 'ad the job of rounding up blokes wot 'ad decided to leave the army . . .'

'You mean deserters?' Woodend asked.

'If yer like. Anyway, they used to raid the pubs that blokes like me used regular, but they never got their 'ands on ole Ozzie.'

Wally Booth hadn't been quite so lucky. He'd been caught by the Squad one afternoon in 1944 and handed over to the army, but before then he'd had what he would probably have described himself as a 'good run'.

On arriving back in London in '42, Booth had immediately contacted 'Greyhound Ron' Smithers – a man who'd earned his nickname not for being fleet of foot, but because of his weakness for the dog track, and who had been the kingpin of the black market at the time. Smithers had welcomed his new recruit with open arms, and for the next two years Booth had distributed forged ration tickets, shifted lorry loads of stolen eggs, and sold petrol which, if it hadn't 'fallen off' a lorry, had certainly been siphoned from one.

Even after his recapture, Booth was not forced to fight for King and country. The army had decided he'd never have the makings of a soldier, so had simply charged him with desertion and locked him up in the glass house for two years.

Released in 1946, Booth had once again joined Smithers's gang, which was still going strong, though now – with more and more things coming off the ration – it had largely moved out of the black market and into the protection racket.

Woodend lit a cigarette, and scanned the list of Booth's known associates. He saw Greyhound Ron's name and recognized two or three others, but never having worked in the Serious Crimes Squad himself, most of them were unknown to him.

So where should he start his investigation? he asked himself.

It was possible that one of those named on this list had been drinking with Booth when he met his death, and – after battling with whatever conscience he had – would feel compelled to come forward and name the killer. Possible, but unlikely – especially if the man who had actually *caused* Booth's death had been a face.

Woodend reached over to his already overflowing ashtray, and angrily stubbed out his cigarette.

The simple fact was that he didn't really *care* who had killed Wally Booth. But he *did* care about who had killed Pearl Jones, and he was far from ready to leave the investigation of her death in the hands of DCI Bentley.

The door of the Wolf's Lair suddenly swung violently open, and the chief inspector stormed through it like a full-blown tornado.

'Did you tip her off?' he bawled at Woodend, across the room.

'Tip who off, sir?'

'The darkie! Mrs Victoria bloody Jones. Did you tell her I was going to have her picked up?'

'No, sir.'

'Well, that is strange, isn't it?' asked Bentley, who had drawn level with Woodend's desk, and now seemed to be fighting hard against the urge to smash his sergeant in the face. 'Because, you see, Sergeant Woodend, when DC Cotteral got to her house, she was nowhere to be found.'

'She could have gone out shoppin',' Woodend suggested.

'Do you think I'm a complete bloody idiot, Sergeant?' Bentley demanded.

Yes, sir, Woodend thought.

'No, sir,' he said aloud.

'Because actually it *did* occur to me, when Cotteral phoned and told me that she wasn't answering her door, to think that she might have gone shopping. It also occurred to me that since Cotteral had a search warrant in his pocket, it would be a pity to waste it. So I told him to jemmy the door, and go inside. But, as it turned out, he didn't *have to* jemmy it, because the door wasn't locked.'

'I see,' Woodend said.

'Do you, indeed?' Bentley hectored. 'And can you guess what I told Cotteral to do once he *was* inside?'

'You told him to go straight upstairs, and have a look through her bedroom chest of drawers?'

'I told him to go straight upstairs and have a look through her bedroom chest of drawers,' Bentley agreed. 'And guess what? The chest of drawers was empty! So what do you conclude from that, Sergeant?'

'That's she's gone away.'

'Exactly! And is there any significance to the fact that she didn't lock her door before she left?'

'Yes, sir.'

'And what significance might that be?'

'Nobody leaves their front doors unlocked – especially in an area like Canning Town.'

'And why is that?'

'Because they know that if they do, they'll find the house stripped when they get back.'

'So?'

'So she isn't *going* back.'

'Sherlock Holmes is not dead,' Bentley said, with heavy sarcasm. 'He lives on, in the form of Detective Sergeant Charlie Woodend.' He leant over, and put his hands on Woodend's desk. 'Look me in the eyes, and tell me you weren't the one who tipped off Victoria Jones,' he ordered.

Woodend did as he'd been instructed. 'I did not tip off Victoria Jones,' he said.

'Then who *did*?' Bentley wondered.

'I don't know,' Woodend said.

But he was certainly going to do his damnedest to find out.

Nine

T hroughout the length and breadth of London, much the same things were happening everywhere – men were already at work, women were busy cleaning their houses, and children were sitting behind their desks at school. But Balaclava Street was in this way – as in so many others – different. On this street, the men slept late, dragging themselves from their pits just in time to reach the pub's front door for opening time, the women wouldn't have recognized housework if it had hit them in the face, and the children went to school only when their parents were threatened with fines by truancy officers.

And yet, Woodend thought as he walked up the street, there was, in the middle of all this decay and desperation, a small oasis of tidiness and order – the home that Victoria Jones had made for herself and her dead daughter.

He drew level with Lene's house, and was just reaching for the door knocker when the door itself swung open.

'Shaw yer coming up the shtreet,' Lene said.

Of course she had, Woodend thought, and noted that though she kept her purple beret on, even when she was at home, she had no such qualms about her false teeth.

Lene led him into her front parlour. There was an armchair positioned right by the window, and though the window itself was sparkling clean, the rest of the room smelled of neglect and indifference.

'Yer mished all the excitement,' Lene told him, as she offered him a seat on her ratty two-seater sofa.

Woodend sat down gingerly, but not gingerly enough to avoid a cloud of dust and dubious odours from engulfing him.

'The excitement?' he repeated. 'You're talkin' about the policeman, are you?'

'Wot policeman?'

'The one who went into Mrs Jones's house, about an hour ago.'

'Oh, 'e was a copper, was 'e?' Lene asked. 'I didn't know that.'

'So who did you think he was?'

'I fort he might 'ave been a burglar.'

'So you called the Old Bill, did you?' Woodend asked, already suspecting he knew the answer.

'I didn't call them *as such*,' Lene admitted.

'Meanin' you didn't call them *at all*?'

Lene shrugged indifferently. 'It wasn't none of my business, was it?' she asked. 'Besides, if I 'ad called 'em, I'd just 'ave been wasting police time, 'cos when he came out of the 'ouse 'e was carrying no more in 'is 'ands than 'e 'ad when 'e went in,' she added, in her own defence.

There was something not quite right about this conversation they were having, Woodend thought – something about the woman's whole attitude which jarred.

And then he had it!

Lene, whose entire life revolved around watching what went on outside her window, should have been thrilled to learn that the man who had entered Victoria Jones's house was a policeman. She should have been absolutely bursting with questions about why he had gone to the house, and what he had found there.

But she wasn't.

Which could only mean one thing – that Cotteral's visit had been little more than an anticlimax. That something far more exciting had preceded it.

'Would you like to tell me about what happened *before* the copper turned up?' he asked Lene.

'Gawd Almighty, I fort yer'd never ask,' Lene replied. 'What 'appened was that that big black car wot I told yer about come back again.'

'The one driven by the man who watched Pearl?'

'That's right. Only, it didn't park furver down the street, like wot it usually does. This time, it pulled up right in front of that darkie's 'ouse.'

'An' was the same man in it?'

'There was *two* men, this time. And I don't fink neiver of 'em was the man wot usually comes.'

'What did they look like?'

'They was big blokes, wiv their 'ats pulled down over their eyes.'

'So how do you know one of them wasn't the man who usually comes?'

''E's smaller. There's a few inches between 'is 'ead and the roof of the car, but these two was scraping it with theirs.'

I wish all witnesses were like you, Lene, Woodend thought.

'What did these two men do?'

'They knocked on the door, o' course, and when the Jones woman answered it, they barged straight in.'

'You're sure about that, are you, Lene? You're absolutely certain that she didn't *invite* them in?'

'Invite 'em in? I should say not! The first one pushed straight past 'er, an' nearly knocked 'er flying. Then the second one sort o' jostled 'er inside, and closed the door behind 'im.'

'An' what happened next?'

'About ten minutes later, the door opened again, and one of the men stepped out onto the pavement. 'E 'ad a suitcase in 'is 'and, 'e puts the suitcase in the boot, then gets inside the car and starts the engine. Once it's running, 'e gets *out* again, and looks up and down the street, like 'e's making sure there's nobody about. Then 'e makes a "come on" sign with 'is 'and. That's when the uvvers come out of the 'ouse.'

'Mrs Jones an' the second man?'

'Course, it was them. 'Oo did you *fink* I'm talking about? King George and Queen Elizabeff?'

Woodend grinned. 'No, that would have been unlikely,' he admitted.

'Anyway, this second bloke is 'olding on to the darkie's arm. 'E ain't exactly *dragging* 'er, if yer see what I mean. It's more like 'e's guiding 'er. 'E leads 'er over to the motor car and opens the back door. 'E points into the car, and she gets inside. 'E follows 'er, and then the one in front drives away.'

'So you think she was reluctant to go with them, but not *that* reluctant?' Woodend suggested.

Lene looked at him as if he'd suddenly started speaking to her in an exotic foreign language.

'Yer wot?' she asked.

'She wasn't exactly keen on gettin' in the car, but she didn't fight against it, either,' Woodend rephrased.

'No, she didn't fight against it,' Lene agreed. 'If yer ask me, she was too bleeding terrified to fight.'

The Royal Albert public house was on Rotherhithe New Road. With its sign hanging over the main entrance and the name of the brewery etched in its frosted-glass windows, it was, in theory, like any other pub in the area. In practice, however, the only people who entered it were those who had been invited to do so, and the two men standing in the doorway – one big, and the other *very* big – were there to ensure that this practice continued to be observed.

When Woodend showed the two men his warrant card, and asked to speak to Greyhound Ron, the bouncers looked less than impressed.

'Mr Smivvers is a very busy man,' one of them said.

''E don't even 'ave the time to speak to chief superintendents, never mind detective *sergeants*,' the other added.

'I could get a search warrant,' Woodend pointed out.

The bouncers thought this was hilarious. 'Ain't you 'eard?' the bigger one asked. 'Mr Smivvers is *fireproof*.'

It was probably true, Woodend thought. He had, earlier in his career, taken a conscious decision to avoid having anything to do with the Serious Crime Squad himself, because it was well known – though impossible to prove – that just as big-time criminals like Smithers offered their "protection" to small businesses, there were men high up in the Met, who, for a fee, would protect the protectors.

'I'm not here tryin' to nail Smithers,' he said.

The bouncers laughed again. 'Well, I'm sure 'e'll be very relieved to 'ear *that*,' the bigger one said.

''E's been losing sleep at nights at the fort of you turning up at his door, one day,' the other added.

Woodend smiled. 'I do like a good comedy double act,' he said.

The bigger bouncer smirked. 'We aim ter please,' he said.

'But if I wanted to see clowns in action, I'd go to the circus an' see the professionals,' the sergeant added.

The big bouncer's smirk vanished. ''Ang on, are yer saying we're a pair o' clowns?' he demanded.

'I'm sayin' that I want to see Greyhound Ron,' Woodend

replied. 'An' while I can't *make* him see me, I *can* make you *ask* if he'll see me.'

'You reckon?' the big bouncer asked aggressively.

'I reckon,' Woodend agreed. 'Because while your boss might be fireproof, I could burn the pair of you easily, if I put my mind to it.'

'That sounds like a fret,' the bigger bouncer said.

'Does it?' Woodend asked. 'Well, you should know, because makin' threats is somethin' you *are* good at.'

The bouncers exchanged glances, then the bigger one said, 'Wot 'ave I got ter tell 'im yer want to see 'im about?'

'Tell him I want to see him about Wally Booth.'

The bouncer nodded, almost as if that was exactly what he'd *expected* the sergeant to say.

'Wait 'ere,' he told Woodend.

Greyhound Ron Smithers was sitting at a table in the corner of the bar of the Royal Albert. There was a brassy blonde talking to him as Woodend walked in, but Smithers jerked his thumb in the direction of a door at the back of the room, and the blonde obediently headed towards it.

Given his nickname, Woodend had expected him to be a slightly less seedy version of the thousands of punters who crowded into the White City to watch the dogs run, but Smithers bore no resemblance to them at all.

He was a big man, in his late thirties or early forties, and was dressed in a sharp suit, which, whilst it might have just stepped over the line separating good taste from flashiness, was undoubtedly top quality. He had thick black hair, and his dark eyes were either intelligent or cunning – or perhaps both. His nose was slightly out of kilter, his mouth tight and his chin square and forceful. Overall, he gave the impression of being a handsome man – if handsome in a *brutal* sort of way.

Smithers gestured Woodend to take a seat.

'I wouldn't normally waste my time talking to—' he began.

'I know,' Woodend interrupted, 'I've already had all that patter from your two goons stationed outside.'

'Wot patter?'

'That you're a very busy man, that you only usually speak to coppers above the rank of chief superintendent, etc., etc. So since you *are* such a busy man, can we take it as read that

I feel highly honoured to have been granted an audience with you, an' then just get on with the business in hand.'

'I will say this for yer – yer've got some balls on yer!' Smithers said.

'Two of them, to be exact,' Woodend replied. 'I used to kid myself they were world-championship size, but the police doctor tells me they're only slightly larger than average.'

For a moment it looked as Smithers was about to lose his temper, then he smiled and said, 'My boys tell me you're investigating Wally Booth's murder.'

'That's right.'

'How do yer fink I can help?'

'Simple – you can help by tellin' me who did it.'

'What makes yer fink I know?'

'It's your *business* to know. An' even if you don't actually know *now*, you could soon find out, because the killer is either a member of your gang or somebody closely *connected* with the gang.'

'Why are yer so certain 'e's one of *my* "business associates"?' Smithers asked. 'Maybe 'e's one of Toby Burroughs's blokes. Yer 'ave 'eard of Toby, I take it?'

'Oh yes, I've heard of him,' Woodend agreed.

There wasn't an officer serving in the Met who *hadn't* heard of Burroughs. Toby had been in the game even longer than Smithers had, and his firm was the only serious rival to Greyhound Ron's.

'Yeah, maybe it *was* one of Toby's boys who bumped off Wally,' Smithers said, seeming to warm to the idea. 'It would make sense, wouldn't it?'

'It would make no sense at all,' Woodend replied. 'The Waterman's Arms is on your firm's territory. Burroughs's "business associates" know better than to try an' show their faces there.'

'All right, if one of them didn't do it, maybe Wally was killed by a civilian – an ordinary punter,' Smithers suggested.

'In that case, where's the second body?' Woodend wondered.

'Yer what?'

'If an ordinary punter had killed one of your lads, he'd have been dead himself before he had time to reach the door. But there was only one body in the pub when the coppers arrived – Booth's! Which can only mean, when you think about it,

that whoever killed Wally must have been much more important to your firm than Wally was himself.'

'Do yer seriously fink I'd let one of my boys get topped
wivout doing somefink about it – even if that somefink didn't
necessarily involve the law?' Smithers asked.

'If I knew you better, I might be able to give you an answer
to that,' Woodend said, 'but since we've only just met, I've
no idea.'

'Bullshit apart, what is it that yer *really* want?'

'I thought I'd already made that plain. I *really* want the
guilty man.'

'And yer don't just want 'im – yer want to collar 'im in a
hurry.'

'That's right.'

'Why?'

Because the sooner I can close this case, the sooner I can
get back to the one that really *matters*, Woodend thought.

'I want him collared in a hurry because I've got my guv'nor
breathin' down my neck for a result,' he said aloud.

'That guv'nor would be DCI Bentley, would it?' Smithers
asked.

'You know it would.'

'If yer like, I could get the word to Bentley that yer need
a bit more elbow room,' Smithers suggested.

'I *don't* like,' Woodend told him firmly.

Smithers sneered. 'Oh, you're that kind of copper, are yer?
The by-the-book, holier-than-thou variety.'

'Not exactly,' Woodend said. 'I've cut a few corners in my
time – but I've always been choosy about which corners they
were.'

'So if I was to offer yer some money not to bovver me no
more – say, for sake of argument, a couple of grand – yer'd
turn it down, would yer?'

Two thousand pounds was a small fortune to a detective
sergeant, Woodend thought. Even high-ranking officers, like
Commander Cathcart, didn't come anywhere near earning that
much in a year.

'If you were to offer me a couple of grand, I'd have to
assume you were tryin' to hide a much bigger secret than the
name of Wally Booth's killer,' he said.

Smithers laughed. 'Yer right,' he agreed. 'An' if I *did* 'ave a big secret to hide, I wouldn't even *bovver* trying to bribe *you*. For a couple o' grand, I could buy myself a monkey much higher up the tree.'

And the depressing thing was, what he was saying was probably true, Woodend thought.

'I'd like to know what you think about another matter,' he said.

'What uvver matter?'

'Pearl Jones.'

'The coloured girl wot was killed the night before last?'

'That's right.'

'Why should I know anyfink about 'er?'

'Because her throat was slashed with a razor.'

Smithers chuckled. 'Oh, now I get it,' he said. 'Because a razor was involved the murderer must have been a "businessman".'

'Exactly.'

'Razors went out of fashion before the War. The only people wot still carry them are a few of the old-timers – men like Toby Burroughs.'

'You never miss the chance to point the finger at Toby Burroughs, do you?' Woodend asked.

'Would you miss the chance, if yer were in my position?' Smithers countered. 'What businessman wouldn't love to see 'is main competitor banged up for a few years?'

'Whatever happened to the concept of honour among thieves?' Woodend wondered, almost to himself.

Smithers looked down at his watch. 'Time for yer to go,' he said. 'But before yer leave, I'd like to give yer a bit of advice. And it's this – if yer want to do well for yerself in the Met, it's best not to rock the boat too much.'

'Even if that means lettin' the villains go free?' Woodend asked.

'Yes, even if it means that some of the villains – certain *selected* villains – go free,' Smithers said. 'Tell me, Sergeant, do yer ever wonder why some top coppers in the Met spend so much of their time being wined and dined by some of the top "businessmen"?'

'Because they feel they have to do *somethin'* to earn their bribes?' Woodend suggested.

Smithers looked disappointed with the answer. It was almost,

Woodend thought, as if the question had been set as a test of his knowledge and intelligence and – in Smithers's eyes – he had failed it miserably.

'We both know that there are a fair number of bent coppers on the Force,' the gangster agreed, 'but a lot of the ones wot I go out clubbing with are straight as a die. Try again.'

'If it's not that, then you must all be part of the same funny handshakes brigade,' Woodend said, knowing that this wasn't the answer Smithers was looking for, either.

'Some of my social acquaintances in the Met *are* members of my Masonic lodge,' Smithers conceded. 'But that's not it eiver.'

'Then what *is* the answer?'

'Yer might fink fings are in a hell of a mess out there now,' Smithers said, gesturing towards the street, 'but yer can't even *begin* to imagine how bad they'd be wivout people like me around.' He paused for a second. 'Now don't get me wrong,' he continued, in an almost avuncular manner. 'It's not actually your fault that you can't imagine it.'

'Isn't it?' Woodend asked.

'No, it ain't. You're at the bottom of the 'eap, looking up. But your brass are the top of the 'eap, and they've got a much clearer view of the situation as it really is. So they see me as an ally – at least, they do *some* of the time – because they know that we're involved in the same struggle. Because they know that if we weren't *both* here – the coppers and the top businessmen – everyfink would fall apart in no time at all.'

Ten

D C Cotteral was slouched over his desk. He had wrapped a rubber band in an intricate weave around the outstretched fingers of his right hand, and was now slowly moving one finger at a time, in order to see what effect that would have on the overall structure.

'It's good to see you're keepin' busy,' Woodend said.

Cotteral looked up. 'Oh, I am,' he agreed. 'This isn't as easy as it looks, you know. If you don't get the tension just right, you'll snap the elastic and end up with a nasty case of rubber-band-lash.'

Woodend glanced across at the Wolf's Lair. The door was open, and there was no sign of Bentley.

'Where's the guv'nor?' he asked.

'Don't you know?' Cotteral asked.

Woodend shook his head, and Cotteral smirked.

'Funny he didn't tell you where he was going,' the detective constable said. 'I thought DCIs *always* made it their business to keep their bagmen apprised of their movements.'

But not this particular DCI with this particular bagman, Woodend thought – and you know that as well as I do, Cotteral, you little shit.

'I'm not in the mood for playin' games,' he said aloud.

'Aren't you, Sarge?' Cotteral asked. 'I am surprised, especially after what the guv'nor said this morning, just before he left for his half-day conference.' He wiggled his fingers again, putting even more tension on the rubber bands. 'Now what *were* Mr Bentley's exact words?' he pondered. 'Oh yes, I've got it now. "I'm sick to death of that smart-arse Woodend and his bloody games." That's what he said. I think he's rather annoyed with you.'

If he'd needed any further indication that his own position on the DCI's team was precarious, he'd got it now, Woodend thought. His star had never hung *very* high in Bentley's sky, but for Cotteral to dare to put the boot in like this, it must have gone into freefall and be plunging rapidly towards the earth.

'So you're sayin' the guv'nor's gone to a half-day conference?' he asked Cotteral.

'That's right.'

'About what?'

'I think it's called "Modern Law Enforcement – a dynamic approach to policing London in the second half of the twentieth century",' Cotteral said, his smirk widening.

'And he's wastin' a whole *half-day* on that crap?'

'Well, you've got to admit, it's better than working for a living.'

Woodend felt an anger, which had been nestling in the pit of his stomach for two days, start to bubble up.

'So who's investigatin' the Pearl Jones case?' he demanded.

'The guv'nor is – when he gets back.'

'An' have there been any developments in the case *at all*? Have they found the mother yet?'

Cotteral had finally put too much strain on the elastic band, and now it snapped.

'Ouch!' the constable said, waving the hand in the air, to take away the slight sting.

'Have they found the mother?' Woodend repeated.

'The mother? No, I don't think they *have* found her.'

'Then don't you think you should get off your arse an' start lookin' for her yourself?'

Cotteral gave Woodend a look which fell somewhere between extreme contempt and extreme pity.

'Mr Bentley doesn't like the men working under him using their own initiative,' he said. 'He sees it as challenging his authority. So if you want to get on with him, you do what he tells you to do, *when* he tells you to do it.'

'Don't rock the boat,' Woodend said, echoing Greyhound Ron Smithers's words.

'Well, exactly,' Cotteral agreed. He reached for another rubber band from the box on his desk. 'And if Mr Bentley gives you no instructions at all, then you find a way to amuse yourself until he does.'

'That isn't how things are supposed to work in the police force,' Woodend said.

'Maybe not,' Cotteral said. 'But it's how they *do* work. If you want to get on, you have to play the system as you find it. I'm an expert at that, and if I was a betting man, I'd put money on my making sergeant *long before* you make inspector.'

One day, Woodend promised himself, I'll have my own team. An' when that day comes, I'll award the Golden Boot up the Backside to any member of it who can't come up with an idea that I haven't spoon-fed him.

He sat down at his desk, picked up the Wally Booth file, and ran his eyes over the list of Booth's known associates. The last time he'd looked at the file, he'd thought that getting any of them to cooperate with the investigation would be difficult. Now, after his meeting with Smithers, he decided it was nigh on impossible. Because if Greyhound Ron didn't want to talk himself, he certainly didn't want any of his 'business associates' to talk – and unless they felt the urge to end up dead, like Booth, he wouldn't get a peep out of them.

So what's the point of even pursuing the case any further? he asked himself. Especially when he had *better* things to do with his time.

He stood up.

'I'm goin' out,' he told Cotteral.

'What shall I tell the guv'nor if he wants to know where you are?' asked the detective constable, who had now devised a much more elaborate system, using *two* rubber bands and *both* his hands.

'You can tell him exactly what I've just told you,' Woodend said curtly. 'That I've gone out.'

Word of Victoria Jones's flight – enforced or otherwise – seemed to have got around the neighbourhood, and the door of 36 Balaclava Street was wide open. Woodend didn't look inside. He didn't need to, because he knew that anything that could be nicked would already have been nicked.

Bentley should have posted an officer to guard the place, Woodend thought, but now it was too late. Any evidence the house might have contained would have been stolen or destroyed.

Two women, their hair in curlers, and with untipped cigarettes drooping from their lips, were standing in a doorway on the opposite side of the road. When Woodend started to cross the street, they exchanged glances, but made no effort to move.

'Are you the Old Bill?' one of them asked.

Woodend nodded.

'I said 'e was,' the woman said to her companion.

'Then why ain't 'e wearing a suit?' the other woman asked, as if Woodend weren't there at all.

It was a good question, even if it wasn't addressed to him, Woodend thought.

And the answer, he supposed, was that he'd never really felt comfortable in a suit, because, back where he came from, they were only ever worn at weddings and funerals. Of course, a time might come, once he'd been promoted – *if* he'd been promoted, he corrected himself – when he'd probably have to swap his sports jacket for a suit. But that was long in the future.

'She's got a point, though, ain't she?' the first woman asked Woodend. 'Wiv the money wot you're pulling in, I'd have fort you could *afford* a nice blue suit.'

That was a bit rich, coming for a woman dressed in a pinny so stained it practically told her life history, Woodend told himself.

But all he said was, 'I'm DS Woodend. An' you are . . .?'

'Mrs Wilson,' said the first woman.

'Mrs Gort,' the second supplied.

'I was wonderin' if you two ladies saw what happened over there,' Woodend said, pointed at Victoria Jones's house.

''Appened over there?' Mrs Wilson repeated, as if she had no idea what he was talking about.

'The burglary.'

''As she been burgled?' Mrs Wilson said, with mock surprise. 'Well, we didn't see nuffink, did we, Effel?'

'Not a bleeding fing,' Mrs Gort agreed. 'She used to 'ave some nice stuff, though, didn't she?'

'The question is, where did she get all that nice stuff from?' Woodend said.

'Beats me,' Mrs Wilson told him. 'As far as I could tell, she never did nuffink to earn a crust.'

'Did she have visitors?'

'Yer mean, was she on the game?'

'I mean, did she have visitors of any kind?'

The two women exchanged glances.

'A few darkies, now and again,' Mrs Wilson said. 'But they wasn't out on the razzle. They was *religious* darkies.'

'How could you possible know that?'

'Well, for a start, they only come on Sundays, and always at just about the time the churches was turning out. And yer could tell from the way they was dressed – the men in stiff collars and ties, the women in 'ats – that they'd all been out praising the Lord.'

'Anyway, 'ole families of 'em come sometimes,' Mrs Gort chimed in. 'Piccaninnies and all. They never let them piccaninnies play out on the street, neiver – and if that's not religious, I don't know what is.'

'What can you tell me about Mrs Jones's daughter?' Woodend asked.

'Why d'yer want to know about 'er?' Mrs Wilson wondered.

'Because she's been murdered.'

'Murdered! Get on wiv yer,' Mrs Gort said.

'It was in the paper,' Woodend assured her. 'Didn't you see it?'

'Don't read no newspapers,' Mrs Wilson said. 'Can't seem to find the time.'

Can't seem to make the effort, more like, Woodend thought.

''Ow was she killed?' Mrs Gort asked.

'Her throat was cut,' Woodend said. '*Now* will you answer my question?'

'She was a nice girl – for a darkie,' Mrs Gort said.

Mrs Wilson sniffed. 'If yer ask me, she 'ad ideas well above 'er station,' she said. 'Parading up and down the street in that fancy school uniform of hers, like she was better than the rest of us. Still,' she continued, shivering slightly, 'I wouldn't wish wot's 'appened to her on anybody.'

Mrs Gort had been looking up the street, and now she tugged on her friend's sleeve and said, 'We'd best go inside, Lil.'

'Best go inside? What are yer talking about?' Mrs Wilson asked. 'I ain't finished talkin' to this copper, 'ave I?'

''E'll 'ave enough on 'is hands, wivout us,' Mrs Gort said, glancing nervously up the street again.

This time, Woodend looked too, and saw what Mrs Gort had seen.

Two big men were rapidly approaching, and though they were obviously a team, one was walking on the pavement, and the other on the road, at least four feet from his pal.

'Bleeding 'ell, I see just what you mean, Effel,' Mrs Wilson said. And then, in what probably wasn't intended to be a parody of good manners but certainly came out as one, she continued, 'If yer'll excuse us, Sergeant, we 'ave urgent matters wot we need to attend to indoors.'

The women stepped back into the house, and closed the door firmly behind them, while Woodend, for his part, turned to face the approaching men.

Though they were not the *same* men he had encountered outside Greyhound Ron's pub, they were virtually indistinguishable from them. The same bulky frames, the same sharp suits, the same arrogant swagger to their walk – and the same certainty in their hard eyes that whatever it was they wanted to do, they would meet with no resistance.

Woodend's mind ran back to the phone call, two nights earlier, in which the anonymous caller had threatened him with trouble if he showed too much enthusiasm in investigating Pearl Jones's murder.

Well, maybe this was the trouble, he told himself.

Without even realizing he was doing it, he had adopted a fighting stance – feet wide apart, hands balled into fists. But he knew none of it would do him any good as long as the two men kept a distance between them – because while he might, conceivably, be able to drop one of them, the other would be on him before he had a chance to take evasive action.

The men came to a halt a couple of yards short of him. The one on the left had a long jagged scar on his cheek. The one on the right had a large brown mole just above his lip. Neither of them would have won any beauty contests.

'Are you Charlie Woodend?' the one with the scar asked.

'I'm *Detective Sergeant* Charlie Woodend, yes.'

The man with the scar shrugged, as if to suggest the title didn't impress him, and that even if Woodend had announced himself as Pope Charlie III, it would have made absolutely no difference.

'The boss wants to see you,' he said.

'The boss?' Woodend repeated. 'Ron Smithers?'

The other man smirked, and his scar puckered. 'Greyhound

Ron ain't what *I'd* call a boss,' he said. 'I've scraped better fings off the sole of my shoe than *Greyhound Ron*.'

Well, if it wasn't Ron Smithers then it had simply to be the other big wheel, Woodend thought.

'We're talkin' about Toby Burroughs, are we?' he asked.

'That's right,' Scarface agreed. 'Mr Burroughs. Like I was saying, 'e wants to see yer.'

'An' what if *I* don't want to see *him*?'

Scarface shrugged again. 'Then yer don't 'ave to.'

'You won't try me make me?'

'No, we ain't 'ad no orders about making you. But if yer do decide to turn 'im down, that's *your* funeral.'

It would interesting to see how Burroughs would react if he *did* turn him down, Woodend thought.

On the other hand, it might be even *more* interesting to hear what it was that the man wanted to say.

'Where's your car?' he asked, making a snap decision.

Scarface chuckled. 'Car?' He turned to his partner. 'I didn't say nuffink about us 'aving no car, did I?'

'Nuffink at all,' his partner agreed, grinning. 'I'm sure I'd 'ave remembered if yer 'ad done.'

Woodend gave a deep sigh. This was the second pair of heavies he'd met in the space of a few hours, and like the first, they seemed almost compelled to put on a comic double act for him.

Where *did* they draw their inspiration from? The music hall? Television? American gangster films?

The two men were still waiting for a response from him.

Woodend sighed again. 'All right, I'll buy it,' he said resignedly. 'How *will* I be travellin' to the headquarters of the feller who's *supposed* to be the most feared man in the whole of London? By bus?'

'No, we'll drive yer there.'

'An' how do you propose to do that, without a car?'

It was clearly just the moment the two men had been waiting for – the crowning moment of their routine.

'We'll take yer in our mobile business unit,' the one with the mole over his lip said.

Eleven

The 'mobile business unit' turned out to be an aged black van. The words ACME WINDOW CLEANING SERVICE had been stencilled in white on the side, and – in case the words themselves were not enough to convince a passer-by of the verisimilitude of the whole operation – there were ladders, sponges, and several enamel buckets nestling haphazardly in the back.

Woodend briefly examined the back of the van, then said, 'You're not expectin' me to travel in there, with all the equipment, are you?'

Scarface laughed. 'Course we're not. That'd be below the dignity of a detective sergeant – specially one wot's as sharply dressed as wot you are.'

The hairy sports coat was going to have to go, Woodend told himself resignedly. Sooner or later, he was simply going to have to invest in a suit.

'So who *will* be ridin' in the back?' he asked.

'Nobody,' Scarface told him. 'We'll all ride in the front, like the good pals wot we've just become.'

The man with a mole over his lip climbed into the driver's side, and Scarface opened the passenger door.

'After you,' Woodend said.

'After *you*,' Scarface insisted.

Woodend climbed in, reflecting as he did so that there were probably better places in the world to be than sandwiched between two thugs.

'So you're both window cleaners, are you?' Woodend asked, as the van pulled away from the kerb.

'That's right,' the driver agreed easily.

'I find that surprisin',' Woodend admitted.

'And why's that?'

'Because you're not exactly dressed for the job.'

'Ah well, yer see, we're wot yer might call the new, modern, managerial-style winder cleaners,' Scarface said.

'An' what does that boil down to in practice?' Woodend wondered. 'That you collect the money for the window cleanin', but don't actually clean any windows?'

'Maybe,' Scarface countered. 'But it's no big strain on the people wot pay us. Shelling out a bob a week ain't never 'urt nobody.'

'But it doesn't get your windows cleaned, either,' Woodend pointed out.

'True enough,' Scarface agreed. 'But at least it makes sure that yer winders don't get *smashed*.'

As long as they were on the busy roads, full of traffic – full of *potential witnesses* – Woodend felt safe, even if he was crammed between two men who made their living out of breaking bones. But the situation changed when they reached Whitechapel, and the driver stuck his hand out of the window to signal that he was about to turn right into an alley.

'Where are we goin'?' Woodend asked, doing his best to hide his growing alarm.

'I told yer, we're taking yer to see the boss,' the driver replied.

'An' he lives up an alley – this kingpin of crime – does he?'

'Course 'e don't. But for yer own protection, we fort it might be better if yer weren't seen going in froo the front, so yer'll be entering the premises by what yer might call the tradesmen's entrance.'

Or maybe I won't be enterin' the premises *at all*, Woodend thought.

Because maybe they'd never *intended* to take him to their boss.

Perhaps, all along, their plan had been to beat the crap out of him, and they simply hadn't wanted to do it under the watchful eyes of the people of Balaclava Street.

He could see another main road at the end of the alley, but before they reached it the driver turned again, into an even smaller alley – and this time a dead end.

He would deal with the driver first, Woodend quickly decided – a forceful hand to the back of the head should be enough to smash his face down into the steering wheel. And at the same time, he'd see what damage he could do to Scarface with his right elbow.

'Relax,' Scarface said, reading the signals. 'If we was planning to give yer a going over, we wouldn't 'ave given yer time to *fink* about it.'

The driver braked in front of a door which had the words 'Las Vegas Club, Staff Only' painted on it.

'We're there,' he said.

Scarface got out of the van, and held the door open for Woodend with all the grace of a professional chauffeur. Then, when the sergeant had climbed out himself, he slid back into the van.

'Won't you be comin' with me?' Woodend asked.

'We'd like to, but we just ain't got the time,' Scarface told him. 'Not wiv a winder-cleaning business to run.'

Woodend watched the van as it reversed back to the alley. He was sweating, he realized, but then – in his situation – who *wouldn't* be?

He opened the back door to the club, and stepped into a long narrow corridor. There were further unmarked doors on either side of him, but he kept on walking until he reached the double doors at the end. Pushing them open, he found himself in a large room with a dance floor at one end and a bar at the other.

Most nightclubs didn't look up to much in the harsh light of day, Woodend thought. Stripped of their subdued lighting, they lost their glamour and became merely seedy. But that wasn't the case here, because this club didn't just create the *illusion* of being expensive and sophisticated – it actually was both those things.

'Welcome to the Las Vegas,' said a voice from across the room.

The man who had spoken the words was sitting at a table in the centre of the room. The table itself was piled high with banknotes – most of them fivers – and he appeared to be in the process of counting them.

'You'll be Toby Burroughs,' Woodend said.

'That's right,' the other man agreed. 'Why don't yer come and join me?'

Toby Burroughs was older than Ron Smithers by a good ten years, Woodend decided as he walked across the room. He was shorter, too – by a good three inches.

Even so, in a fight between the two of them, the sergeant thought he would have put his money on Burroughs. Smithers, it seemed to him, had *become* a hard man through training and self-discipline, but his rival gave off an aura of having emerged from the womb hard. And Woodend couldn't fail to note that while Smithers had surrounded himself with his heavies, Burroughs – despite all the money on the table – seemed to be quite alone.

'Take a seat, Sergeant,' Burroughs said amiably.

Woodend sat. There had to be at least a thousand pounds resting on the table, he calculated.

'Interestin' name that you've given this club of yours,' he said.

'Yes, it is, ain't it?' Burroughs agreed.

'What does it mean?'

Burroughs gave him a long, hard, calculating look. 'Are yer asking me that because yer really want to know the answer – or just 'cos yer shitting yer pants so much that yer saying the first words wot come into yer head?'

Woodend smiled. 'I might have been shittin' my pants a few minutes ago,' he admitted, 'but that stopped the moment your lads drove off.'

Burroughs nodded. 'It's a wise man 'oo knows when there's no need to be scared, and an even wiser 'oo knows when he *should* be,' he said. 'In answer to yer question, Sergeant, I used to call this place the Havana Club, after Havana in Cuba, because, for a gambler, that's where the real action is.'

'Then why did you change it?'

'Because when the government of Cuba falls – and it will fall, given time – people will start looking round for a new gambling capital of the world.'

'An' you think that will be this Las Vegas place?'

'I do. It don't look much at the moment – it's nuffink but a small town wiv a few casinos, in the middle of the desert – but in a few years it'll be the business.'

'So that's why you've changed the name of your club now?' Woodend asked. 'Because you like to associate yourself with winners very early on in the game?'

'Correct,' Burroughs concurred. 'It's been by associating wiv winners early on that I've managed to stay on top.' He

paused for a second or two, then added, 'Have yer been to
see Ron Smithers?'

It wasn't a really a question, and Woodend didn't even
bother to pretend that he thought it was.

Instead, he said, 'You seem to be very well informed.'

'Yes, I am well informed,' Burroughs agreed easily. 'That's
anuvver reason I'm still on top.' He paused for a second time.
'Listen, Sergeant, if yer on Greyhound Ron's payroll, that's a
matter between you and him, and yer'll get no complaints about
it from me. But if that *is* how it is, I'd like to know about it.'

'Why?'

'Because this is my city, and I need to be told wot's
going on.'

'Your city,' Woodend mused. 'I can think of any number
of people who might challenge that – an' Ron Smithers is
certainly one of them.'

'I like to fink of London as a pie,' Burroughs said, philo-
sophically. 'A very *big* pie – big enough for everybody who
wants a slice to 'ave one. But I'm the one wiv the serving
knife – so I'm the one who decides 'ow big each slice will
be. For the moment, Ron's being reasonable about the size of
his slice – but if 'e ever starts getting greedy, yer'll soon see
who's the *real* boss.'

Maybe he was right, Woodend thought.

Or maybe, like so many other dictators throughout history,
he was over-estimating his own power.

'*Are* yer in Ron's pocket?' Burroughs asked.

'No,' Woodend said.

'Then what was the purpose of yer visit to 'is ratty little
pub?'

'I went to see him about a case that I'm investigatin'.'

'And what case was that?'

'I really don't think that's anythin' to do with you.'

Burroughs nodded. 'Fair enough,' he agreed. 'It's your business, not mine. But if I 'ad to put money on it, I'd be willing
to bet it was about the Wally Booth case.'

'No comment,' Woodend said.

'Like I told yer, it's your business.'

'Can I ask *you* a question now?' Woodend asked.

Burroughs thought about it. 'I don't see why not,' he said
finally.

'Do you know anythin' about the murder of a coloured girl on Mitre Street, the night before last?'

Burroughs's eyes hardened. 'Now why would yer want ter ask me about that?' he demanded.

Because Ron Smithers says you're an old-fashioned gangster who still carries a razor around in his pocket, Woodend thought.

'Because, as this is your city, I thought that you might have heard somethin',' he said aloud.

'Are yer on that case *as well*?' Burroughs asked.

'Not any more.'

'Meaning wot?'

'Meanin' that I was on it, but now I've been reassigned.'

'So if yer ain't involved in that particular case no more, why are yer still poking yer big nose into it?'

I could lie, Woodend thought – but why should I?

'From what I learned about her while I *was* still on the case, I've come to the conclusion that Pearl Jones was a really nice kid – a really *good* kid,' he said. 'And I'd like to see whoever killed her hangin' from the end of a rope.'

Burroughs nodded seriously. 'I wouldn't mind seeing that myself,' he said. 'I don't *like* violence.'

Woodend laughed. He didn't mean to do it, but he simply couldn't stop himself.

'*You* don't like *violence*?' he repeated, incredulously.

'That's right.'

'But from what I've heard, your entire empire is built on violence.'

'That was business,' Burroughs said crisply. 'I never cut up nobody 'oo wouldn't have cut up me first, if 'e'd been given the chance. And I've always kept the civilians out of it.'

'Unless they didn't give you exactly *what* you wanted, exactly *when* you wanted it,' Woodend said sceptically.

'Unless they got in the way of my business plans,' Burroughs agreed. 'But to get back to the point, Sergeant, I don't know who killed this coloured girl of yours – but if I did, I'd tell yer.'

He could be telling the truth or he could be lying through his teeth, Woodend thought – and there was no way he could tell which it was.

There was the hoot of a car horn being sounded outside the front door.

'That'll be yer lift, on 'is way round to the back to pick yer up,' Burroughs said.

'Timed it just nicely, hasn't he?' Woodend asked.

'Which means yer can leave now,' Burroughs continued, with the same arrogant dismissal to his tone that Greyhound Ron Smithers had displayed earlier.

Woodend stood up, and walked over to the double doors.

'One more question,' he said, as he was pushing them open. 'Do you still carry a razor, Mr Burroughs?'

Burroughs smiled – and it was probably the most frightening smile that Woodend had ever seen in his life.

'Cross me, and yer'll soon find out,' the gangster said.

DCI Bentley had probably gone straight from his half-day conference to a heavy lunch with some other members of the top brass – a lunch which would undoubtedly be paid for out of the Met's crime-fighting budget. Cotteral had abandoned his experiment with rubber bands in a favour of a construction project involving paper clips, then had abandoned that too, and gone out for a pint.

Left alone in the office, Woodend chain-smoked, and did his best to analyse the day's events.

'There were a lot of questions I needed to ask myself after that meeting with Toby Burroughs,' Woodend told Monika Paniatowski.

'And the first one was whether Burroughs was behind that late-night phone call which warned you off investigating the Pearl Jones murder?' Monika guessed.

'Exactly,' Woodend agreed. 'An' the more I thought about it, the more my head hurt. On the one hand, you see, it was perfectly possible that Burroughs hadn't really wanted to see me at all – that he'd only used seein' me as a pretext to get me away from Balaclava Street, where there was a danger I might learn more about the murder.'

'But, on the other hand, a man as resourceful as Burroughs seems to have been could have come up with any number of other pretexts – none of which involved him directly,' Paniatowski said.

'*Just so. But if the meetin'* hadn't *been a pretext, then what the hell* had *it been?'*

'*He* said *he wanted to know if you were working for Greyhound Ron.'*

'*I know that's what he said, but how likely was it that an important criminal like him would take a personal interest in whether or not a low-rankin' policeman was takin' the occasional bribe from one his rivals?'*

'*Not likely at all,'* Paniatowski admitted. '*So what* was *the real reason for the meeting?'*

'*Pardon?'* Woodend said, as if he hadn't heard.

'*You did eventually find out why he wanted to see you, didn't you?'*

'*Oh yes, it was obvious, once all the other bits of the jigsaw had slotted into place.'*

Paniatowski sighed. '*So tell me?'*

Woodend chuckled. '*Not yet. A good tale's a bit like a good meal – if you serve bits of it out of order, you spoil the taste of the whole thing.'*

'*There are times when I could kill you, Charlie,'* Paniatowski said.

'*Aye, I can be annoyin' on occasion,'* Woodend agreed. '*Anyway, while I was sittin' there, tryin' to make sense of it all, the phone rang. An' who do you think it was?'*

Paniatowski sighed again – *even more heavily this time.* '*I don't know,'* she said. '*Who was it?'*

'*It was a voice from the past,'* Woodend told her.

'Charlie?' said the vaguely familiar voice at the other end of the line.

'Yes?'

'Arthur Cathcart here.'

'Oh, hello, sir.'

Woodend had caught sight of Major Cathcart – now *Commander* Cathcart – from time to time, and they'd even exchanged a few meaningless pleasantries when they'd happened to meet accidentally – but it must have been at least two years, he thought, since they'd had anything that could have passed as a conversation.

'I think we need to have a talk,' Cathcart said.

'All right,' Woodend agreed, mystified.

'But not over the phone. It should be done face-to-face.'

'Would you like me to come up to your office, sir?'

'No!' Cathcart said emphatically. 'No,' he repeated, more softly this time. 'I think it would probably be better, given the *nature* of what needs to be said, if we met somewhere not *too* closely connected to the Job.'

'A pub?' Woodend suggested.

'That would certainly be more suitable,' Cathcart agreed. 'Or better yet, why not come to my place for Sunday lunch?'

'Sorry, sir,' Woodend said, not certain he had heard the commander correctly.

'We throw a buffet-lunch party most Sundays,' Cathcart said. 'It's very informal, and it's really quite a jolly crowd.'

'Whenever I have the opportunity, I like to spend my Sundays with my wife,' Woodend said.

'It's perfectly understandable that you would,' Cathcart agreed. 'And, naturally, when I invited you, I was also inviting her.'

'I'm not sure . . .' Woodend began.

'We're old comrades-in-arms, Charlie,' Cathcart reminded him. 'And really, I'm quite ashamed of the way I've been neglecting you since we were demobbed.'

'I never expected you to . . .'

'I mean to say, I've never even *met* your wife. Joan, isn't it?'

'That's right.'

'And you've never met mine.'

'Even so . . .'

'What's the matter? Do you think it will make you feel uncomfortable to be rubbing shoulders with the brass?'

'The thought had occurred to me,' Woodend admitted.

Cathcart laughed. 'Well, you needn't worry on that score, Charlie. Sundays are part of my *other* life – the part that doesn't involve police work. In fact, you'll be the first copper I've ever invited.'

'It's very kind of you, sir . . .'

'Is that a yes?'

'I'll have to ask Joan.'

'And if she's happy with the idea, can I take it as a yes then?'

'I suppose you can,' Woodend said cautiously.

'Jolly good! So I'll look forward to seeing you both on Sunday,' Cathcart said.

And then he hung up.

Twelve

It was a quarter to four when DCI Bentley finally returned to the office. Once inside, he walked straight over to Woodend's desk with the careful steps of a man who was sober enough to know that he'd had too much to drink, but drunk enough to believe he could successfully conceal the fact from other people.

'How's your murder investigation going, Charlie?' he asked with unaccustomed bonhomie.

How's *yours* going, you fat idle bastard? Woodend thought.

'I'm makin' some progress, sir,' he lied.

Bentley nodded his head sagely, as if to acknowledge having just heard some profound statement from his sergeant.

'Good, good,' he said. 'Excellent, in fact. You know, Charlie, you and me, we may have had our differences in the past, but I still think that you've got the makings of a bloody good copper in you.'

'Thank you, sir,' Woodend said.

Though he was only too well aware that, as the effects of the drink began to wear off, Bentley's newly discovered golden opinion of him would start to fade away, too.

'There's just . . . just one thing,' Charlie,' Bentley continued, opening and closing his eyes in an effort to make them focus properly.

'What's that, sir?'

'What's what?' Bentley asked, puzzled.

'The "just one thing", sir.'

'Oh, yes. That. Over lunch, I had time for a few quick words with one of the directors of the brewery.'

'Which brewery?'

'You know! It's the . . . the . . .' Bentley said, as he tried to recall the name, and failed. 'The one that owns that pub, the . . . whatever the devil it's called.'

'The Waterman's Arms?' Woodend suggested.

'That's right, I knew it was *something* like that. The Waterman's Arms.' Bentley paused to draw a few shallow breaths, then continued. 'Apparently, according to this chap, the place is still closed down.'

'Well, it is the scene of a crime, sir,' Woodend pointed out.

'It . . . it may, as you say, be the scene of crime, but keeping it closed is costing the brewery a lot of *money*. They don't like that. And . . . and there's no reason why they should.' Bentley paused again, this time to collect his thoughts. 'Is there any reason why the Waterman's Arms *shouldn't* re-open?' he asked.

'Not really,' Woodend said.

Nor was there, he thought. The forensics team had arrived at the pub long after the scene had been hopelessly contaminated by fleeing potential witnesses, and if they couldn't find anything then, it was highly unlikely they'd be able to find anything new now.

'Maybe you'd better check it over again yourself, personally, before we finally give them permission to open up,' Bentley suggested.

'Oh, I don't think that will be necessary, sir.'

The chief inspector blinked, and Woodend realized he was going through one of those sudden mood swings that drunks are always prone to.

'So you think that won't be necessary, do you?' Bentley asked, with a new, harsh edge to his voice.

'That's right, sir, but if you feel it would be—'

'Let me tell you something, Sergeant. What *you* think doesn't matter a tuppenny damn. Round here, it's what *I* think that matters.'

'Yes, sir, I quite accept—'

'So instead of lecturing me on what is and isn't necessary, you'd do well to get yourself off to the pub and see if it *can* be opened again. Got that?'

'Got it, sir,' Woodend said.

The Waterman's Arms was entered from a narrow alleyway which ran from the road to a series of steps (which, themselves, led to a small jetty on the river), and just taking a walk down the alley made Woodend feel as if he were stepping back in time.

He knew all about the watermen, after whom the pub was named. They had made their money by ferrying people across the Thames, back in the days when there had been far too few bridges spanning the river to meet the needs of an expanding city. They'd been a tough breed, and – having to row for twelve hours a day, in all weathers, and often against the tide – they'd needed to be. In the middle of the previous century they'd been able to supplement their incomes by claiming finder's fees for fishing dead bodies out the river, but that practice had been stopped when the authorities had noticed that the number of corpses had increased dramatically, and assumed – quite rightly – that the watermen had given up waiting for victims of drowning, and had begun to create a few of their own.

All of which made it more than likely that Wally Booth hadn't been the first man to die in the Waterman's Arms by a long chalk, Woodend thought, as he drew level with the pub.

The official notice, pinned to the door of the Waterman's Arms, stated that the establishment was closed until further notice, on the orders of the Commissioner of the Metropolitan Police.

Not that such a notice was really necessary, Woodend thought, because the regular customers would not only *know* it was closed, they would know whose angered fist had been *responsible* for closing it.

He took the pub's front-door key out of his pocket, and inserted it in the lock. Then, as he felt the mechanism begin to click into place, he began to wonder whether it was worth the effort of actually going inside.

The only reason he was there at all, he reminded himself, was because a drunken chief inspector had irrationally told him he *should* be there.

And since he had no expectations of finding anything interesting inside, what was the point of wasting any more of his time?

'Hang about, Charlie,' said the voice in his head which was comparatively new to him then, but over the coming years would grow to be a more or less constant companion. 'You don't actually know for certain that you *won't* find somethin' in there, now do you?'

'Don't I?' Woodend wondered aloud.

'Of course you don't. It's not beyond the bounds of possibility, is it, that a man like you – a fresh an' brilliant young detective – will come across a vital clue that the jaded forensic team have overlooked?'

Woodend grinned. 'I've got two points to make,' he told the voice. 'The first is that I'd better learn to stop talkin' to myself before somebody sends the men in white coats to take me away.'

'An' what's the second?' the voice asked.

'I've got to give up these delusions of grandeur concernin' my detectin' skills, because if I don't, my head will swell up so much it won't fit through this door or any other.'

'So you're *not* goin' in?' the voice asked, disappointedly.

Woodend sighed. 'I'll go in,' he conceded. 'I suppose I might as well, since I'm here already.'

Then he pushed the door open, and stepped inside.

The pub was pretty much as he'd expected it to be. There was sawdust on the floor, and several spittoons placed strategically around the room, in order that customers would not have to walk far to expectorate. There was a counter which ran the whole length of the far wall, with a painted mirror behind it and the brass foot-rail – which had robbed Wally Booth of his life – at its base. There were tin adverts, mounted on the walls, for products that had long ceased to exist, and heavy wooden tables which bore the scars of generations of cigarette burns.

This boozer would hardly have changed at all since the time the great Charles Dickens might have visited it, Woodend thought. And closing his eyes, he could picture the weather-beaten watermen, knocking back pints of bitter, paid for in aching muscles, before going home to the hovels where their families eked out their miserable existence.

It had been a good idea to come inside, he thought, if only to immerse himself, for a moment, in the world that Dickens himself had once inhabited. But opening his eyes again, he saw none of the clues that the persuasive voice in his head had suggested he might find there.

He turned around, and walked back towards the door.

And it was then that he heard the noise!

It was a deadened, heavy noise. Not the scampering of a

frightened rat, but rather a slight movement made by something considerably heavier. And it was coming from behind
the bar.

He turned again.

'Police!' he said. 'You'd better come out.'

It was perhaps five or six seconds before the man who'd
been crouching behind the counter reluctantly stood up.

He was, Woodend estimated, roughly five feet eight or five
nine inches tall, and was around forty years old. He was
wearing the same kind of suit as the ones worn by Greyhound
Ron Smithers's bouncers and Toby Burroughs's collectors, but
it had been less expensive when new, and now was showing
distinct signs of wear.

'Who are you?' Woodend demanded.

'Smiff,' the man said. 'John Smiff.'

'Well, that's certainly original,' Woodend told him. 'An'
what are you doin' here, Mr *Smith*?'

The other man shrugged. 'I was walking past when I saw
the door was wide open, so I just come in.'

'The door wasn't wide open – it was *locked*,' Woodend
corrected him. 'But then that doesn't really present much of
a problem to a man with a set of skeleton keys in his pocket,
now does it?'

'I swear to you, I wasn't doing nuffink,' 'Smith' whined.

'Tell that to your brief,' Woodend advised him. 'Maybe
he'll be able to convince the court it's the truth – but I very
much doubt it.'

'Yer *arresting* me?' 'Smith' asked, as though it was the
most outrageous thing he'd ever heard.

'I don't see why I shouldn't,' Woodend replied. 'Given the
circumstances, it seems like the right thing to do.' He took
his handcuffs out of his pocket and held them in the air for
'Smith' to see. 'Would you come round from behind the bar
now, please?'

With a great show of reluctance, 'Smith' did as he had been
ordered, but when he was halfway between the bar and
Woodend, he came to a sudden halt.

'Look . . . er . . . ain't there nuffink we can do to make this
bit o' unpleasantness just go away?' he asked.

'Nothin' that *I* can I think of,' Woodend said.

'Smith' reached into his pocket. 'It's like this, Sergeant,' he said, 'I've 'ad a bit of luck at the dog track, which means that I just 'appen to 'ave a few quid on me, and . . .'

Woodend shook his head. 'Careful,' he warned. 'You don't want to go addin' attempted bribery to the charges, now do you?'

The next few moments passed in a blur.

One second, 'Smith' was standing perfectly still. The next he was lunging towards Woodend, and screaming, 'Bastard!' at the top of his voice. His hand, now clear of his pocket again, was holding not the promised cash but a very unpromising cosh, and as he got within striking range, he swung it at the sergeant's head.

Woodend did his best to feint to the side but he was not quite fast enough. The cosh failed to strike its intended target, but it did land heavily on his shoulder, and a pain shot along his arm right to his fingertips.

'Smith' took one step backwards, to give himself more space for a second assault. Woodend, his head swimming and his eyes refusing to focus properly, lashed out blindly with his right foot.

The boot connected with something solid. Smith let out a loud 'oof', then sank to his knees – almost in slow motion – moaning, 'Ohmygod, ohmygod,' softly to himself.

For an instant, Woodend contemplated following through with a second kick – to the other man's chest, this time – but then he realized there was no need, because it was clear that 'Smith', who was gingerly, and experimentally, touching his genitals, would be in no position to cause any more trouble for quite a while.

Woodend flexed the fingers of his right hand, and was surprised at how a movement in one part of his body could cause so much pain in so many other parts. But though it hurt like hell, he was almost sure that nothing was broken.

'Smith' looked up at him, his eyes filled with agony.

'Yer've . . . yer've bloody well gone and castrified me,' he complained, through clenched teeth.

'The word you want is *castrated*, you ignorant bastard,' Woodend said, and then, as a new wave of pain shot along the length of his arm, he added, 'An', if I have done, it's no more than you bloody deserve.'

He walked around the still kneeling man, carefully bent his own knees, and pulled 'Smith's' arms behind his back.

'Listen, there's still a chance that we can work somefink out between us,' the other man gasped, as Woodend slipped the handcuffs over his wrists. 'I'm sorry that I 'urt yer, and I'm more the willing to pay for it. Suppose I was to offer yer fifty quid, all in used oncers? What would yer say to that?'

'I'd say I've met any number of hopeless optimists in my time, but you really take the biscuit,' Woodend replied, as he clicked the cuffs in place.

'What d'yer mean?'

'I mean you've got about as much chance of me takin' your offer as a dog turd has of bein' crowned Queen of the May.'

'I might be able to stretch to an 'undred quid,' 'Smith' said hopefully.

Woodend rose to his feet, and then grasped 'Smith' by the arms and assisted him into a standing position. His own arm, he noted as he did so, still hurt like buggery.

He transferred his hands to 'Smith's' shoulders, and turned the other man around, so that they were facing each other.

'John Smith, I am arrestin' you on the suspicion that you were engaged in an act of burglary on these premises, an' on the bloody *certainty* that you have attacked a police officer in the course of his lawful duty,' he said. 'Or to put it in the vernacular – you're well an' truly nicked, my son.'

Thirteen

The man who was still insisting on calling himself John Smith leaned heavily – and somewhat theatrically – on the interview-room table and said, 'My knackers are on fire. I need medical attention.'

'Aye, I know how you feel,' Woodend said, with mock sympathy. 'I've got this throbbing pain in my shoulder that I wouldn't mind the quack givin' the once-over, an' all. So it's a real pity, isn't it, that neither of us have time to go an' see a doctor at the moment?' He slid his packet of Capstan Full Strength across the table. 'Why don't you stop complainin' an' have one of these? It'll help to ease the pain.'

'Smith' took one of the cigarettes, and Woodend lit it for him.

'Name?' the sergeant asked.

'I've already told yer, it's John Smiff.'

Woodend shook his head. 'No, it isn't,' he said. He lit up a cigarette himself, and gulped down the acrid smoke greedily. 'Listen,' he continued, 'since we both know that the criminal-records department is goin' to match your fingerprints up to your real name sooner or later, why not save some time, an' tell me now?'

The prisoner gave the matter some thought – it seemed to be a painful process.

'All right,' he said finally. 'The name's Machin. Jimmy Machin.'

'That's very good, Jimmy,' Woodend said encouragingly. 'Now, the next step is for you to tell me exactly what you were doin' in the Waterman's Arms.'

'What do yer fink I was doing? I'm a tea leaf, ain't I? The reason I went into the pub was to pinch somefink.'

'Somethin'?' Woodend repeated, rolling the word around in his mouth thoughtfully. 'Like what, for example?'

Machin shrugged. 'Well, yer know . . .'

'No, that's the point, I *don't* know,' Woodend replied. 'That's why I'm askin' you to tell me.'

'I fort there might be some cash lying around.'

'Really?'

'Yeah.'

'You saw the notice on the door . . . you can read, can't you?'

'Course I can bleeding read!'

'You saw a notice sayin' that the police had closed the place until further notice, an' you seriously thought there was a chance that the brewery would have been stupid enough to leave *money* inside?'

'Well, I didn't fink there was *too much* of a chance of it,' Machin admitted. 'But there's uvver fings yer can nick from pubs, as well as gelt.'

'True,' Woodend agreed. 'But you'd have looked a right bloody idiot walkin' down that passageway with a piano on your back, now wouldn't you?'

'There was booze!' Machin said.

'Yes, there was. Pubs are famous for havin' booze in them. If you wanted a bottle of whisky, an' you had to decide between goin' to a pub an' a furniture store for it, you'd choose a pub every time.'

'There's no need to be sarcastic,' Machin said sulkily.

'Why wouldn't I be sarcastic, when all you're doin' is feedin' me a load of old cobblers?' Woodend asked. 'An' before you start tellin' me any more of your lies, just remember one thing – I've seen your skeleton keys.'

'What's that supposed ter mean?'

'They're works of art, are them keys. A beauty to behold. Only a real artist would have a set of keys like that.'

Machin's chest swelled with pride.

'They are good, ain't they?' he said. 'I made them myself, yer know.' Then, growing wary again, he added, 'But wot does that prove?'

'It proves you weren't after booze.'

'Come again?'

'Most of your common-or-garden toe-rag criminals will turn their hands to anythin' when the need arises. But you're an artist – an' artists are different. You wouldn't catch Leonardo

da Vinci whitewashin' a shithouse wall – an' you wouldn't
catch a good keyman like you breakin' and enterin' when all
he could expect to come out with is a bottle or two of whisky.
It's a question of pride an' professional standards, isn't it?'

'Oo's this da Vinci bloke wot yer talkin' about?' Machin
asked. ''E's not that Wop wot runs the rackets down in
Limehouse, is 'e?'

'How long have you been workin' for Greyhound Ron
Smithers?' Woodend asked, out of the blue.

'Yer wot?'

'It's a simple enough question, I would have thought, but
there's no real need for you to answer it. An' shall I tell you
why there's no real need?'

'If yer like.'

'You see, I've already figured out that if you *weren't* workin'
for Ron Smithers, there's no way that you would have been
in the Waterman's Arms when Wally Booth got killed.'

'Oo says I *was* in the Waterman's then?'

'Nobody says it *directly*. But they don't need to – because
your own actions give you away.'

''Ow do yer mean?'

'Maybe I should explain the lines I'm thinkin' along,'
Woodend suggested. 'The way I see it is that ever since the
murder occurred, you've been tellin' yourself there was
absolutely nothin' in the pub to connect you with it. Tellin'
yourself – but not really *believin'* it. An', in the end, you were
worryin' so much that you decided you had to do somethin'
to resolve your doubts once an' for all. So you went back to
the pub, to check. You'd probably convinced yourself that
there was no risk in doin' that – an' there wouldn't have been,
if I hadn't walked through the door at just the wrong time.'

Machin folded his arms. 'I ain't got nuffink more to say.'

'You didn't mean to kill Wally Booth. I know that,' Woodend
said coaxingly. 'When you lost your temper with him, all you
meant to do was knock him down. It was pure chance that he
fell the way he did, an' died as a result. An' believe me, the
Director of Public Prosecutions will understand that just as
clearly as I do. You'll go down for manslaughter, not murder,
an' with any luck, you'll be out again in three years.'

Machin uncoiled his arms, and stared down at his hands.

'If I . . .' he began.

Then his mouth snapped shut, as it were on a spring.

He was fighting the impulse to confess, Woodend thought – but it was a losing battle. And tottering on the brink as he was, it would only take the very gentlest of pushes to make him come clean.

'You could get at least *five* years simply for attackin' me, Jimmy,' he said. 'Just think of that. Five long years! But if you're prepared to put your hands up for Wally Booth's death, I'll see to it that the other charges are dropped.'

The door to the interview room suddenly swung open, and a young uniformed constable entered.

'Yes, what is it?' Woodend said irritably, as he silently cursed the constable's timing.

The constable nodded in the direction of the prisoner. 'His solicitor's here, and is asking to see him.'

'You've made a mistake, you bloody idiot!' Woodend said angrily. 'It can't be *his* solicitor. *His* solicitor doesn't even know he's here, because he hasn't spoken to anybody but me since I arrested him.'

The constable glanced across at the prisoner again. 'Are you James Archibald Machin?' he asked.

'That's me,' Machin confirmed.

'Sorry about that, Sarge,' the constable said, 'but this is the bloke the solicitor wants to see, all right.'

'Just because he's asked to see you, it doesn't mean that you have to agree to it if you don't want to,' Woodend told his prisoner. 'An' really, under the circumstances, it might be best *not* to see him. Because once a lawyer's involved – makin' trouble left, right, and centre, as they do – the DPP might decide to go for a murder charge after all. On the other hand, if we can get this whole business neatly wrapped up between the two of us . . .'

Machin folded his arms across his chest again. 'I demand to see my solicitor,' he said firmly.

Well, shit! Woodend thought.

The solicitors who made a precarious living out of defending petty criminals like Jimmy Machin were easily identifiable as a group. They could be picked out, even from a distance, by the shabby suits they wore, and the yoke of bitterness and cynicism which seemed to weigh them down. They had all but failed in their chosen profession, and showed, by their every action and every word, that they were well aware of the fact.

The man standing in the corridor at that moment was of an entirely different breed – not a legal rat scuttling around in the bowels of the judicial system, but a proud lion sitting atop it. *His* suit had been made by one of the more expensive tailors on Savile Row, and the watch that he was gazing at so pointedly would have cost a detective sergeant at least six months' pay.

Woodend held out his hand to the solicitor.

'I'm DS Woodend, sir,' he said. 'I'm the officer who arrested – an' who's been questionin' – your client.'

The other man nodded brusquely, but ignored the proffered hand.

'And I'm Edward Tongue,' he said. 'I'm the solicitor whose job it will be to unscramble the mess that you've undoubtedly left my client's mind in.'

Woodend did his best to avoid disliking people at the first meeting under normal circumstances – but in Tongue's case he was more than willing to make an exception.

'Jimmy must have been doin' a *lot* of breakin' and enterin' recently, if he can afford to hire a feller like you,' he said.

Tongue gave him a fishlike stare. 'I will not even dignify that comment with an answer,' he said.

'An' even if he *has* got the money to pay you, I'm still surprised that you'd lower yourself to defend a guttersnipe like him.'

'No comment.'

'But what's got me really puzzled – as I mentioned to the constable back there in the interview room – is that you even *knew* that Jimmy had been arrested. How *did* you know, Mr Tongue?'

Tongue sneered. 'You seem to have got things entirely the wrong way round, Sergeant,' he said. '*You* don't put *me* through the third degree. What happens is that we wait until you're in the witness box, when *I* give *you* a grilling.'

'You're a real cocky sod, aren't you?' Woodend said.

'I take great exception to being addressed in that manner,' Tongue told him, 'and if it happens again, I shall report you to your superiors.'

'Is that right, you bag of piss an' wind?' Woodend asked pleasantly. 'Well, when you do report me, make sure you spell my name right.'

When Woodend entered the bar of the Conway Club, Tom Townshend was already holding court in front of a bunch of admiring younger reporters, but the moment he saw the detective sergeant approaching, he imperiously waved them away.

'Must be nice to be looked up to like that,' said Woodend, with a mock-admiration that was, in fact, only *half* mocking.

Townshend shrugged. 'Fame is a fleeting thing, Charlie, and any man who takes his own fame seriously is a fool. Those chaps look up to me now because I'm at the top of my game, but the moment I pass my peak, they'll have absolutely no difficulty at all in finding someone else to admire.'

'Are you really as cynical as you seem, Tom?' Woodend wondered.

'The cynicism you see on the surface is merely the tip of the iceberg of disillusion which floats heavily below,' Townshend replied. 'What can I do for you, Charlie?'

'I wanted to thank you for gettin' that picture of Pearl Jones printed in your paper.'

'And your thanks are very much appreciated. But you could have delivered them just as easily by phone.'

'That's not quite the same, though, is it?' Woodend asked.

'No, it probably isn't,' Townshend agreed. 'And, of course, on the phone it's much more difficult to ask for *additional* favours.'

Woodend sighed. 'Am I that obvious?'

'Yes – though perhaps it is less your poor acting abilities which give you away than it is the edge of desperation which goes with them.'

'Edge of desperation?' Woodend repeated, looking round to make absolutely certain that Townshend wasn't talking to someone else.

'That's what *I'd* call it,' Townshend replied. 'Though you, I suppose, would choose some more *comfortable* term – like drive, initiative, or determination – to wrap it up in.'

Woodend forced a grin to his face. 'You certainly don't pull your punches, do you, Tom?' he asked.

'Would you want me to?' Townshend countered.

No, Woodend thought, I wouldn't.

And what his old friend had said was quite right – he *was* desperate.

He was desperate to bring Pearl Jones's killer to justice – if only because no one else seemed to give a damn about her.

But he was also desperate, if he was being completely honest, to demonstrate that he really *could* handle a major case – to prove, if only to himself, that his decision to join the police had been the right one.

'I wouldn't need your help if I was gettin' the backup I need from the Yard,' he said bitterly. 'But I'm not.'

'And I'm not in the least surprised,' Tom Townshend said. 'Do you know what your problem is, Charlie?'

'You mean I've got other problems, apart from my desperation?' Woodend asked, doing his best to lighten the tone.

'Dozens of them,' Townshend said. 'But the one I want to discuss at the moment is the problem of your being a decent, honest, *principled* bloke in a world that has largely given up being decent and principled. Worse than that – you're a knight in shining armour, riding out on a white charger to slay dragons, just at a time when everybody else has decided to pretend that dragons don't exist.'

'An' that's a problem, is it?'

'Yes, because you still expect the same standards from others that you expect from yourself. But you won't get them. Most people – and especially most policemen – are complete arseholes.'

'I wouldn't go so far as—'

'And if you refuse to see that, Charlie, then you'll never learn how to deal with them effectively.'

Once, not so long ago, they had been comrades and equals, Woodend thought. Now Townshend seemed so much older – so much more in control – than him.

Why was that?

Because Tom Townshend was now a top-flight reporter, and he was still a humble detective sergeant? Because Townshend had grown more cynical since the old days, while he had merely grown more naive?

Whatever the reason, it was not a happy thought.

'So what, exactly, is it that you'd like me to do for you?' Townshend asked.

'Two things,' Woodend told him, sounding – at least to himself – crisper and more authoritative now. 'Firstly, I want you to dig up everythin' you can on Victoria Jones – especially in matters relating to her finances.'

'Why should Mrs Jones's finances be of any particular interest to you?' Townshend wondered.

'Because she doesn't work, but she lives well, an' her daughter went to an expensive school. Because if I can find out where her money comes from, I'm guessin' it will open a lot of doors, an' answer a lot of questions.'

'You may be right,' Townshend agreed. 'And how do you propose that I get this information?'

'Takin' a look at her bank account might be a good start.'

Townshend pretended to look shocked. 'Bank accounts are private and confidential. I wouldn't even begin to know how to get access to someone else's.'

Woodend grinned. 'Wouldn't you? Then I probably imagined readin' that story the other week – the one in which you revealed where that crooked stockbroker had stashed all the money he'd stolen from his clients.'

Townshend returned the grin. 'All right, I may have a *few* tricks up my sleeve that can help you,' he admitted. 'What's the other thing you want to know about?'

'Edward Tongue.'

'Now there's a thoroughly nasty piece of work,' Townshend said. 'Our Edward started out in life with all the advantages. He went to a good school and a good university. He could have built himself a distinguished career in the law, if he'd put his mind to it. Instead, he decided to get very rich, very quickly.'

'In other words, he sold his soul?'

'Yes, he did. But to be fair to him, he made sure he got a good price for it. Employing him can be *very* expensive.'

And yet he was representing Jimmy Machin, Woodend thought.

'What kinds of people does Tongue work for?' he asked.

'Dodgy property developers, slum landlords, bent stockbrokers like the one in my article – people of that ilk.'

'Gangsters?'

'Them, too. I believe he's on a retainer from Toby Burroughs.'

'An' Ron Smithers?'

'Might be. I haven't heard about it, but that doesn't mean he isn't, because while it's true that Smithers and Burroughs are bitter rivals, that wouldn't deter our Edward from working for both of them, if there was money to be made out of it.'

So it probably was Smithers who was paying Tongue to handle Jimmy Machin's case, Woodend thought.

But why would he do that? Why spend a lot of money on defending a minor criminal?

Because Machin was not the *only one* involved in Wally Booth's death!

Because Greyhound Ron was up to his neck in it, as well!

Fourteen

The dark clouds hanging heavily over the Victoria Embankment oppressed all that lay below them. They frowned down on New Scotland Yard, which seemed to shiver under their disapproval. They imbued the river with the colour of suicidal greyness. And even the wind, which was wont to announce its arrival from across the water with a howl, had been subdued into no more than a whimper that morning.

From the window of his office, Woodend watched the rounded bundles of heavy clothes scuttling along the Embankment, and thought he knew just how the people wrapped up inside those bundles must feel.

It was one of those mornings which might have been specifically designed to weigh down the human soul, he decided – one of those mornings when it was almost impossible to envision a silver lining hiding beyond the clouds, and oh so easy to believe that the whole Earth had descended into perpetual winter.

'Buck up, Charlie, it might never happen,' said a cheery voice from somewhere behind him.

DCI Bentley? Woodend asked himself.

It certainly *sounded* like Bentley's voice. But, of course, it couldn't *be* him.

And then he turned and saw – to his amazement – that it was.

But this was not the old Bentley, the drunken sot who had lumbered aggressively around the office the previous afternoon, the mangy wolf for whom an angry snarl came as naturally as breathing.

This was a new Bentley. A happy, beaming one – a Bentley who looked capable of gazing out of the window onto the mournful Embankment below and seeing in it the promise of the spring to come.

'Somethin's happened, hasn't it, sir?' Woodend guessed. 'Somethin' significant?'

'You could say that,' Bentley agreed. 'Yes, I think you could definitely say that without fear of contradiction.'

'Have you got a break in the Pearl Jones murder?'

'The Pearl Jones murder?' Bentley repeated, as if he had no idea what his sergeant was talking about. Then he shook his head. 'No, no progress there, I'm afraid. But the Wally Booth murder's a different matter entirely, Charlie boy! Machin's prepared to hold his hands up for it – but he insists that you're there in the room when he makes his statement.'

'Why would he want *me* to be there?' Woodend wondered.

Bentley shrugged. 'Who knows the way that little toe-rag's twisted mind works? Who even *cares*?'

'It doesn't make any sense,' Woodend muttered, almost to himself.

'Maybe he wants you there because he secretly fancies you,' Bentley said, his good humour unabated by Woodend's concern. 'Maybe he's only insisting you're there because Tongue *told* him to insist. I couldn't give a damn, because the important thing is that he's willing to come clean. Isn't that right?'

'Yes, I suppose it is,' Woodend agreed dubiously.

There were four of them at the table, Woodend and Bentley on one side, and Machin and Tongue on the other.

The solicitor, with a leather-bound folder open in front of him, seemed calm, relaxed, and totally in control of the situation. His client, on the other hand, looked unnaturally wooden. It was rather, Woodend thought, like watching a ventriloquist and his dummy at work.

'My client wishes to make his statement now,' Tongue said. 'Should you wish to question him at any point while he is making it, I will not raise any objections.' He turned to Machin. 'Go ahead, Jimmy.'

The prisoner cleared his throat. 'I met Walter Booth in the Waterman's Arms at approximately two-fifteen on Thursday afternoon,' Machin said. ''E seemed very angry about somefink, but when I asked 'im what the matter was, 'e told me to mind my own bleeding business.'

The first half of that statement was as dull and flat as a

routine police report, Woodend thought. The second half, in contrast, was a first step in the process of establishing Booth as the aggressor in what had followed.

'Carry on,' he said.

'As the afternoon wore on, Booth's mood got worse and worse. I fort of leaving 'im to stew in 'is own juice, but I knew 'e'd be offended if I walked away, and the last fing I wanted was any trouble.'

'He was drunk, was he?' Woodend asked.

'No, 'e wasn't. 'E'd certainly 'ad a couple o' drinks during the afternoon, but 'e was 'olding it well enough.'

'You're sure about that?'

'As sure as I'm sitting here.'

Strange, Woodend thought. *Very* strange.

Given that Machin was attempting to construct a version of the events that was favourable to himself, it would surely have been in his interest to grasp – with both hands – the suggestion that Booth had been drunk.

So why hadn't he?

It was almost as if he knew that the post-mortem report stated the dead man had had very little to drink.

'What happened next?' Woodend asked.

'Just before closing time, Booth really started to lose 'is rag. 'E accused me of sleeping wiv 'is girlfriend, which I assured 'im I never 'ad. Then 'e turned violent. 'E 'it me two or free times, but I didn't do nuffink in return. It was only when I saw 'e was reaching for a bottle that I realized I 'ad to defend myself.'

'But even then, you exercised restraint, didn't you?' Woodend suggested. 'Even then, you did no more than push him away.'

'The mood 'e was in, pushing him away wouldn't 'ave done no good,' Machin said. 'So I punched 'im.'

'Where?'

'In the face.'

And that was *another* detail which was not generally known, but *had* been in the post-mortem report, Woodend thought.

'That's when Booth fell over backwards, is it?'

'That's right, Sergeant. As he went down, 'e 'it 'is 'ead on the brass rail, and that was wot did for 'im.'

'There's no mention in your record of your ever havin' been an associate of Wally Booth's,' Woodend said.

Machin glanced at his lawyer for guidance, but Tongue's eyes flashed back the message that he was on his own.

'We ... er ... Wally and me 'ad only become mates quite recent,' Machin said. ''E'd seemed like a nice bloke – until that partic'lar day.'

'Who else witnessed the fight?'

'I'd ravver not say.'

'It's in your own interest to give me their names,' Woodend pointed out. 'They're the ones who can corroborate your statement.'

'Do wot?'

'They can confirm that things happened just like you say they did.'

'Even though I never meant to kill Wally, I know it was wrong wot I did, and I'm willing to take my punishment for it,' Machin said. 'But what I *ain't* going to do, under no circumstances, is grass up my mates.'

'How would it be grassin' them up, if they played no part in the events?' Woodend wondered.

'My client is well aware that since his "mates" chose to leave the scene of the crime before the police arrived, they could be charged with obstructing justice,' Tongue said. 'And that is something he wishes to avoid.'

'How about if we could promise that no charges would be laid against them, Jimmy?' Woodend asked. 'Would you be willin' to give us their names then?'

'I ... er ...' Machin began.

'My client has made his position in this matter quite plain,' Tongue interrupted. He closed his leather folder. 'That's all, gentlemen.'

'I'd just like to know—' Woodend said.

'I'm sure you would,' Tongue agreed. 'However, Mr Machin has made his statement, and now has no more to say.'

'He might have made the statement, but there are still a number of questions that haven't been—'

'Leave it out, Sergeant,' DCI Bentley ordered. 'We've got what we wanted, so just leave it out.'

The drinking session in the Black Lion had been DCI Bentley's idea.

'We've got a result,' he'd told the rest of the team, when

he and Woodend returned to the office. And when the cheering and whistling died down, he continued, 'And what do we do when we get a result, DC Cotteral?'

'We go out for a lunchtime piss-up, sir,' the DC answered.

'We go out for a lunchtime piss-up,' Bentley agreed.

So there they were, at a table almost over-spilling with drinks.

Bentley stood up. 'When you're looking at me, you're looking at a man whose stock around the Yard has shot up considerably as a direct result of this morning's work,' he said to his team. 'Now, as all you know, I've never have a bad word to say about any of my fellow chief inspectors . . .'

There were more whistles and whoops, and DC Cotteral said, 'Not much you haven't, guv'nor!'

Bentley smiled, indulgently. 'But I will say this,' he continued, 'the bastards had grins stretched right across their poxy faces when the case was handed to me, rather than to one of them. And why was that? Because they didn't think there was a cat in hell's chance of cracking it. But we proved them wrong, didn't we?'

The constables banged their glasses on the table, and shouted, 'Yes, we certainly bloody did.'

'In this job, getting a result is always down to a team effort,' Bentley continued. 'But sometimes there's one particular member of the team who stands out – and that's the case here.' He raised his glass. 'So here's to Charlie Woodend, who not only made a case that even *I* wasn't quite sure *could be* made, but managed to do it in only two days.'

Glasses were clinking, and hands slapped Woodend on the back and patted him on the shoulder.

'Nice one, Sarge!' Cotteral said.

Nice one, Woodend repeated – silently and bleakly.

For now, at least, he had his boss's approval and his colleagues' admiration. This should have been a moment of crowning glory – but it wasn't, because though he *had* got a result, he was far from believing that it was the *right* one.

'When I'd been questionin' Jimmy Machin the previous afternoon, I'd been convinced I was talkin' to Wally Booth's killer,' Woodend told Paniatowski. 'An' then I walked out of the interview room an' ran straight into that bastard Tongue, who not

*only cost more than Machin could ever afford to pay, but had
turned up to defend a client who nobody even knew was under
arrest. An'* that's *when I started havin' my doubts.'*

'And the more you thought about it, the less convinced you
were,' *Paniatowski said, signalling for another round of drinks.*

'Exactly,' *Woodend agreed.* 'The doubts had blossomed
overnight, an' after I'd heard Machin's confession they'd grown
so big they were completely blockin' out whatever warmin'
glow of triumph I might have felt.'

'You never wanted the case in the first place, Charlie,'
Paniatowski reminded him.

'I know, I know.'

'In fact, what you actually* did *want was to get rid of it as
soon as possible – so that you'd be free to investigate the
Pearl Jones murder.'*

'There's no disputing that.'

'So what was your problem?'

'There wasn't just one problem – there were two! The first
was that I didn't like to see justice being perverted, even if
the victim of that perversion in this case was a habitual criminal, who, for all I knew, might well have blood on his hands,
even if that blood wasn't Wally Booth's.'

'And the second?'

'The second was that I didn't appreciate being used as a
pawn in someone else's game, which was what – I was almost
sure – I had been.'

'No, you wouldn't like that,' *Paniatowski agreed.* 'You
wouldn't like that at all.'

Woodend became aware of the fact that Bentley was calling
for yet another round of drinks, and stood up.

'Off for a slash, Charlie?' the chief inspector asked.

'That's right, sir,' Woodend lied.

'You young coppers!' Bentley called after him, with comic
disgust. 'You might be faster on your feet than us old-timers,
but when it comes to a true test of a man's physical prowess
– holding his drink – we leave you standing.'

Woodend stepped out into the corridor. It was the phone,
not the toilet, that he felt a strong urge to use, and even as
he was searching for coins with his right hand, he was reaching
for the receiver with his left.

He asked the operator for the *Daily Globe*, and when he was connected he said he wanted to speak to Tom Townshend.

'Have you found out anything for me yet, Tom?' he asked, the moment Townshend came on the line.

'Found out anything?' the journalist replied. 'What do you think I am, Charlie, a bloody miracle-worker? Do I *need* to remind you that it's less than twenty-hours since you asked me to start rooting around?'

'Which is more than enough time for an ace reporter like you to have come up with results,' Woodend countered.

'You're right, of course,' Townshend agreed complacently. 'Most men would still be floundering around in a swamp of uncertainty, but Thomas Townshend, the Pride of Fleet Street, has already begun to drain that swamp – and to discover what lies beneath it.'

Woodend laughed. 'The richer you get, the more flowery you become,' he said. 'Listen, Tom, the *Globe* may pay you by the word, but I don't – so get to the bloody point!'

'You don't pay me *at all*,' Townshend reminded so. 'You're a *charity* case. So shall I tell you what I've got so far, Oliver Twist?'

'If you wouldn't mind.'

'Well, for a start, I can't give you any details of Victoria Jones's bank account, because she doesn't have one.'

'You're sure about that?'

'I'm sure.'

'Then how does she pay her bills? How did she buy all that expensive stuff I saw in her house?'

'She pays cash.'

'An' where does the cash come from?'

'Now that,' Townshend said, 'is another question entirely, and one which – for the moment – I don't have an answer to. But what I *can* tell you is that her daughter's school fees are paid by the Meadows Educational Trust. Does that name ring any bells with you?'

'No,' Woodend admitted. 'It doesn't.'

'That's hardly surprising, because it's a small trust – a very small one indeed.'

'How small?'

'The only reason it exists at all – as far as I can tell – is to provide a scholarship for Pearl Jones.'

'So who's behind it?'

'It's administered by a solicitor, who is, in turn, instructed by a firm of chartered accountants. What I don't know yet is who instructs *the accountants*.'

'Can you keep diggin'?' Woodend asked hopefully.

'Now that I've got the scent firmly in my nose, you just try and *stop* me,' Townshend replied.

Woodend hung up, and returned to the bar. Though he'd only been gone for a few minutes, the team seemed considerably rowdier than when he'd left them, and Bentley in particular was well on the way to being drunk.

'Here he is again – the man of the hour,' the chief inspector said, slurring his words slightly. 'We've . . . we've been talking it through, Charlie, and we've decided that when we finish here, we'll go to a little drinking club I know in Soho.'

And bollocks to the Pearl Jones murder, eh, you lazy bastard! Woodend thought angrily.

'If you don't mind, sir, I'd prefer to go home and get my head down for a few hours,' he said.

For a moment, it looked as if Bentley was about to take offence at having his offer turned down, then he said, 'Good idea, Charlie. You've been working hard. You go home and have a good long rest.'

But as Woodend left the pub, going home was the last thing on his mind.

On every other day of the week, Greyhound Ron Smithers either ate lunch with his business associates or made do with a sandwich at his desk, but on Fridays he had a permanently booked table for one at the Savoy Grill. He valued this time alone, and liked the fact that the waiters who deferred to him did not do it through fear, as most people did, but simply because he was such a good tipper. So he was far from pleased when, just as he was sipping his coffee and liqueur, the man in the hairy sports coat pulled a chair and sat down beside him.

'How did yer know I was 'ere?' Smithers hissed.

Woodend smiled. 'You're a criminal, Ron. The Met likes to keep track of you, an' all your regular haunts are noted down in your record.'

'My boys are just outside,' Smithers said, threateningly.

'Yes, I'm sure they are,' Woodend agreed. 'An' I dare say that they could throw me out easily enough, if they put their minds to it. But if they did do that – if they caused a scene – then you'd never be welcome here again.'

Smithers sighed. 'What do yer want?'

'I want what coppers like me always want – the answers to a few simple questions.'

'Let's get it over with, then,' Smithers said, resignedly.

'Question number one: why have you been havin' me followed?'

'I 'aven't.'

'Of course you have, Ron. How else would you have known that I'd arrested Jimmy Machin?'

''Oo?'

'I'd also like to know how you persuaded him to confess to Wally Booth's murder,' Woodend continued. 'An' it will have taken some *real* persuadin', because he must have known that if he'd just kept his mouth shut, I'd never have been able to make the charges stick.'

'Yer really are talking in riddles today,' Smithers said.

'I'll tell you what I think. I think he wasn't even *in* the pub when Wally Booth died. Now ask me *why* I think that.'

Smithers took a sip of his brandy. 'All right. *Why* do yer think that?' he asked.

'Because if he'd seen what *really* happened in the Waterman's – and coverin' *that* up is what this whole elaborate pantomime is all about – he might have let the true story slip in an unguarded moment.' Woodend paused. 'Anythin' you'd like to say at this point?'

'Plenty,' Smithers told him. 'Firstly, if the Jimmy Machin yer talking about is Jimmy Machin the keyman . . .'

'He is.'

'. . . then while I've 'eard of 'im, I've never actually met 'im. And secondly, ain't it possible that when 'e confessed to Wally's murder, 'e was doing no more than telling the truth?'

'No, it isn't possible,' Woodend said. 'He'd been briefed on exactly what to say, and he didn't say it particularly convincingly. And when I asked him how he'd become mates with Booth – which was a question that he hadn't been coached to answer – he was completely lost for a minute. Anyway, why are you botherin' to pretend you think he might have

done it. You know he *couldn't have* – because if he'd been in
the Waterman's Arms that afternoon, you'd have seen him for
yourself.'

Smithers laughed. 'As traps go, that's a pretty basic one,
ain't it? I *wasn't* in the Waterman's that afternoon.'

'Your lads were.'

'Maybe they were, and maybe they weren't. But while there
are some bosses 'oo like to go out drinking with their boys
– in, for instance, the Black Lion – I'm not one of them. I
like to keep a certain distance from my employees.'

'I still can't see why you went to all the trouble of fittin''
Machin up for the murder, when you didn't have to,' Woodend
admitted. 'It must have been expensive. Tongue alone will
have cost you an arm an' a leg.'

'Tongue?' Smithers said. ' "Silver" Tongue? Was 'e involved
in all this?'

'You know he was.'

'Listen very carefully,' Smithers said. 'It's *possible* I was
in the Waterman's on that afternoon, though I'll deny it if I'm
pushed. And it's possible – *if I was there* – that I saw a fight
break out in which nobody was meant to get seriously 'urt,
but somebody ended up dead. But it really is as simple as
that. There's no conspiracy to uncover – no deep dark secrets
I'm trying to 'ide from you. All that 'appened was that a
simple accident occurred.'

'Well, all that certainly sounds plausible enough,' Woodend
said. 'But if that *is* what happened, how do you explain
Tongue's involvement?'

'I can't,' Smithers told him. 'Because if somebody asked him
to fit up Jimmy Machin, that somebody certainly wasn't me!'

Fifteen

The single-decker bus creaked and wheezed its way along the country lanes like an old donkey which it would have been no more than a kindness to have had put down. The driver, as venerable as his vehicle, crunched the gears with regularity, hooted his horn occasionally, and maintained a low, muttered monologue which seemed to be aimed at no one in particular. Only the conductor, a thin young man with a rash on his neck and a home-rolled cigarette between his fingers, seemed to be enjoying the journey.

It was hard to believe they were only a few miles away from central London, Woodend thought, as he shifted position in an attempt to make himself as comfortable as he could on a seat which had been designed to take a much smaller man.

'Are you all right?' he asked his wife.

'I'm fine,' Joan replied.

But she wasn't. From the moment that they'd left their tiny flat that Sunday morning, she'd seemed entirely wrapped up in her own thoughts. She'd said nothing to him as they'd travelled by the underground to the last station on the line, and left it entirely up to Woodend to discover which bus they had to take for the next stage of their expedition. And though she had always loved the countryside – even in winter – she was making absolutely no comment on it now.

The bus had ground to a protesting halt in several small villages, and people had got off at each stop, so that now the Woodends were the only remaining passengers.

'It's further than I thought it would be,' Charlie said.

And Joan said nothing.

They reached a T-junction, where an even narrower lane ran off the lane they were now on, and the bus stopped again.

'This is it, mate,' the conductor said cheerfully.

'This is what?' Woodend asked, looking around and seeing nothing but bare trees and naked hedgerows.

'This is Thamesview Lane.'

'Are you sure? I don't see any houses,' Woodend said.

The conductor chuckled. 'There ain't no view of the Thames, eivver, but walk for 'alf a mile down that lane over there, and yer'll have both.'

'I suppose we'd better get off, then,' Woodend said to Joan.

'Yes, I suppose we better had,' Joan agreed reluctantly. Then, as she began to descend the steps to the lane, she turned to the conductor and said, 'Can you tell me when the next bus back is, please?'

'They're every two hours,' the conductor replied.

'Every two hours!' Joan repeated bleakly.

The bus slowly pulled away again, and Joan watched its departure with a mournful look in her eye.

Woodend took her hand, and led her towards Thamesview Lane. 'Soon be there,' he said optimistically.

'Hmm,' Joan replied noncommittally.

Woodend sighed. 'Look, I'm sorry it's taken us so long to get here, luv,' he said. 'But it won't always be like this. I've been doin' my sums, an' I think that next year we should be able to afford a little second-hand car – maybe a Wolseley – to do our runnin' around in.'

Joan stopped walking. 'It's not the time it's taking us to get there that's botherin' me, Charlie,' she said.

'No?'

'No! What's botherin' me is why we're goin' there *at all.*'

'We were invited.'

'Yes, but *why* were we invited?'

'Commander Cathcart wants to have a talk with me.'

'An' couldn't he have done that much more easily in the city, one day in the week?'

'Perhaps. But he also said that he wanted to meet you, an' have us meet his missus. Remember, I did serve with him in the War.'

'An' did you save his life or somethin'?' Joan asked.

'Why do you ask that?'

'Because every time I meet one of your old mates from the army, he always seems to have a story about how you saved his life.'

Woodend laughed. 'Everybody saved everybody else's life in them days,' he said. 'Besides, I was a sergeant – it was my duty to look after my men.'

'But you didn't save *Commander Cathcart's* life?' Joan persisted.

'Nay, lass, by the time him an' me ended up servin' together, most of the fightin' was over.'

'Then I still don't see why we've been "honoured" with an invitation to his house for Sunday lunch,' Joan said, but, despite her doubts, she began walking down the lane again.

They turned a corner in the lane, and the Cathcarts' house was suddenly laid out in front of them.

'Bloody hell!' Woodend said.

Joan tugged at his arm. 'I want to go home, Charlie,' she said.

And though he didn't want to admit it, Woodend could quite see her point.

The house was a substantial tile and brick building which just fell short of being a mansion, and it did not so much *stand* on the bank of the river as loom *over* it. There were, Woodend calculated as he counted the upstairs windows, at least twelve bedrooms. And if the house itself was not enough to impress, there were also the gardens which surrounded it, and managed, even in winter, to maintain an air of grandeur and elegance.

'What? No struttin' peacocks?' Woodend said jovially. 'I expected there to be at least a *few* of them.'

'It's not funny, Charlie,' Joan said. 'It's not somethin' you can just laugh away. Look at them cars.'

It was indeed an impressive array, Woodend was forced to concede. There were Rolls-Royces, Bentleys, and Jaguars. There was even a Wolseley, though this particular model was almost large enough to have fitted the modest one Woodend was contemplating buying in its boot.

'Did you hear what I said just now, Charlie?' Joan demanded.

'About it not bein' funny?'

'No – that I want to go home.'

'We *can't* go home, even if you *do* want to. You heard what the conductor said. There won't be another bus along for two hours.'

'I don't care. We'll go back to the bus stop, an' wait for it anyway.'

'Waitin' there won't make it come any quicker.'

'I know.'

'An' there's no bus shelter, or even a bench to sit on.'

'Then I'll stand. I don't mind.'

'What exactly is it that's botherin' you, luv?' Woodend asked solicitously. 'Is it all them flashy cars?'

'No,' Joan replied. 'It's not the cars themselves – it's the folk that can afford to run them.'

'The folk who've come to lunch?'

'Exactly.'

'Do you think they're better than us?' Woodend asked.

'No, of course I don't,' Joan said, though with not quite as much conviction as her husband would have liked.

'Then what *is* your problem?'

Joan took a deep breath. 'You're right,' she said. 'I shouldn't have a problem. After all, you're a decorated war hero . . .'

'Give over,' Woodend said awkwardly.

'. . . an' I'm a real little peach of a woman.'

'You'll get no argument from me on that score.'

'So let's go to this party an' enjoy ourselves.'

'That's my girl,' Woodend said.

Given the grandeur of the house, Woodend would not have been entirely surprised if they'd been met at the door by a butler kitted out in full livery. But instead, his ring on the door bell was answered by Commander Cathcart himself, accompanied by a strikingly attractive and very elegant woman in her mid-thirties.

'How nice that you could make it, Charlie!' Cathcart said – and he did sound genuinely pleased. He turned his attention to Joan. 'And this, I take it, is Mrs Woodend?'

'Yes, it is,' Woodend confirmed.

Cathcart held his hand out to Joan. 'I'm delighted to meet you at last, Mrs Woodend – or may I call you Joan?'

'Please do,' Joan said.

Cathcart performed another slight twist, so he was looking at the woman next to him. 'And this is *my* wife, Margaret.'

The woman laughed. 'Arthur is such a stuffed shirt that he will insist in introducing me that way,' she said. 'I'd be grateful if you'd ignore him, and call me Peggy – like everyone else in the whole world does.'

Cathcart grinned, perhaps a little ruefully.

'I'll try again,' he said. 'This is my wife, *Peggy*. Shall we go inside?'

Cathcart led them through a large hallway into an even larger lounge.

At one end of the lounge, there was a large oak table on which had been placed half a dozen kinds of glasses and a seemingly endless variety of drinks. Behind the table stood a crisply uniformed waiter. His eyes were as alert as those of any sentry on duty in a war zone, and his general demeanour suggested that when it came to a desire to please, he could leave a puppy dog standing.

At the other end of the room was another long table, covered with a white linen tablecloth. It was piled high with plates, but the promised buffet had, as yet, to appear. The space in the middle of the room was occupied by perhaps two dozen people, all well dressed and all exuding an air of self-assurance which could only have been inherited.

If Joan made a dash for the door now, he would not entirely blame her, Woodend told himself.

But worse was yet to follow.

'Drinks first!' Cathcart announced. He was clicking his fingers – only lightly, but enough to have the waiter scurry across the room in record time. 'What would you like, Joan?'

'I'll have a sweet sherry, please,' Joan said.

For an instant, Cathcart's eyes fluttered. 'I'm not sure we have a *sweet* sherry, as such,' he said, 'but I happen to know we have a rather fine old amontillado, if that will serve instead.'

'That would be lovely,' Joan replied, in a voice which managed to blend the confused with the totally miserable.

'And what about you, Charlie?'

'I'll have a beer, if you've got one.'

Cathcart laughed. 'I should *say* we've got beer, old chap,' he said. 'Barrels of the stuff. I'll tell you later why that is. And now we've got the serious business out of the way, why don't we leave the ladies alone to get to know one another properly, while we find a quiet corner where we can talk about the old days?'

Woodend saw the look of panic well up in Joan's eyes, and said, 'If you don't mind, sir, we'd appreciate a few minutes to get our bearings.'

'Get your bearings!' Cathcart repeated. 'What nonsense! We've got a lot of fat to chew over which would bore the ladies half to death, and you've no need to worry about Joan, because Margaret – Peggy, I should say – is perfectly capable of keeping her amused. Isn't that right, darling?'

'Of course it is,' Peggy agreed, with a smile.

Cathcart placed a hand firmly on Woodend's shoulder, and steered him away from the women.

They did not move far – no more than a few feet. But then, Woodend assumed – though knowing nothing about it – in cocktail-party circles a few feet was all you *needed* to move in order to signal that you were having a private conversation.

'I'll always be grateful for the privilege of having spent time in Berlin in '45,' Cathcart said. 'I can't say it was a particularly *pleasant* experience, but an *experience* it certainly was.'

'I know what you mean,' Woodend said, but his thoughts were not really on Cathcart, but on the woman Cathcart had forced him to abandon.

Joan looked distraught, but if Peggy Cathcart had noticed that, it certainly wasn't showing in her animated expression and extravagant gestures.

Woodend strained his ears in an effort to hear what was being said, and found that, despite the surrounding hubbub, it wasn't too difficult.

'I sometimes feel that while Arthur and I both love this house dearly, it's really rather selfish of us to live here,' Peggy Cathcart was saying.

'Selfish?' Woodend heard Joan echo. 'How do you mean?'

'Perhaps "selfish" wasn't quite the right word,' Peggy conceded. 'What I really meant, I suppose, was *inconsiderate*.'

'Who to?'

'To our visitors, of course. We invite our friends to lunch with gay abandon, not giving a second's thought to how long it will take them to get here, or how difficult it is to find the place. I can't tell you how many people have arrived late, simply because they've spent hours lost down these country lanes of ours. Of course, I don't imagine you had that difficulty, not with your Charlie driving. He looks like a man who knows *exactly* where he's going, and I expect he didn't take a *single* wrong turning.'

Poor Joan, Woodend thought, wondering if she'd have the nerve to admit that they hadn't actually come by car.

'No, we had no difficulty at all,' Joan agreed. 'But then, Charlie didn't *have to* know the way.'

'Didn't he? Why ever not?'

'Because the bus driver did.'

'Did I say something unintentionally amusing?' Cathcart asked Woodend sharply.

'No, sir, I was just remembering something funny that happened yesterday,' Woodend lied.

And he was thinking, That's my girl! That's the woman I married.

Peggy was laughing, as though she thought Joan had made a rather clever joke. But then, when she realized the other woman was serious, her look turned to one of absolute horror.

'You came by *bus*?' she asked incredulously.

'Not all the way, no,' Joan said. 'We did the first half of the journey on the tube.'

'So you don't *have* a car?' Peggy asked, as if she could still not quite get her head around the idea. 'Oh, Arthur's such a fool! He should have *known* that, and sent a car to pick you up.'

'We wouldn't have wanted to put anybody to that much trouble,' said Joan, who looked as if she was beginning to wish she'd just nodded when Peggy had asked if the finding the place had been easy.

'I'm rapidly coming to the conclusion there are only two kinds of women in this world,' Peggy said. 'Sweethearts like you, who "don't want to put anybody to that much trouble", and bitches like my friends and me, who are *so* used to putting other people to trouble that half the time we don't even realize we're doing it.'

'Is that right?' Joan said vaguely.

'And now I've shocked you, haven't I?' Peggy asked.

An' she's not the only one you've shocked, Woodend thought.

'Well, yes, I was a bit surprised,' he heard Joan admit. 'You see, while I've heard men call women "bitches" once or twice – usually when they've had too much to drink – I don't think I've ever heard a woman use the word about herself – an' certainly not about *other* women.'

Peggy laughed again. 'Then clearly you don't hang out with the same kind of bitches as I do,' she said. 'But let's change the subject, shall we?'

'Yes,' Joan said gratefully. 'I think that *might* be for the best.'

'So what shall we talk about? Why don't you tell me how you feel about living in London?'

'It really is very polite of you to spend so much of your time with me, Mrs Cathcart . . .' Joan began.

'Peggy! Call me Peggy!'

'. . . an' I want you to know that I do appreciate it. But wouldn't you rather be chattin' to some of your other guests?'

'Look around you at the women in this room,' Peggy Cathcart said. 'Do they remind you of me? Or do they remind you of you?'

'Well, of you, obviously.'

'Exactly. And that's the trouble with them.'

'The trouble?'

'I've grown up with them – or with their sisters or cousins, which is much the same thing. I know all about their attitudes, and the ways their minds work. So even as I'm asking them a question, I already know what the answer's going to be. And that's most awfully boring.'

'Listen, I know you're tryin' to be kind—' Joan said.

'See the woman over there?' Peggy interrupted, pointing.

'Yes?'

And Woodend saw her, too. She was as tall and elegant as Peggy, and was wearing a cocktail dress which had probably cost as much as a small cottage in Whitebridge.

'I'm going to ask her how her plans for Christmas are going,' Peggy Cathcart told Joan. 'And she's going to tell me that it's hell in Harrods these days, because the assistants are useless, it's full of people who should really be shopping *elsewhere*, and anyway, it doesn't offer anything like the quality it used to. She may also say – and this is more of a guess on my part – that at least she and her family will avoid the worst of the actual Christmas period, because they'll be away in Switzerland, on a skiing holiday.'

'Look, there's no need to . . .' Joan protested.

'Oh, come on, don't spoil my bit of fun,' Peggy said, and

then she took Joan by the arm, and led her across to where the woman in the smart cocktail dress was standing.

'Do you think I'm right about that, Charlie?' Woodend heard Cathcart ask.

'Right about what, sir?'

'That if we'd had the political will, we could actually have stopped the Russians from taking over so much of Berlin?'

'Maybe,' Woodend said.

And from the corner of his eye he saw that Peggy had now led Joan away from the woman in the smart cocktail dress, and the two of them were huddled in a corner, giggling like schoolgirls.

'You seem to be having difficulty concentrating with all this noise,' Cathcart said.

'Well, it is a bit distractin',' Woodend admitted.

'Then maybe it might be better if we adjourned to the garden before we start talking about really important matters, don't you think?' Cathcart said.

And though it sounded like a suggestion, it was very clearly an order.

'That's fine with me,' Woodend said.

And he meant it. He had no qualms about leaving Joan alone any longer. In fact, he thought, she seemed to be coping with the situation better than he was.

'What I didn't know at the time – an' didn't find out until considerably later – was that while all this was goin' on, a very different kind of meetin' was takin' place back in London,' Woodend told Paniatowski. 'It was a significant meetin' in all kinds of ways, not the least of which was that it was the first time in years that Toby Burroughs an' Greyhound Ron Smithers had come face to face.'

'Come face to face,' Paniatowski repeated. 'But weren't they bitter rivals?'

'They were. An' not just at a business level. They hated each other with a passion. Toby Burroughs had told me that he was quite happy to let Ron Smithers have his share of the London pie, you remember, but that was a lie. The simple fact was that there was nothin' he could do about it, and while both men would have loved to take over the other's gang, neither of them was strong enough to pull it off.'

'So where did this meeting take place?' Paniatowski asked.
'Somewhere public, I'd imagine.'

'Very *public*,' Woodend agreed. 'Tower Bridge. They both arrived mob-handed, but on different sides of the river. Then, while the minders stayed at the ends of the bridge, the two bosses walked to the middle, which was where an invisible line ran, dividin' Toby's territory from Ron's.'

'Is that what the meeting was about? Territory?'

'No, it was about Jimmy Machin.'

'Why would Burroughs be interested in Jimmy Machin?' Paniatowski wondered.

Woodend grinned. 'You're almost *askin'* the right question – but not quite,' he said.

'So what *is* the right question?'

'Who asked for the meetin' in the first place?'

'All right, who asked for the meeting in the first place?' Paniatowski said obediently.

'Smithers did. Now ask me why.'

'Why?'

'Because he knew Machin hadn't killed Booth. An' how did he know that?'

'Because he was there himself when Booth was killed?'

'Exactly. He'd almost confessed as much when I confronted him in the Savoy Grill. You remember what he said? "It's possible I was in the Waterman's on Tuesday afternoon, though I'll deny it if I'm pushed. An' it's possible – if I was there – *that I saw a fight break out in which nobody was meant to get seriously hurt, but somebody ended up dead. But it really is as simple as that. A simple accident occurred".'*

'Did *he* see a fight break out – or did he *start* one?' Paniatowski asked.

'That's somethin' we'll never know,' Woodend said. 'Though given his reputation for both temper an' violence, it wouldn't surprise me at all if he was the one who killed Booth.'

Paniatowski took a thoughtful sip of her vodka. 'I still don't see why he wanted the meeting with Burroughs,' she said. 'After all, since he'd already dealt with the business by getting Machin to confess . . .'

'But that's the point! He hadn't! The other thing he'd told me in the Savoy Grill was that if somebody was usin' Tongue *to fit up Machin, it certainly wasn't him. And for once, he was telling the truth.'*

'*So he thought that Burroughs was responsible for the fit-up?'*

'*Yes.'*

'*Why?'*

'*Because although Machin wasn't actually on Burroughs's firm, he'd at least done some work for him in the past.'*

'*And so Smithers wanted to know why Burroughs – his deadly enemy – had gone out of his way to do him a favour?'*

'*He was* burstin' *to know – mainly because he wanted to find out what Burroughs expected in return.'*

'*And what* did *Burroughs expect in return?'*

'*Nothin'. In fact, he said that he knew absolutely nothin' about the fit-up.'*

'*Was he telling the truth?'*

'*Maybe,' Woodend said, enigmatically.*

'*And if he* wasn't *telling the truth – if he* was *behind it – what was his motive? What possible reason could he have had for saving Smithers's bacon?'*

Woodend's grin broadened. 'You're the new detective chief inspector,' he said. 'You tell *me.'*

Sixteen

Woodend and Cathcart strolled through the garden until they reached the natural barrier of the river.

Woodend looked around him – at the swans gliding majestically by; at the weeping willows which would be truly magnificent in a few short months; at the jetty projecting out into the water, to which an expensive motor boat was moored.

'So what do you think of the old place, Charlie?' Cathcart asked. 'Are you impressed by it?'

'Who wouldn't be?' Woodend asked.

Cathcart grinned. 'But if you're as good a copper as I think you are, you'll also have been wondering how I can possibly afford to run it on my salary.'

'No . . . I . . .' Woodend began.

'Charlie!' Cathcart said sternly.

'It had crossed my mind,' Woodend admitted.

'My wife's maiden name was Bairstow. What's the first thing that *you* think of, when you hear that name?'

'Bairstow's Best Bitter,' Woodend said, automatically.

Cathcart laughed again. 'Knowing your penchant for strong ale, I'd have been disappointed if you'd said anything else. Bairstows own not only the brewery, but two hundred and fifty public houses as well. And my wife, as the only child of the late Harold of that ilk, owns *Bairstows* – lock, stock, and beer barrel.'

It was Woodend's turn to grin. 'It's every Northern male's fantasy,' he said.

'What is?'

'Marryin' a woman who owns a brewery.'

'But that's not *why* I married her,' Cathcart told him, suddenly serious.

'No, no, I'm sure it isn't,' Woodend said hastily.

'Do you remember that talk we had, back in Berlin, when

you asked me if I was married, and I replied – rather awkwardly – that getting married was something I'd never quite got around to doing?' Cathcart asked.

'Yes, I do,' Woodend replied.

'I wasn't being quite honest with you at the time. Or perhaps I wasn't being quite honest with myself. The fact is that there are some things you never expect to do in your life, Charlie, and, in my case, one of those things was falling in love. But then I met Margaret, and the moment I caught sight of her, I was lost. She seemed to float across the room, rather than walk as mere mortals do. I thought at first I was just imagining her. And then I realized my poor, pathetic imagination was incapable of conjuring up such a perfect picture of loveliness.'

'She's . . . er . . . certainly a good-lookin' woman,' Woodend said awkwardly.

'And now you're embarrassed,' Cathcart countered.

'No, I . . .'

'Of course you are, and I don't blame you for it for a moment. *Anybody* would be embarrassed at hearing a middle-aged man going on like a love-sick schoolboy. I want to apologize for putting you in such an awkward position.'

'Think nothin' of it,' Woodend said.

Cathcart coughed, perhaps to cover his own embarrassment, then said, 'Anyway, I didn't bring you out here to witter on about myself. It's *you* I want to talk about.'

'Is it, sir? What *about* me?'

'I feel responsible for you, Charlie.'

'There's no need to.'

'Yes, there is – at least, looking at things from my perspective there is. If we hadn't had our little chat in that jeep in Berlin, you probably wouldn't be here now.'

'That's true enough.'

'I suggested you joined the Met because I felt it would be good for *you*, and *you* would be good for it – and though you may not have realized it, I've been following your career with interest.'

'Have you?'

'I have indeed. And I have to tell you now that you've more than justified the confidence that I showed in you back in Berlin.'

'Thank you, sir.'

'I was the one who pushed through your promotion to DCI Bentley's team,' Cathcart continued. 'How are you getting on with Bentley, by the way?'

'All right.'

'All right! That doesn't exactly tell me much, does it?'

'No, sir, I don't suppose it does.'

'Then let me put matters another way. Do you – or do you not – consider him a good copper?'

'We all have our blind spots, an' DCI Bentley's no exception,' Woodend said, picking his words carefully.

'Which is another way of saying that he's a fat, lazy, drunken bastard who never looks for a complicated answer when there's a simple – if wholly erroneous – one lying within his easy reach.'

'I wouldn't put it quite like that, sir.'

'I'm sure you wouldn't. And, given your position in the pecking order, you're very *wise* not to. But, you see, I outrank him, and so I can say what I like.' Cathcart took a pack of cigarettes out of his pocket, and offered one to Woodend. 'To be honest, Charlie, I had initial doubts myself about placing you with Bentley. But that posting was the one that became available at the time, and I decided that you'd probably rather work with him than wait a year or so for another opportunity to arise. Was I right?'

'On balance, yes, you were,' Woodend said. 'Can I ask you what this is all *really* about, sir?'

'I've been hearing rumblings about you coming into conflict with Bentley over one of your recent cases,' Cathcart said, slightly uncomfortably. 'According to these rumblings, you don't like the way your guv'nor's been conducting the investigation, and you've made no attempt to keep those feelings hidden.'

'I've made *every* attempt to keep my feelings hidden – but I'm just not very good at it,' Woodend told him. 'An' just to be clear about this, you are talkin' about the Pearl Jones case, aren't you?'

'I don't know any of the details of your dispute with Bentley, Charlie – and, to be honest with you, I'm not sure I really *want* to,' Cathcart said evasively.

'But you do know *somethin'* about the case I'm talkin' about, don't you?' Woodend persisted.

'I may vaguely have heard a few of the details in passing. This Pearl Jones was a coloured girl, wasn't she?'

'An' by that, do you really mean that she was *just* a coloured girl, sir?' Woodend asked.

'Of course not,' Cathcart protested.

'Good! Because that particular coloured girl had more balls than the two of us put together. An' somebody – some vicious bastard! – robbed her of all her hopes an' dreams by slittin' her throat.'

'You've taken it hard,' Cathcart said sympathetically. 'And not just hard, but personally. Still, knowing you as I do, I can't say I'm surprised about that.'

'The point I'm tryin' to make is that while *you* might not think of her as *just* a coloured girl, that's the way DCI Bentley sees her – which means that he's not about to bust a gut to bring her killer to justice,' Woodend said.

'So a clash between you and Bentley is inevitable?'

'I'm afraid so.'

'And there isn't a way in which you can honourably back down?'

'I haven't thought about it that way, to tell you the truth. But even if there was, I wouldn't take it.'

Cathcart nodded. 'Again, I suppose that's pretty much what I should have expected you to say. Look, Charlie, I'll try to protect you as much as I can . . .'

'I'm not askin' for that.'

'I know you're not, but we're old comrades, and old comrades watch each other's backs. Even so, this isn't the War any more, and while I would have been prepared to give my life for you back then, I'm not prepared to give up my career for you now. If you go down, you go down alone.'

'Understood,' Woodend said.

'That said, if you keep me in touch with developments – preferably without getting *too* specific about the details – I'll do what I can. I may not be able to stop a bullet for you – but at least I should be able to warn you it's on the way.'

'Thank you, sir,' Woodend said.

Cathcart checked his watch. 'The food should be on the table soon.'

'Then maybe we'd better . . .'

'But to tell you the truth, I don't much fancy a lavish buffet lunch. Why don't the two of us slip off quietly to a pub – one of *Margaret*'s pubs, preferably, since it will be keeping the business in the family – and have a couple of pints and a sandwich instead?'

'I'm not sure Joan would like that,' Woodend said.

'Margaret will look after Joan. I'm willing to wager they're already getting on like a house on fire.'

'Even so . . .'

'What are you, Charlie – a man or a mouse?' Cathcart asked, and without giving Woodend time to reply, he continued, 'Look, I'm your boss, and I *insist* on us going out. So if you get into any trouble with your missus later, you can always blame it me.'

'All right,' Woodend agreed reluctantly.

But he was thinking, If you believe that that kind of excuse will work with *my* missus, then you really don't know Joan Woodend.

'I'm sorry about missin' the buffet, but Major Cathcart insisted we went to one of his wife's pubs for lunch,' Woodend said, as he and Joan walked back down the lane towards the bus stop.

'Yes, I expect he *did* insist,' Joan replied noncommittally. 'He looks like a man who expects to get his own way. Still, he *was* kind enough to apologize to me for it, just before we left.'

And what, exactly, did she mean by that? Woodend wondered. That the apology had made everything all right? Or that it had just added insult to injury?

'An' *while* he was apologizing, he offered to arrange a lift back into town for us,' Joan continued.

'Did he?' Woodend asked, still treading carefully while he tried to establish which way the wind was blowing.

'He did – though I imagine it was Peggy who put him up to it.'

'An' what did you say?'

'I told him it was very nice of him to think of us, but we'd quite enjoy the walk to the bus stop – an' besides, we'd bought return tickets.'

The signs weren't looking good, Woodend told himself.

'I'd never have gone with him if I hadn't thought you'd be

all right on your own,' he said. 'But you seemed to be gettin'
on so well with his wife.'

'So you were watchin' us, were you?' Joan asked.

'Not exactly *watchin'*,' Woodend said uncomfortably,
'though I may have glanced across at you occasionally.'

'An' did you happen to hear what we were talkin' about?'

'Not really. I might have caught the odd word or phrase –
it was hard not to – but as far as . . .'

'But you *did* see us go over an' talk to Veronica?'

'Who?'

'The woman in the expensive cocktail dress.'

'Yes, I think I did notice that.'

'An' did you notice how, after we'd finished talkin' to her,
we almost collapsed in a fit of giggles?'

'Yes, I assume that was because she'd reacted just like Mrs
Cathcart . . .'

He dried up, realizing that he'd said too much.

'Just like Mrs Cathcart said she would?' Joan supplied.

'Well, yes.'

'So you heard more of our conversation than you were
lettin' on to?'

'I suppose so,' Woodend admitted.

'Anyway, you're quite right,' Joan continued. 'Peggy asked
her how her Christmas preparations were goin' and she said,
"Oh God, don't ask. I swear, I don't know where Harrods
find their assistants from these days. They're positively simian,
my dear. And the shoppers themselves are even worse. I'm
sure most of them would feel much more at home making
their purchases in some fusty little department store in the
suburbs."'

Woodend laughed, both at the accent she was assuming and
the verve with which she played the role.

'Very good,' he said.

'Thank you,' Joan replied, in a tone which suggested that
while she was pleased he'd liked her impression, she was not
yet quite ready to forgive him for the desertion. 'Would you
like to hear more?'

'Yes, I'd love to.'

'"Not that it really matters *what* the assistants or other
customers are like,"' Joan continued in the same plummy
accent, '"since there's practically nothing there to buy any

more. I think the pre-War concept of quality has disappeared
for ever. I imagine – sigh! – we'll all just have to get used to
putting up with mass-produced rubbish. But I suppose one
shouldn't complain, because when things are at their blood-
iest, we'll be sunning ourselves in the Caribbean."'

'Mrs Cathcart had that part wrong, at least,' Woodend
pointed out.

'Did she?'

'Well, yes,' Woodend said, realizing he'd made another
mistake but accepting there was no way of pulling back from
it now. 'She said they'd be goin' skiing, didn't she?'

'You *were* listenin' carefully, weren't you?' Joan said.

'All right, I admit I was worried about you,' Woodend
conceded. 'An' if it had really looked like you were sinkin',
I'd have waded in an' pulled you out. But after the first few
minutes, you seemed to be doin' fine.'

'I *was* doin' fine – after those first few minutes,' Joan said.
'In fact, I really started to enjoy myself.'

'So you an' her had a really good time together?'

'For a while.'

'What do you mean – for a while?'

'Well, Peggy couldn't spend her whole time with me, could
she? She was the hostess. She had certain social obligations
to fulfil.'

'So what did you do when she'd gone off to talk to other
people?' Woodend asked, intrigued.

'I talked to other people myself. What did you *expect* me
to do? Hide myself away in some corner?'

Well, yes, that seemed *exactly* what you were likely to do
at one point, Woodend thought.

'An' what did you think of these people you talked to?' he
asked aloud.

'Allowin' for the fact that they don't have the slightest idea
of what it's like to live like ordinary folk, some of them were
rather nice.'

'An' the rest?' Woodend couldn't resist asking.

'Oh, the rest of them were nothin' but a bunch of stuck-up
snotty bitches,' Joan said, without heat.

Stuck-up snotty bitches! Woodend thought. That was Peggy
Cathcart's influence!

'Still, I suppose it's not their fault they're like they are,'

Joan continued. 'They can't help havin' been born under-privileged.'

'Under-privileged!' Woodend repeated. 'Are you sure you've got quite the right word there?'

'Absolutely,' Joan said firmly. 'Havin' been born with silver spoons in their mouths, they've been denied the chance to see the world as it really is.'

Woodend chuckled. 'You're a marvel.'

'*I* know that,' Joan said. 'I'm just surprised it's taken *you* so long to realize it.' She paused for a second. 'So are you goin' to tell me what you an' Mr Cathcart were talkin' about in the garden?'

'He said he wanted me to know that he had my best interests at heart,' Woodend told her.

'Meanin' what, exactly?'

'It means that, as far as he's concerned, he's plucked me out of the mire, an' that brings with it a certain responsibility.'

'That's a bit patronizin', isn't it?'

'I suppose it is, if you look at it one way,' Woodend agreed. 'But to understand men like Major Cathcart—'

'Commander Cathcart,' Joan corrected him.

'He'll always be *Major* Cathcart to me,' Woodend replied. 'Anyway, as I was sayin', to understand men like him – to see what's drivin' them – you really have to get into the mind of the officer class.'

'An' what will I find, once I'm in there?' Joan wondered.

'You'll find men who look on themselves as natural-born leaders, an' feel that they have a duty to develop an' foster the talents of those folk below them who they've chosen to adopt as their protégés.'

Joan sniffed. 'It *still* seems a bit patronizin' to me,' she said. 'Are you sure it doesn't bother you at all, Charlie?'

'He means well,' Woodend replied. 'Anyway, as a future leader myself, I hope one day to have protégés of my own.'

'Well, I'm certainly glad you feel that way about him,' Joan said, 'because the last thing I would want would be for you to feel uncomfortable when we have the Cathcarts round to dinner.'

'When we have *what*?'

'The Cathcarts round to dinner,' Joan repeated. 'I wouldn't normally invite people without consulting you first, but unfortunately, Charlie, you weren't there *to* consult.'

No, I wasn't, Woodend thought, I was in the pub with the major – and I'm paying for it now!

'You've invited them round to our pokey little place?' he asked, still not quite able to grasp the magnitude of what his wife had done in his absence.

'What's the matter, Charlie? Do you think they're better than us?' Joan asked, deliberately echoing the words he had used himself, a few hours earlier.

'Well, no,' Woodend replied awkwardly.

'Then what's your problem?'

The problem was that he noticed the way Cathcart had looked down his nose at Joan when she asked for a *sweet* sherry. The problem was that he was afraid Joan was unable to decipher the code which these people talked in, and instead of reading the hidden messages had taken everything they'd said at face value.

'You don't even like Major Cathcart,' he said.

'True,' Joan agreed. 'But as with them stuck-up women, it's probably not his fault that he's the way he is. An' I *do* like Peggy.'

'I'm sure you do. An' I'm sure that she's very nice. But I expect that Mrs Cathcart . . .'

'Peggy.'

'. . . I expect that Peggy told you they've got a very full social calendar at the moment, didn't she?'

'Yes, she did.'

'Well, there you are, then.'

'But they do have *one* free evening next week – an' that's when they're comin' round to dinner.'

Seventeen

It was as they were waiting for the rickety bus to take them back into London that Woodend sneezed for the first time.

'Bless you,' Joan said automatically. Then she took a closer look at her husband, and asked, with mild concern, 'Are you all right, Charlie?'

'I'm fine,' Woodend replied.

'Are you sure about that?

'Yes.'

'I only ask because you're *hardly ever* ill.'

'Well, there you are, then.'

'But when you *are* ill, you're probably the world's worst patient. And do you know why that is?'

Woodend grinned, and was surprised to find that even such a minor movement made his facial muscles ache.

'Well, *do* you know?' Joan challenged.

'Is it because I just lie there in my bed an' expect you to wait on me hand an' foot?' he asked.

'No, it isn't. It's because you absolutely refuse to accept there's anythin' wrong with you, an' continue to carry on as normal. An' what's the result of that?'

'I only make myself worse?'

'That's right. An' then I *do* have to wait on you hand an' foot. Not because you want me to – you're in no state to *want* anythin' very much by that stage – but because you're in such a mess there's no choice in the matter.'

'Fair point,' Woodend agreed. 'The next time I'm feelin' ill, I promise you I'll take it easy right from the start. But I'm not ill *now*.'

'That's what you always say when you're startin' to feel proper poorly,' Joan sniffed disdainfully.

*   *   *

On the underground stretch of the journey home, Woodend's legs began to feel as if they'd had heavy weights attached to them, and by the time the couple reached their flat, his entire body was aching and hot.

'You put the kettle on, an' I'll slip down the road an' pick up Pauline Anne from her mate's house,' he told his wife.

'You'll do no such thing, Charlie,' Joan said. 'Just look at yourself! You're positively sweatin' buckets.'

'I do feel a bit hot,' he admitted.

'I'll go an' pick up Annie,' his wife said firmly, 'an' you – my lad – will get yourself straight off to bed.'

It was never wise to argue with Joan when she was in this kind of mood, Woodend knew from past experience, and anyway, truth to tell, he didn't really feel as if he had the strength to.

He lumbered heavily into the bedroom, and stripped off his clothes – which should have been a quick enough operation, but somehow wasn't. That done, he climbed into bed, and immediately fell into an uneasy sleep.

He is lying down. There is no one else in the bed with him, but he senses that there is someone else in the room.

He tries to open his eyes, and realizes that his eyelids have been glued to his cheekbones. His raises his hands, and slowly – painfully – peels the eyelids back with his fingers.

This is when he sees her standing there – a pretty half-caste girl.

'Hello,' she says with a smile. 'I'm Pearl Jones.'

She is wearing a red dress which is rather short, and has a neckline which, while it doesn't exactly plunge, certainly swoops down far enough to offer promise. This is the dress, he recognizes, that will eventually become her shroud.

There are so many questions he wants to ask her, but the one that immediately comes out of his mouth is, 'Does your mother know you've got that dress?'

'Don't you like it?' Pearl asks, pouting and feigning childlike disappointment.

'It's very nice,' he says, not wanting to hurt her feelings, but knowing that he is going to have to be honest. 'Very nice indeed. It's just that somehow it simply doesn't belong on a kid like you at all. That's why I asked if your mother knew about it.'

Pearl smiles again, slightly mischievously this time. 'You've met her,' she says. 'What do you think?'

Victoria Jones is a God-fearing woman, who goes to church regularly and doesn't drink, Woodend reminds himself.

'Of course she doesn't know about it,' he says.

'Of course she doesn't,' Pearl agrees.

'So what were you doin', wearin' it on the night that you . . . on the night that you . . .?'

'On the night that I died?' Pearl asks. 'Because I do know I'm dead. Or rather, you know I'm dead.'

'I'm not followin' you,' Woodend confesses.

'I'm not really here,' Pearl says. 'I'm in the morgue. And you should have learned by now, Charlie, that even the dead can't be in two places at once.'

'I don't understand,' Woodend says, almost pitifully.

'Of course you don't,' Pearl agrees. 'But you're not at your best, so that's only to be expected. Let me see if I can help you.'

She raises one arm in the air, above her head, then brings it down in a sharp arc before straightening it out again. And when it comes to a stop, she punches the air underneath with her free hand.

'What am I doing, Charlie?' she asks.

'Don't know,' Woodend mumbles.

'Come on, Charlie!' Pearl says, with an anger which he recognizes – even now – as not hers, but his own. 'You're a bright feller – a detective sergeant in the Metropolitan Police. And you know all about charades – you had your

cousin Ethel's kids in stitches when you played
it with them last Christmas. So what have I
just been doing?'

'Mimin'?'

'Yes! But what was I mimin'?'

'Don't know.'

'I'll do it again, but only the once,' Pearl
says sternly.

She repeats the action, and this time he
understands it.

'Question mark,' he says.

'That's right,' Pearl agrees. 'Question mark.
That's all I really am - questions that have
been bouncing around in your head for some time
- questions that you still haven't found an
answer to.'

'An' one of them is the question about the
dress?'

'Naturally, it is. Remember, I'm no more than
a schoolgirl. But not just any schoolgirl,
Charlie - I'm one who works hard, obeys her
teachers, and hopes to go to Oxford. So why
would I even want a dress like that?'

'Somebody suggested to me, at the scene of
the . . . of the . . .'

'Of the crime? Say it, Charlie. At the scene
of the crime! Where my body lay - my throat
savagely slashed through, my life's blood
staining the uneven ground? Say it - it certainly
can't hurt me now!'

'Somebody suggested, at the scene of the crime,
that the reason you were wearin' the dress was
probably because you were on the game.'

'Yes, people can be just horrid about you,
can't they - especially when you're dead and
you can't defend yourself. But you don't believe
I was on the game, do you, Charlie?'

'No, I don't.'

'So why did I need the dress?'

'You needed it as a disguise. Because you wanted
to pretend to be something that you weren't.'

'Very good, Charlie! But that really raises more questions than it answers, doesn't it? And the biggest one of all is, why would I want to pretend to be something I wasn't?'

'I don't know,' Woodend screams. 'I just don't bloody know!'

'You shouldn't let yourself get upset when you're not feeling well,' Pearl says, in a kindly manner. 'Let's try something a little easier, shall we?'

'All right.'

'Do you think my mother loved me?'

'I'm sure she did. She had photographs of you all over the sideboard. An' you should have seen the look of anguish that came to her face when I showed her the picture they'd taken of you at the morgue.'

'I'm sure it must have been heartbreaking. But then – almost immediately – she changed, didn't she? She said she didn't recognize the girl in the picture at all. She insisted that whoever it was, it definitely wasn't me. Isn't that right?'

'Yes.'

'And what could have made her act in such an unmotherly way?'

'I don't know.'

'Come on, Charlie, you can find an answer if you really put your mind to it,' Pearl says – and now there is a hint of impatience in her voice.

'Fear!' Woodend croaks. 'She was frightened.'

'But who was she frightened for? For me?'

'No.'

'Why not for me?'

'Because you were already dead.'

'Then it could only have been fear for . . .?'

'For herself!'

'I knew you'd get there in the end,' Pearl tells him. 'But why was my mother afraid?'

'Because . . . because she thought she might be the next one to die.'

'Obviously. But again, why did she think she might be next?'

'Because the killer was punishin' her for somethin' she'd done to him?'

Pearl clicks her tongue disapprovingly.

'You disappoint me, Charlie,' she says. 'The words you've just used might have come out of your mouth, but it wasn't you speaking them. It's that idiot DCI Bentley I seem to be having a conversation with now.'

'I know,' Woodend admits. 'And I'm very sorry.'

'So let's take a couple of steps backwards, and see if we can make more sense of it,' Pearl suggests. 'If I'd been murdered to punish my mother, she wouldn't have been afraid that she'd be killed herself, would she?'

'No.'

'Why not?'

'Because the point of the punishment would be to let her go on livin', knowin' that she'd been at least partly responsible for your death.'

'Exactly. And if she was the one who the killer wanted dead, why not just kill her, and leave poor innocent little Pearl out of it?'

'Are you sayin' that if she had been killed . . .'

'Or has been killed, Charlie, because you don't know, do you, whether she's still alive or not?'

'. . . or has been killed, it's for an entirely different reason to the one that led to your death?' Woodend asked.

'I'm not saying anything, Charlie,' Pearl replies. 'How can I, when we've already established that I'm not really here?'

He could hear two voices. They sounded as if they were coming through a wad of cotton wool, but they were still clear enough for him to be able to tell that one of them was a woman's voice, and the other a man's.

'He's burnin' up, Doctor,' the woman said, worriedly.

'It's only to be expected, and it's all to the good,' the man replied. 'This is a very nasty case of the flu your husband has come down with, and the best thing for him is just to lie there and sweat it all out.'

'But I feel so helpless!' said the woman – who Woodend had now identified as Joan. 'Isn't there *anything* I can do to make it easier for him?'

'Nothing at all,' the doctor assured her. 'But there's absolutely no need for you to worry about him. All he needs is complete rest for a couple of days, and he should be right as rain.'

When Woodend opened his eyes, the light streaming in though the window made them prickle. But that didn't matter, he told himself. The important thing was that it was morning, and he should already be at work.

'Where's Pearl?' he asked.

'Pearl?' the doctor repeated. 'Is she your daughter?'

'No, she's . . . she's . . .' Woodend said, and then discovered that he wasn't entirely sure *who* she was at the moment. 'She was . . . she was here,' he concluded lamely.

'Well, I can assure you that she's certainly not here now, and if I were you, I'd forget all about this Pearl of yours for a while,' the doctor said. Then he turned to Joan, and mouthed, 'Delirious.'

The man was a complete idiot, Woodend thought woozily.

'I have to get up,' he said. 'I've got to go to the Yard.'

'You're stayin' right there in bed, Charlie,' Joan said, placed a restraining hand on his chest.

As if that could stop him, Woodend thought. Joan was no lightweight, but the idea that she could keep a man of his size down when there was a job to done was plainly ludicrous.

And then, to his amazement, he found that she could – that he simply didn't have the strength to resist her.

'Go to sleep now, Charlie,' Joan said softly. 'You need to go to sleep.'

'Can't sleep,' Woodend told her. 'Not sleepy at all.'

But, without even realizing it, he was already beginning to doze off.

Eighteen

The overnight rain had frozen into a wafer-thin sheet of ice, turning the Thursday-morning Embankment into one of nature's booby traps. Most of the people on their way to work treated this temporary hazard with proper respect, abandoning their usual broad strides in favour of a cautious shuffle, but the big man in the heavy overcoat did not seem aware that there was any danger at all – hardly seemed aware, in fact, that he was even *on* the Embankment.

'Three days!' Woodend kept repeating to himself, as he approached Scotland Yard. 'I've wasted three days. In bed!'

His woollen scarf – which Joan had insisted on wrapping tightly around his neck before she allowed him out – had begun to itch almost from the moment he left the flat, but he had been so preoccupied that he had not even thought to loosen it.

'Three days. Three *whole* bloody days!'

It was possible that Victoria Jones had died sometime in those three days, though *if* she had, he still had no idea why she should have done.

'*Are you sayin' that if she* has *been killed, it's for an entirely different reason to the one that led to your death?*' he'd asked the dead Pearl, in his delirium.

And the dead Pearl had not, of course, provided any answer. Three days!

Whatever clues there were to Pearl's murder – if there were any *at all* – would have grown stale in three days. Or worse, might have disappeared completely.

It wasn't fair to either the dead girl or her mother that he should have been struck down by the flu bug – but then, when had life ever been fair?

Two days had been plenty of time to make a full recovery, he told himself, as he climbed the stairs to his office – after two days he should have ignored the doctor's advice and got back into harness.

But by the time he reached the landing his lungs were on fire, and there was at least a part of him which acknowledged that if he had got up the day before, he'd have been back in his sick bed by now.

The office was empty, save for DC Cotteral, who had abandoned his interest in paper-clip sculpture, and now he was conducting an experiment in abstract art which involved releasing drops of ink from his fountain pen at various heights, and then studying the pattern they made on his blotting paper.

'Good to see you back on your feet again, Sarge,' he said cheerily. Then, with a broad wink, he added, 'Course, we don't really know *why* you were off your feet in the first place, now do we?'

'I had the flu,' Woodend said.

'So you say. But it wouldn't surprise me if, instead of having the *flu*, you'd been hammering the bedsprings with some *floo*zy for the last three days.'

How long had Cotteral been working on that particular line, Woodend wondered. Ever since Joan had phoned in to say that he was sick?

'Get it, Sarge?' Cotteral asked. '*Flu* and *floozy*?'

'I get it,' Woodend said.

He should have expected no better, he told himself. Cotteral had to fill his time with something, and since catching murderers was *unthinkable*, why not fill it by thinking up weak jokes?

'Where's the guv'nor?' he asked.

'Now there you've got me,' Cotteral admitted. 'I don't actually know where he is at the moment. But I *do* know that he said he'd be in later in the morning.'

'An' how's the case goin'?'

'The case?' Cotteral repeated, as if he had no idea what the sergeant was talking about. 'Oh, you mean the little darkie's murder?' he asked, as enlightenment dawned.

Woodend wondered what kind of disciplinary sanction would be imposed on him if he spattered DC Cotteral's idiot face all over the wall. By rights, he thought, he should be given a medal for it.

'Yes, I mean the little darkie's murder,' he said.

'There's been no progress at all, really,' Cotteral said lazily. 'We're still waiting for the big break.'

'How about the mother? Victoria Jones? Have you got any leads on where she might be?'

'Well, yes, we have, as a matter of fact,' Cotteral said, with a sudden seriousness. 'We think that she's hiding in a coal cellar somewhere, especially after dark.'

'Why would you think that?'

A grin started to form at the corners of Cotteral's mouth. 'Because we can't find her, Sarge.'

'You're not makin' any sense,' Woodend told him.

'Don't you know the old joke?'

'What old joke?

'Question: what's the hardest thing in the world to find?'

'I've no idea.'

Cotteral laughed. 'Answer: a nigger, in a coal cellar, at midnight.'

'You make me puke,' Woodend said.

'Don't you think it's funny, Sarge?' Cotteral asked, half-surprised, half-offended.

'No, I bloody don't!'

'But I thought you were one of us now.'

It was the phone, ringing on his desk, which prevented Woodend telling Cotteral that since he'd never had any particular ambition to become an idle, bigoted toe-rag, the chances that he would *ever* become one of them were very slim.

He picked up the phone. 'DS Woodend.'

'You knew what was going to happen, didn't you, you bastard?' demanded the man at the other end of the line. 'You *knew* you were making me walk across an unmarked mine-field – and you didn't bloody care!'

The voice sounded so cracked – so utterly pathetic – that it took Woodend several seconds to identify it. And even when he did come up with a name, it was such an improbable one that he almost sure he'd made a mistake.

'Tom?' he asked tentatively. 'Tom Townshend? Is that you?'

'Why do you even need to *ask* who it is? Or have you sent *so many* poor sods out on suicide missions that you've begun to lose count of them?'

'I really have no idea what you're on about, Tom,' Woodend protested. 'Can we meet up somewhere an' talk about it?'

'If it was left up to me, the next time we met would be at your funeral,' Townshend said bitterly. 'And the only reason I'd put in an appearance there would be so I could dance on your grave.'

'Listen, Tom—' Woodend began.

'But it *hasn't* been left up to me, has it?' Townshend interrupted. 'I've been told we've *got* to have a meeting. This morning!'

'Told? *Who* told you?'

'I'll see you at the northern end of the Broad Walk in Green Park, in an hour from now.'

'I'm not sure I can just drop everything here and—'

'Be there!'

'I have to know what's happened, Tom,' Woodend said worriedly. 'You need to explain . . .'

But he was talking to a dead line.

The plane tree stood directly behind the park bench. Its solid trunk seemed impervious to the cold, but its smaller branches suddenly began to shiver, as if, so it seemed to Woodend, they had only recently discovered their own winter nakedness.

'Own winter nakedness!' he repeated, this time aloud – and with mild self-disgust. 'Leave poetry to them what's got the trainin' an' aptitude for it, Charlie. You just concentrate on catchin' villains.'

But the fact that the stark image *had* come to him, unsought, merely showed that the feeling of bleakness – which had enveloped him while talking to Tom Townshend on the phone – was still with him.

The sight of Townshend himself – even from a distance – did nothing to help dispel the mood. He was sitting on the bench with the collar of his overcoat turned up around his ears, and his hat pulled down so tightly that it almost covered his eyes. He seemed to be a much smaller man than the one who Woodend had talked to so recently in the Conway Club.

While Woodend was standing there, watching and worrying, the cigarette in his right hand burned so far down he could feel the heat of it on his fingers. He performed the impressive trick of taking a fresh Capstan from its packet one-handed, then lit the new cigarette from the old one, threw the stub away, and began to walk towards the bench.

On the phone Townshend had seemed desperate to have a meeting, but now, when he heard Woodend's approaching footsteps, he did not look up – and even when the sergeant stopped directly in front of him, he kept his eyes fixed firmly to the ground.

'Whatever's happened to you, I never meant it to,' Woodend said. 'I had no idea at all that you'd be runnin' any risk. I give you my word on that, as an old comrade.'

Townshend did finally raise his head – just enough for Woodend to see some of the bruising on his face.

'Why is it, Charlie, that when you're a young man, with so much to live for – so much to look forward to – you throw yourself into the heat of battle without even a second's hesitation?' he asked.

He didn't sound angry, as he had done earlier – and as Woodend had expected him to now. Instead, his voice was filled with deep sadness, almost as if he were in mourning.

'And why is it that later in life,' Townshend continued, 'when so many of the good times are already far behind you – when you know it's all downhill from now on – that the fear finally comes?'

'I don't know,' Woodend admitted. 'Maybe it's because the less you have left, the more you learn to cherish it.' He took a deep drag of his cigarette, then said, 'Tell me what happened, Tom.'

'I can't help you any more,' Townshend said. 'From now on, Charlie, you'll have to fight the battle on your own.'

'If that's all you needed to say to me, you could have done it over the phone,' Woodend pointed out.

'I know.'

'So what was the point of draggin' us both all the way out to the park, on a shitty day like this?'

'It was just the way it had to be.'

Woodend quickly scanned the area around the bench. A woman, warmly wrapped up, was pushing her brand-new baby in a brand-new pram. A tramp, swathed in even more layers of clothing than the woman, was picking up the cigarette end that the sergeant had recently discarded. And standing in a clump of trees, a hundred yards away, was a man in a green duffel coat holding his hands up to his eyes.

No! Woodend thought. *Not* holding his hands up to his eyes – holding something *in* his hands up to his eyes.

Binoculars!

'We're bein' watched by the feller who's standin' in that clump of trees,' he told Tom Townshend.

'Yes, we are,' Townshend agreed.

'How long has he been there?'

'I don't know.'

'All right, then, let me put it another way – how long is it since you first *noticed* him there?'

'I didn't notice him at all. I had no idea where he'd be – but I knew he'd have to be *somewhere*.'

'*Why* is he here?'

'Can't you work that out for yourself?'

Yes, Woodend thought, he probably could.

'He's here because somebody decided that it wasn't enough for you to just *tell* me you weren't goin' to help me any more – you had to be *seen* to be tellin' me?' he guessed.

'Yes, that's exactly why he's here,' Townshend agreed.

'Well, since he *is* watchin' us, we might as well give him somethin' *interestin'* to watch,' Woodend said.

He threw his cigarette on the ground, grabbed Townshend by the lapels of his overcoat, and jerked the journalist roughly to his feet.

'For God's sake, what are you doing, Charlie?' Townshend gasped. 'Are you trying to scare me? Because if you are, you're wasting your time. I couldn't be more terrified than I am already.'

'I can see that for myself,' Woodend said softly. 'An' believe me, that's not my intention, Tom. All I'm tryin' to do is put on a good show for your mate over there.'

'I don't understand,' Townshend said.

'If I just walk away, he'll never know what you've actually said to me. But if I rough you up a bit – an' then storm off in a temper – it'll be obvious that you've delivered just the message you were *supposed to* deliver.'

He released his grip on the other man's lapels, and pushed Townshend roughly back onto the bench.

'Jesus Christ, that hurt,' the journalist groaned.

'It was *meant* to hurt,' Woodend told him. 'We're bein' observed by a professional, an' if I'd tried to fake it, he'd have *known* it was faked.' He lit up another cigarette. 'Who did this to you, Tom?'

'I don't know.'

'Are you sayin' you didn't recognize them?' Woodend asked, waving his hands angrily in the air for the benefit of the man with the binoculars.

'That's right, I didn't recognize them,' Townshend agreed.

'You're lyin',' Woodend told him. 'You know the face of every major villain in London. That's your job.'

'The . . . the reason I didn't recognize them was because they were wearing masks,' Townshend stuttered.

Woodend shook his head. 'No, they weren't.'

'I swear to you . . .'

'An' the *reason* they weren't wearin' masks was because they wanted you to know who they were – an', more importantly, they wanted you to know who it was that had sent them.'

'You're right, of course,' Townshend agreed weakly. 'I *do* know who sent them. But I daren't tell you.'

'Then what *can* you tell me?'

'Nothing! I can't tell you a bloody thing!'

'What did they *say* to you?' Woodend persisted.

'They told me it was about time I started minding my own business.'

'An' what did they mean by that?'

'I don't know.'

'You're lyin' again.'

'They . . . they told me to stop trying to find out who was behind the Meadows Educational Trust.'

'Have you found any more about the trust than you knew the last time we talked?'

'No. And that's the truth, Charlie! But even if I *had* found out more, I wouldn't tell you now.'

'Under the circumstances, I can't say I blame you,' Woodend said. 'Is the watcher still there?'

'He's still there,' Townshend confirmed.

'I'll leave in a minute,' Woodend told him. 'But before I do, I'm goin' to have to hurt you again, so you'd better brace yourself.'

'Do you have to?' Townshend groaned.

'You know I do. It's for your own protection.'

'Then make it quick.'

Woodend lashed out with his right hand. Townshend never saw the blow coming, but when it struck his cheek, his head rocked.

'Well, *that* should certainly convince the watcher,' Townshend said, with what passed, on his battered face, for a grin.

'I'm sorry I got you into this, Tom,' Woodend said, looking down at him. 'If I'd known how deep it ran, I'd never have asked you to help.'

Then he turned, and stormed away like an angry man who had been frustrated at every turn – which, given the circumstances, wasn't a hard show to put on.

Nineteen

As he'd left Tom Townshend and Green Park behind him, Woodend hadn't even stopped for a moment to wonder where he would go next – because he'd already known he would be heading for Balaclava Street. The place seemed to have a hold on him. It exerted a magnetic – or perhaps even magical – pull that was hard to resist. Now, back in Canning Town and standing on the sordid street where hopes and dreams died before they had even begun to come into bud, he asked himself why he had bothered.

He didn't know what he expected to find there. He didn't *really* know if he expected to find anything at all. But since DCI Bentley's official investigation clearly wasn't going anywhere – and Tom Townshend's enquiries had been brought to a sudden, terrified halt – he had to do *something* himself.

Or to put it another way, he thought despondently, he had come back to Balaclava Street because he had no idea *where else* to go.

He walked slowly from one end of the street to the other; past the door of Victoria Jones's looted house; past the window behind which Lene sat watching her own narrow world go by; up to the pub where – contrary to what the DCI had claimed – Victoria Jones had *not* spent her days drinking, and where her daughter, Pearl, had *never* rung her to say that she all right.

He supposed that what he'd secretly been hoping for (*so* secretly that he'd even been keeping it from himself) was that someone would approach him and provide him with the lead which would get the investigation rolling again: a neighbour, who had written down the registration number of the big black car which had, early one morning, spirited Victoria away; a friend of hers from church (another *darkie* Christian, as her neighbours might say), who would be able to tell him where she got her money from; a snotty-nosed kid, a talking dog – anybody, or anything, which could give him the break he needed.

When he *was* finally approached, it wasn't by any of these. Instead, it was by three hard-looking men, who walked towards him with a firmness of purpose which left no doubt in his mind that he was their intended target.

He waited until they were a few feet from him, then raised his hand and said, 'Stop right there.'

'Or what?' one of them asked – but they had stopped anyway.

'Or I'll breathe all over you.'

'Come again?' the man said, as if he suspected he'd misheard.

'I'm just gettin' over a very bad case of the flu,' Woodend warned. 'An' let me tell you now, you wouldn't want my germs.'

And he was thinking, These aren't local lads at all. They've been brought in from outside.

Which was not good news – because London gangsters generally cleaned up their own mess, and it was only when they had a particularly nasty job they needed doing that they brought in outsiders.

'Did you hear dat?' said the man who was clearly the leader of the trio. 'He just threatened to breathe all over us! What we've got here, lads, is a bobby who can do a comic turn! I like dat.' He turned to the man on his left. 'Don't *you* like dat, Paulie?'

'Oh, I do, Eddie,' the other man agreed obediently. 'I enjoy a good laugh, me.'

'How about you, Jack?' Eddie asked the third man.

'I tink the bobby's a regular riot.'

They were Liverpudlians, Woodend realized.

And that was more bad news – because there no harder gangs in the whole country than the ones based in Liverpool.

'But ja know what's an even funnier joke?' the man called Eddie asked Woodend. 'I've gorra a pistol in my pocket, an' if you don't do exactly what I tell you, I'm gonna blow your bloody head off.'

Eddie didn't want to shoot him – Woodend was sure of that – because the Liverpudlian knew that once he'd killed a copper, he was a marked man.

No one would protect him. No one would hide him. The moment he pulled that trigger, he was putting a rope around his own neck.

So Eddie didn't *want* to shoot him – but if things didn't turn out how he'd planned them to, if he lost his nerve for a moment – then he just well *might*!

'Let's hear your patter, then,' Woodend suggested.

'My patter?'

'The little speech that you've got worked out in your head.'

'Oh, *dat* patter,' Eddie replied, with a grin. 'Well, it's like dis, Sergeant. We've come all de way down to the big city to teach you a lesson you won't forget in a long time. Now if you make us do it here, where there's witnesses, it's gonna be a very rough lesson. But if you let us take you into a back alley – if you cooperate with us, like – we might go a bit easier on you. So which is it to be?'

Eddie was lying, Woodend thought. The beating would be just as harsh *wherever* it was administered. But the longer it was postponed, the more chance there was that the three thugs would drop their guard for a moment.

'I'll cooperate,' he said.

'A wise choice,' Eddie told him. 'I tink you'd berra turn round now, Sergeant. And do it slowly.'

Woodend performed a slow turn, and the moment he was facing the other way he felt strong hands grip his arms tightly.

Anyone who was watching would know exactly what was going on, he told himself.

But would they care?

Would they call the police station?

No chance!

In the eyes of most of the occupants of Balaclava Street, beating up a copper was almost a public service.

With Eddie behind them – and his pistol no doubt pointing at the sergeant's head – Woodend and the two other Liverpudlians walked a few yards down the street, and then turned into a narrow alley.

'Shall we do it here?' Paulie asked.

'No,' Eddie replied. 'Let's take him round to der back street. It'll be wider, so we'll have more room to do de business.'

As they wheeled around the corner, Woodend saw that Eddie

had been right. The back street was *much* wider than the alley, wide enough to accommodate what the council called 'the sanitary engineers' vehicle' and everybody else – well aware that its sole purpose was to collect the large pails (often swilling over with faeces) from the street's outside toilets – referred to as the 'shit cart'.

But while there was more space for Eddie's crew, there was also more space for him, Woodend thought. Because though he accepted the fact that he was going to take a beating – and probably a very bad one – he was not going to go down without a fight.

'Dis'll do as well as anywhere,' Eddie said, when they had walked a few yards up the street.

Paulie and Jack stopped, did a half-turn, and – without relinquishing their grip on his arms even a little – flung their prisoner against the wall.

Woodend gasped as he felt the breath forced out of him. But no real damage had been done. Not yet!

Eddie marched up and down in front of the other three men, like an officer inspecting his troops.

'Before we do what we're here for, I've been told by the feller who sent me to ask you a few questions,' he said.

'An' who *is* "the feller" who sent you?' Woodend wondered.

'We don't want to go into names. Let's just call him "a concerned friend", shall we?' Eddie suggested. 'Can I ger on wid de questionin' now?'

If Woodend could have shrugged, he would have done, but he was still held in a vice-like a grip which made such a gesture impossible; so he simply said, 'If that's the way you want to play it.'

'It *is* de way I want to play it,' Eddie told him.

'Then ask away.'

'What your "friend" wants to know is why, when he went to all de trouble of phoning you up to warn you off de darkie girl's case, you didn't listen.'

'I must have had the phone held up to my left ear, an' that's the one that I'm deaf in,' Woodend said.

'Still de comedian,' Eddie said. 'I wonder if you'll still find it funny when you're crawlin' around on the ground, looking for dat *left ear* of yours.'

'What else did my "friend" say?' Woodend asked.

'De other ting that he wanted me to ask you was if you was really as stupid as you seem to be.'

'An' why would my friend think that I was stupid? Just because I wouldn't listen to him?'

'No – because you wouldn't listen to *anybody*. He says dat even an idiot like you should have worked out by now that nobody wants the case solved – and dat includes your bosses in the big cop-shop on de river.'

It was time to make his move, Woodend decided.

He let his body go limp – as if he were almost on the point of collapse – and said, 'Listen, Eddie, you don't have to do this, you know.'

'Did I say you could call me "Eddie"?' the other man demanded.

'No, but . . .'

'Then call me *sir*.'

Woodend gulped. 'You don't have to do this, sir.'

'But I *do* have to do it,' said Eddie, who was still parading up and down in front of him. 'I've already been *paid* to do it.'

'But . . . but if you went back to the man who sent you . . .'

'Your concerned friend?'

'Yes, if you went back to him, an' you told him that you thought I'd already learned my lesson . . .'

'Not quite so full of yourself now, are you?' Eddie asked. 'Face it, Charlie, you're going to take a hammering,' he grinned again, 'so you might as well just sit back and enjoy it.'

'Please . . .!' Woodend begged.

And then he tensed his body – and lashed out with his right foot.

He would have liked to have kicked Eddie in the groin, but the angles were all wrong for that, so instead he aimed at his left kneecap.

Woodend felt his boot connect, and heard Eddie scream out in agony. A heavy thud followed almost immediately, which was probably the sound of the Liverpudlian hitting the ground, but he didn't see Eddie fall, because he'd already turned his attention to Paulie and Jack, and was attempting to swing them round so that their heads banged together.

It didn't work.

He'd never really thought it would.

These men were professional hard cases, and had given more beatings than he'd had hot dinners.

There was a sudden explosion of pain in the pit of Woodend's stomach, and as he sank to slowly his knees, gasping for air, he felt a blow to his head which made his vision blur.

'Don't hit him any more!' he heard Eddie call out. 'He's mine!'

Eddie rose slowly to his feet, placed his left foot on the ground, and winced. He tried again, and seemed to find it more bearable this time. Satisfied he could just about walk, he took a flick knife out of his pocket and hobbled over to the kneeling man.

Very gingerly, Eddie bent his knees again, so that his head was on the same the level as Woodend's.

'You shouldn't have dat to me,' he said, through clenched teeth, ''cos now I'm really going to hurt you. Now, I'm gonna take your eye out.'

The sudden and dramatic appearance of the large black van took all four men by surprise.

One second it wasn't there at all, the next it was speeding down the back street with its engine roaring. It seemed, for an instant, as if it would keep on going until it had ploughed them all down, then the driver hit the brakes and the van came to a screeching, juddering halt.

The doors flew open, and three men emerged. They were all carrying clubs in their hands, and had nylon stockings over their heads.

'What's happening? Who de bloody hell are you?' Eddie yelled.

But by the time he had finished speaking, the first of the new arrivals – a man in a green duffel coat – had almost drawn level with him, and instead of answering the question, he simply swung his club.

The club found its target, hitting the side of Eddie's skull with a dull but sickening thud – and Eddie went down again.

Paulie and Jack, who had already released their grip on Woodend, moved into the centre of the street, where they would have more fighting space. But even as they stood awaiting the onslaught, they must have known that their knuckledusters were no match for the wicked-looking clubs of their three advancing enemies.

The fight was short and bloody. Paulie, attacked from two sides, was the first to go down. And then it was three against one, and though Jack did manage to land a single punch before he succumbed himself, the outcome had never been in doubt.

The man in the green duffel coat walked around the fallen Liverpudlians in what appeared to be partly a tour of inspection, and partly a lap of honour.

'That'll teach yer not to come sticking your oar in where it's not welcome, won't it, you Scouse bastards?' he said, almost conversationally.

Then he kicked Paulie – hard – in the ribs.

Paulie groaned, but barely moved at all.

'These toe-rags are making the street look untidy,' Duffel Coat said. 'Get 'em in the back of the van.'

One of his men grabbed Paulie by the ankles, the other grabbed Jack. They dragged the two men along the street, and as they did so the backs of the Liverpudlians' heads went bang-bang-bang along the cobblestones. Once they had deposited the first two in the van, the men came back for Eddie.

Duffel Coat crouched down in front of Woodend.

'Yer fort yer was a gonner there, didn't yer?' he said.

'No, I always knew that the cavalry would turn up at the last minute,' Woodend replied.

And then he tried to smile – which hurt.

'Let me 'elp yer up,' Duffel Coat suggested, putting this hands under Woodend's armpits and levering him to his feet.

It was a painful process, but once he was up, Woodend found that he could *stay up* without assistance. And though his gut was still on fire, at least now his vision had cleared.

'Do you need us ter take yer anywhere, or can yer get there under yer own steam?' Duffel Coat asked.

'I can manage on my own,' Woodend said. 'Who are you?'

'The last bloke wot asked me somefink like that got a club round the 'ead,' Duffel Coat said.

And though – given the way the nylon stocking distorted his features, it was hard to say for sure – Woodend was *almost* certain that he grinned.

'What are you goin' to do with them three Liverpool lads?' he asked. 'Kill them?'

'Nah,' Duffel Coat said. 'Nuffink like that. We'll just wrap 'em in a nice neat parcel, and send 'em 'ome to mum.'

He walked back to the van, and just before he got in, he turned again. He stood rooted to the spot for a moment – as if assessing whether or not Woodend really could manage on his own – then gave a cheery wave and said, 'Mind 'ow yer go.'

It was those few seconds of standing still which had really given him away, Woodend thought.

Up to that point he'd had his suspicions about the man, but no more. After all, he argued to himself, there were probably thousands of men in London – perhaps even scores of thousands – who wore green duffel coats. And if only by the law of averages, the chances were that a good number of them would be roughly the same height and build as this man.

But how many of the men of similar height and build would adopt exactly the same *stance* when sizing up a situation as he had? And what was the likelihood of Woodend running into two of them, barely more than an hour apart?

The van drove away, and Woodend found himself wondering if Duffel Coat had followed him from the park, or if he'd only been called in when it became obvious that reinforcements would be needed.

Twenty

'What are you working on, Sergeant?' DCI Bentley asked.

Woodend looked up from a desk, artfully strewn with documents and reports, which, if they were not in fact meaningless in themselves, were certainly meaningless to him.

'I'm just catchin' up on my backlog of paperwork, while I've got the chance, sir,' he said.

Bentley nodded approvingly. 'Excellent. I've always said that well-maintained paperwork is the sign of a tidy mind – and that a tidy mind is the sign of a good policeman.'

Quite right, Woodend thought. Who cares whether you catch any criminals or not, as long as all your 'i's are neatly dotted an' all your 't's clearly crossed?

'What about the rest of you?' Bentley asked the three detective constables who were the other current occupants of the office. 'Have there been any developments on that little darkie's murder yet?'

Two of the constables contented themselves with simply shaking their heads, but DC Cotteral said, 'We're still working on it, sir.'

'Is that right?' Bentley asked. 'Well, might I suggest that you work on it a little *harder*?'

'Sure thing, guv,' Cotteral agreed readily.

'I have to go out for the afternoon, and the chances are that I won't see you again until tomorrow morning,' the DCI continued. 'But when I *do* see you, you'd better not come to me empty-handed. Solid leads is what I want. Solid leads is what I *demand*.'

His words didn't ring true, Woodend thought. It was almost as if Bentley was play-acting – and doing so solely for *his* benefit.

What was it Eddie, the Liverpool thug, had said?

'*Nobody wants the case solved – and that includes your bosses in the big cop-shop on the river!*'

So maybe he'd had it wrong about the investigation all along. Maybe it wasn't just idleness or bigotry that was slowing it up. Maybe there was *another* reason for the sluggishness – one he couldn't even begin to guess at.

'Remember, boys,' Bentley said from the doorway, 'it's a solid lead I want – something I can really get my teeth into.'

Then he stepped through the door, and was gone.

And as Bentley's footsteps echoed down the corridor, Woodend's mind turned to thoughts of the man in the green duffel coat.

'I was very grateful for what he'd done for me,' Woodend explained to Paniatowski. 'As it was, I was hurtin' quite a lot, but if he hadn't *intervened, it would have been a bloody sight worse. But what I still couldn't understand was* why *he'd intervened.'*

'*I should have thought that was pretty obvious,' Paniatowski said.*

'*Would you?' Woodend asked. 'Then please explain it to me.'*

'*Well, the man who'd sent the Liverpudlians after you wanted you off the Pearl Jones case. Agreed?'*

'*After what they'd said to me, there's no disputin' that.'*

'*And whoever was behind the man in the green duffel coat wanted you to stay* on *the case.'*

'*It's as simple as that, is it?' Woodend asked.*

'*I think so.'*

'*Then how do you explain what happened to Tom Townshend?'*

'*Sorry?'*

'*Two hours before the man in the green duffel coat rescued me so I could continue investigatin' the murder, he beat the shit out of Tom precisely* because *he was part of that same investigation. Now how do you make any sense out of that?'*

'*I can't,' Paniatowski admitted.*

'*No, I didn't think you could,' Woodend said, his smile back in place. 'But there* is *an answer, an' when it comes to you, you will let me know, won't you?'*

* * *

Woodend raised his head, and glanced around the office. Even though Bentley had gone, the three detective constables were all on the phone, making a great show of trying to come up with the lead that their guv'nor had demanded. Yet Woodend couldn't help thinking that that was all it was – a show!

So there they all were, he told himself – four men sitting in an office, three pretending that they *were* working on the Pearl Jones case, and one pretending that he *wasn't*.

When Woodend arrived home at seven o'clock, it was to be greeted by the smell of furniture polish and freshly cut flowers, which was no surprise at all to him, since that night was *the* night on which Commander and Mrs Arthur Cathcart were coming round for *the* meal.

'So how does the place look?' Joan asked him, the moment he stepped into the living room.

Woodend glanced around him, which, given the size of the flat, didn't really take him very long.

'It looks grand,' he said. 'What are we givin' them for supper?'

'Dinner, Charlie,' Joan corrected him. 'We're givin' them *dinner*.'

'Dinner, then,' he agreed.

'We're havin' Lancashire hotpot.'

He'd been expecting her to say steak or fish. It had never occurred to him that she would be offering her guests the typical Lancashire mill workers' meal of meat and vegetables, which owed its popularity mainly to the fact that it could be left stewing all day, while the whole family was out at work.

'Is there somethin' wrong with givin' them hotpot?' Joan asked, sensing his misgivings.

'Nay, lass,' Woodend said, unconvincingly.

'You think there is,' Joan countered. 'I can see it in your eyes. But what you have to understand, Charlie, is that posh food would be no treat for them. They're so used to it, they'll have it comin' out of their ears. But they'll never have had Lancashire hotpot – so it'll be a nice change for them.'

'You're one in a million,' Woodend said admiringly.

And so she was, he thought.

Most wives in her position would have been intimidated by the thought of the Cathcarts coming round to eat, but Joan had not only taken the whole thing in her stride – she had been the one who'd actually arranged it.

'You seem to be movin' a bit stiffly, Charlie,' Joan said.

And how many women, just before their important dinner party, would have noticed *that*? Woodend thought with affection.

'I'm all right,' he said. 'Is there anythin' I can do to help?'

'No, you just put your feet up for a while.'

'I don't need to . . .'

'You've probably been sweatin' over a hot criminal all day, an' now you need to put your feet up!' Joan said firmly.

'Well, just for the sake of domestic tranquillity, I'll not argue with you any more,' Woodend told her, as a pain shot across his midriff.

It was at twenty past seven that Joan's veneer of confidence began to show the first signs of cracking.

'I think you were right, Charlie – I should have cooked somethin' else for them,' she told Woodend.

'*I* never *said* you should have cooked somethin' else,' Woodend pointed out. 'An' anyway, I'm sure they'll enjoy what you *have* cooked them.'

'Maybe we should have taken them out to a restaurant,' Joan fretted.

As if we could ever afford the kinds of restaurants that *they're* used to goin' to, Woodend thought.

'I told you, they'll love your food,' he said. 'An' if they don't . . .'

'Yes?'

'Well, they can just get stuffed, can't they?'

'Thank you, Charlie,' Joan said, with a weak smile.

'What for?' Woodend asked.

His wife shrugged. 'I don't really know. For just bein' *you*, I suppose.'

At twenty-five past seven, Joan began moving the vases of flowers around, and would probably have rearranged all the furniture, too, if Woodend hadn't stepped in and stopped her.

'It's just that the flat looks so *small*,' Joan said.

'It *is* small,' Woodend told her. 'An' shiftin' around the sofa isn't goin' to make it look any bigger. Besides, this is where we *live*, *not* who we *are*.'

'Sometimes I think I've married the wisest man in the world,' Joan said.

'An' sometimes you think you've married a bloody idiot,' Woodend countered.

'That's true as well,' Joan agreed.

At half past seven on the dot, the door bell rang.

'You answer it, Charlie,' Joan said, in a panic.

Woodend opened the door, and saw Peggy Cathcart standing on the threshold. At her own luncheon party she'd been wearing an elegant cocktail dress. Now she was wearing a cheap – if slightly daring -- frock.

Woodend wondered if she'd deliberately dressed down, so as not to intimidate them – and *if* she had, whether he appreciated the gesture or not.

'Where's the commander?' he asked. 'Parkin' the car?'

Peggy looked embarrassed. 'I'm afraid Arthur won't be coming after all,' she said. 'He was called to a very important meeting at the last minute.'

Had he been called to a meeting, Woodend wondered – or had he *arranged* a meeting himself, in order to avoid what he probably suspected would be a very awkward social situation?

'Well, it's a great pity the commander can't be here, but these things happen,' he said aloud.

'Maybe they do, though I'm still furious that he *allowed* it to happen,' Peggy replied. 'But I'm certainly not going to let his absence spoil *my* fun.'

Peggy looked surprised that there was no first course to precede the hotpot, but she made such a quick recovery that Woodend was almost certain that Joan hadn't noticed. And the commander's wife certainly attacked the food which was placed in front of her with real gusto.

Over the meal – and mainly in answer to Joan's questions – Peggy talked about her life. She told of foreign cruises and embassy receptions, of sitting on the boards of museums and attending the final day of racing at Royal Ascot. She was both witty and modestly brief, but the more she spoke, the more Joan seemed to shrink into herself.

'Well, you certainly seem to have led an interestin' life,'

Joan sighed, as Peggy mopped up the last of her stew with a piece of bread.

'Do you really think so?' Peggy asked.

'Well, yes.'

'Well, I don't. I think it's been all been so mind-numbingly predictable. Oh, I admit the idea of a cruise *sounds* glamorous if you've never been on one, but really, it doesn't take you long to realize that when you've seen one stretch of sea, you've seen them all.'

'But what about goin' to Royal Ascot for the races? What about meetin' the King an' Queen in the Royal Enclosure?'

'You don't *meet* the King and Queen,' Peggy said. 'You're *presented* to them.'

'Isn't that the same thing?'

'No, it most certainly is not. You stand in a line, and when they draw level with you, you curtsey. And if you're *very* lucky, they say a few words to you. It's supposed to be a great honour . . .'

'It certainly seems like one to me.'

'. . . but how much of an honour can it *be*, when you know – if you really bother to stop and think about it – that the moment they've passed down the line, they've forgotten all about you?' Peggy paused. 'Do you know what I'd really like to do?'

'What?'

'I'd like to work for some kind of charity in the East End. I'm sure that would be much more interesting and rewarding than sitting on stuffy museum boards, trying to decide whether or not to buy yet another piece of Greek sculpture.'

'Then if that's what you want to do, what's stoppin' you from doin' it?' Woodend wondered.

'Charlie!' Joan hissed, warningly.

But Peggy seemed not to mind the question at all.

'*Arthur*'s what's stopping me,' she said. 'He thinks it would be *inappropriate* – which is one of his favourite words.'

An' maybe that's why he isn't here now, Woodend thought – because while it was appropriate enough for him to invite us to his house, it was *inappropriate* for us to invite him to ours.

'Arthur thinks that – given my background – I wouldn't be able to handle the conditions I'd come across in the East End,'

Peggy said. She paused again, then continued, 'Please don't get me wrong – Arthur's a sweet man, a perfect husband, and I love him to pieces. But I do think that sometimes he under-rates my ability to deal with difficult situations. And possibly he also feels, because he *is* such a conventional soul, that my getting my hands dirty in such a disreputable area would somehow damage his own position.'

'*For God's sake, Charlie, you're going to be the head of the family,*' Cathcart had said to Woodend, in that jeep in Berlin. '*Your wife will do what's necessary for you to get on in life.*'

Woodend noticed a slight flickering of the eyes when Peggy saw the fresh-fruit salad that Joan was serving as a sweet, but she attacked this offering, as she had the hotpot, with apparent enthusiasm.

'I'm feeling awfully guilty about the fact that we seem to have spent the whole evening talking about me,' Peggy said, as Joan cleared away the dishes. 'So let's put a stop to that right now, shall we? Why don't you tell me something about your work, Charlie?'

'You'll not get him to talk about that,' Joan said, returning from the kitchen. 'Charlie never brings his cases home with him.'

'Besides, I would have thought you got enough police talk from your own husband,' Woodend added.

'Oh, Arthur *never* talks about his work,' Peggy told him.

'Well, there you are then, we're two of kind,' Woodend said.

But that wasn't quite true, was it, Woodend thought.

They were both policemen, that was true enough, but they were *far* from being two of a kind – and if recent proof of that were needed, he had it in Commander Cathcart's absence from this meal.

'But even if Arthur *did* talk about his work, I don't think I'd find it particularly interesting,' Peggy said.

'No?'

'Of course not. Arthur's an administrator. It so happens that he works for the police, but he could just as easily use the same skills he employs in the Yard to run a dull insurance company or a dreary bank. Your job's quite different, Charlie. You get to see life as it is really lived – in all its glory and all its depravity. You're surely not going to deny that, are you?'

'No,' Woodend agreed, 'I'm not.'

'Which is precisely the reason why it would be so fascinating for me to hear all about it.'

'I'm not sure . . .' Woodend began.

'It wouldn't do any harm to tell Peggy just *a little* about what you do, would it?' Joan asked.

His wife's words knocked Woodend slightly off balance. It was not just that they were unexpected in themselves. It was also the tone – which somehow managed to turn what could have been a simple question into almost a plea.

He found himself wondering just what was going on – and then the answer came to him in a flash.

Joan's new friend *claimed* to be having a good time, but Joan herself was wondering how that could possibly be true – how a woman used to cruises and royal events could actually enjoy herself in this humble flat with a detective sergeant and his wife. But now, Peggy had expressed a real interest in something – and Joan was desperate to give her what she wanted.

'What particular part of my job would you like me to talk about?' he asked, bowing to the inevitable.

'You could tell us about your current case, couldn't you, Charlie?' Peggy suggested brightly.

No, he bloody well couldn't, Woodend thought, because even making allowance for the fact that her husband was in the 'job', she was still a civilian.

'Yes, tell us about your current case!' Joan said enthusiastically.

Woodend wondered if there was any way around his dilemma – any way to please his wife without stepping over his own carefully defined limits.

'I could tell you about a case that's *fairly* current,' he said, picking his words with some care. 'It's not one I'm directly involved in, though I do have some general background knowledge of it.'

Peggy looked a little disappointed, and then she smiled and said, 'I'm sure that will be perfect.'

'But there'll be no names, an' no details that I think will give too much away,' Woodend cautioned.

'Of course not,' Peggy said solemnly.

'There was the case of this girl who was found murdered on a bomb site recently,' Woodend said, testing the water.

If, in response, Peggy said, 'You're talking about the Pearl Jones investigation, aren't you?' it would stop right there, Woodend promised himself.

But all she *did* say was, 'Yes?'

'You haven't read anythin' in the newspapers on the case that I'm talkin' about?' he probed.

'I don't think so,' Peggy told him. 'To tell you the truth, I really don't look at the newspapers very often.' She turned to Joan. 'I mostly read the fashion magazines. Aren't women like me *so* superficial?'

'This girl I'm talkin' about was still at school,' Woodend continued. 'A very bright girl, by all accounts . . .'

He told his tale, editing it as he went – and making no mention *at all* of either what had happened to Tom Townshend or what had happened to him. It was his hope, for Joan's sake, that he could still give Peggy some flavour of the work, even if many of the details were necessarily missing.

And then a strange thing happened. He was halfway through his narrative when he realized, to his own surprise, that he'd actually begun to enjoy himself.

When he'd finished, Peggy said, 'So there are two things you really need to know, aren't there?'

'Are there?'

'I think so. The first is where the girl had been immediately prior to her ending up on the bomb site.'

'An' the second?'

'The second – and I think the more important of the two – is what happened to make a seemingly respectable girl like her suffer the kind of fate which is normally reserved for violent criminals.'

'You're all there with your cough drops, aren't you?' Woodend said admiringly. Then he noticed the look of jealousy which had appeared in his wife's eye, and he quickly added, 'But then, I imagine the same thoughts had occurred to you, an' all, lass.'

'Imagine what you like,' Joan said flatly.

*   *.   *

When the evening was finally over, Woodend escorted Peggy Cathcart down to her car, which was parked in the street below.

'Thank you so much, Charlie,' she said, as she opened the door. 'I've really enjoyed myself.'

Then, before climbing inside the car, she kissed him lightly – and unexpectedly – on the cheek.

When he returned to the flat, he found that Joan was sitting – silently and broodingly – in her armchair.

'I thought that went rather well,' Woodend said.

'Did you?' Joan asked, looking up at him. 'Well, I think the whole thing was a complete disaster.'

'What makes you say that? Did Peggy Cathcart turn out not to be the woman you thought she was?'

'She's *exactly* the woman I thought she was – except even more so. She poised, witty, charmin' and intelligent. And she's not content to rest on her laurels – even if them laurels *are* padded an' gold-plated, an' even if that stick-in-the-mud husband of hers tries to block her at every turn. She wants to try out new things. She wants to try out *difficult* things.'

'An' isn't that a good thing?'

'Well, of course it's a good thing, you idiot!'

'Then what's the problem?' Woodend wondered. 'I thought you liked the woman.'

'I *do* like her!' Joan said. 'Though I didn't much like the way she flirted with you.'

'Flirted with me? Don't talk soft. She didn't do that.'

'Yes, she did. An' you fell for it, Charlie Woodend, hook, line, an' sinker. Just look at the way you told her all about that investigation!'

'You *asked* me to do that!'

'Yes, I did – but you didn't have to do it *so* well,' Joan complained. 'An' you didn't have to look so *pleased* about what she said when you'd finished.'

'How do you mean?'

' "It seems to me you have two main problems, Charlie," ' Joan said, in a fair imitation of the other woman's voice. ' "Oh, thank you so much, Peggy," ' she continued, imitating her husband now. ' "Thank you for pointin' that out to me." Isn't that how it went?'

'No,' Woodend said. 'That isn't at all how it went. I was pleased that she'd understood what the problems were . . .'

'I'll just *bet* you were pleased!'

'. . . but only because that showed that I'd explained myself well.'

'Yes, I could see you were takin' *great* care over it,' Joan said tartly.

'An' she certainly didn't tell me anythin' about the case that I didn't already know,' Woodend concluded.

'Well, that's all right, then,' Joan said – though it clearly wasn't.

'Look, you said earlier that you like the woman, but you're certainly not talkin' now as if you do,' Woodend said. 'So if you've changed your mind – if you've decided that you *don't* like her after all – why don't you just come straight out an' say it?'

'But I *do* like her,' Joan said, as tears began to form in her eyes. 'I like her a lot. It's *me* I'm not very keen on.'

Twenty-One

Joan Woodend may have gone to bed angry with herself – and possibly with others – but when she woke up the following morning, she was feeling distinctly sheepish.

And as she watched her husband drink his early morning mug of tea, inevitably accompanied by his second cigarette of the day, she said, 'I made a complete fool of myself last night, Charlie.'

'No, you didn't,' Woodend replied, in as soothing a voice as he could muster so early in the day. 'You were maybe a little *strange*, I'll grant you that, but I'm sure Peggy didn't really notice.'

'Peggy!' Joan retorted. 'Who mentioned Peggy?'

'Well, nobody did, but I just assumed . . .'

'I don't give a bugger what Peggy Cathcart thinks, or doesn't think, about the way I behaved. What I'm talkin' about is makin' a fool of myself *in front of you*. My husband! That's what I did – an' don't you dare pretend I didn't!'

'I think you're bein' too hard on yourself,' Woodend said.

'But the one thing I *was* right about was that Peggy was flirtin' with you,' Joan persisted. 'Not that you should let *that* go to your head.'

Woodend fought back a smile. 'Shouldn't I?'

'No, because what attracted her to you wasn't any of the qualities that I see in you – or even the ones you see in yourself. What attracted her was that you were *different*.'

'Different?' Woodend repeated.

'That's right,' Joan agreed. 'She found herself, for probably the first time in her life, in close contact with a bit of rough – an' I think she found it quite excitin'.'

Woodend gave up the battle to keep his smile at bay. 'Is that what I am?' he asked. '*A bit of rough*? An' there was me thinkin' that since I've been livin' in London I've grown all smooth an' sophisticated.'

'Don't get me wrong, I wouldn't have you any other way,' Joan said, ignoring the comment. 'An' after seein' that poncy stuffed shirt of a husband of hers, I can quite understand why Peggy would find you appealin'.'

'Come on, Major Cathcart's not that bad,' Woodend said, in defence of his old commander.

But Joan was not interested in talking about *Arthur* Cathcart.

'Of course I'm not sayin' she'd ever take it any *further* than mild flirtation,' she continued. 'I'd be perfectly happy leavin' the two of you alone together, for example – at least, I *think* I would – but *flirt* with you was definitely what she did.' She paused, slightly red in the face. 'Anyway, that's not what I wanted to discuss with you.'

'So what *did* you want to discuss?'

'When I went to bed last night, I was burnin' with jealousy over the way Peggy had helped you out with the investigation, an' —'

'She *didn't* help me out,' Woodend protested. 'There wasn't a single thing she told me that I didn't already know.'

'Can you shut up, Charlie?' Joan asked. 'Can you possibly bring yourself to keep that lip of yours buttoned for just a *few* minutes?'

'I'll try,' Woodend promised.

'So there I was, lyin' in bed, tryin' to think of some way that *I* could help you with the case,' Joan said. 'An' then it came to me.'

'*What* came to you?'

'You've no idea where Pearl Jones was prior to the murder, have you?' Joan asked, answering his question with one of her own.

'That's true,' Woodend admitted.

'An' you've no idea why she was wearin' the dress she died in, which – by all accounts – was far too grown-up for her?'

'No, I haven't. An' that dress is one of the things that's been really puzzlin' me,' Woodend agreed.

'So why don't you simply find out who Pearl's best friend at school was, an' ask *her* about it?'

'But is her best friend likely to know?' Woodend wondered.

Joan gave him a look of astonishment – a look which said she was truly amazed at the depths of his ignorance.

'Will she know?' she repeated. '*Of course* she'll know. Girls don't keep secrets from their best friends. They tell them *everything*.'

The girl was walking towards the former Georgian palace which was now an expensive private school. She had pale blonde hair, blue eyes, and light freckles scattered liberally across her cheeks and nose. She carried a leather satchel in her right hand and a hockey stick in her left, and her legs, protruding from below the modest hemline of her navy blue skirt, were almost hockey-stick thin themselves.

She did not look like a particularly adventurous or forceful girl, but she did seem to be a nice one – and she was undoubtedly the *same* girl as the one in the photograph which had been given pride of place on Victoria Jones's sideboard.

When the big man in the hairy sports coat suddenly stepped into the centre of the pavement, effectively blocking her way, she did not show any signs of alarm. Instead, she smiled politely, yet distantly – as she'd probably been taught to – and said, 'Can I help you, sir? Are you lost?'

Woodend held out his warrant card for her to inspect.

'No, I'm not lost,' he said. 'An' yes, I think you can help me.'

The smile froze on the girl's face, but her eyes began to dart around wildly. For a moment, it seemed as if she was about to do a runner, but then she took a deep breath and calmed down a little.

'I can't think of anything that *I* could possibly have to say which might be of use to a policeman,' she told Woodend, in a voice which was relatively steady.

'What's your name?' the sergeant asked.

'My . . . my name?'

'Yes.'

'It's Rachael. Rachael Tompkinson.'

It would have to be something like that, Woodend thought. Just looking at her, it was obvious that she had not been born into a family which named its kids Maisie or Lil – or even Pearl.

'You were Pearl Jones's best friend, weren't you, Rachael?' he asked.

The girl had clearly been expecting the question since the moment Woodend had shown her his warrant card, but even so, when he actually put it into words, it still succeeded in confusing her.

'No, I . . .' she began. 'We weren't exactly . . . what I mean to say is, we knew each other, of course . . .'

Yes?'

'. . . but not *that* well.'

Woodend shook his head sadly. 'You were her best friend – an' she was yours,' he said emphatically. 'An' I'm sure that when she was alive, you promised each other that you'd stick together always, through thick an' thin. But now she's dead, an' since *she* can't do anythin' for *you* any more, you're perfectly willin' to betray her without a second's thought. Isn't that right?'

Rachael Tompkinson looked down at the pavement. 'It's not as simple as that,' she muttered.

'What are you afraid of?' Woodend wondered.

'Nothing. Nothing at all.'

'You helped her to do somethin' that you both knew was wrong, didn't you? And now that she's dead, you're the only one who's left to be punished for it. So you've decided you'll do *whatever it takes* to avoid that punishment?'

'You don't understand,' Rachael said. 'I am being punished. I'm *constantly* being punished.'

'How?'

'I can't study. I can't eat. When I switch off the light at night, all I can see is her face – so I can't sleep, either.'

'You feel guilty,' Woodend guessed.

'Well, *of course* I feel guilty!'

'Why?'

'Because it's partly my fault. I should have tried to stop her – but instead I *encouraged* her.'

'Tell me all about it,' Woodend said softly. 'I promise you, you'll feel a lot better when you have.'

Behind them there was the sound of a bell ringing, and all the other girls who were heading in the same direction as Rachael immediately began to speed up.

'I have to go now,' Rachael said.

'We'll need to talk again – an' soon.'

The girl thought about it for a moment. 'I've got a free

period at ten o'clock. There's a cafe on the corner over there. If you want to . . . if you could . . .'

'I'll be there,' Woodend promised.

In many other parts of the city, the cafes had simple names like Joe's or – if the owner was a little more fanciful – The Drop Inn. A large tea urn was considered the only essential piece of equipment in these places. It was kept in plain view behind the counter, where it hissed and spluttered incessantly, and when the tea was delivered to the table – and placed on the inevitable plastic tablecloth – it was in a thick brown mug.

Such an establishment would never have thrived in an area like this one. To be a success here, a cafe need pretensions – and the one that Woodend found himself in at ten o'clock that morning had them by the fistful.

It was called – for reasons of its own – The Longchamps, and a trellis, covered with artificial ivy, separated and masked the kitchen area from the part of the cafe used by customers.

Except that in this place they probably weren't even *called* customers, Woodend thought. In the Longchamps, they were probably referred to as *guests* or *patrons*.

Tea was served in a delicate china pot, by a lady who, though dressed up like an Edwardian maid, had probably never had to scrub a pan in her entire life. She did not smile at Woodend, as she had at her other customers – at her other *guests* – which he took to be a clear indication that while his business would be tolerated, it was not exactly welcome.

At five past ten, Rachael Tompkinson walked through the door. Though she was clearly concerned about the nature of the meeting she had arranged, she seemed perfectly at home in the location where it was about to take place.

This was her natural stamping ground, Woodend thought. She did not feel even the least bit awkward, though he most certainly did, and though – he was sure – her best friend Pearl would have done.

The smile on her face, as she sat down opposite him, managed somehow to combine uncertainty with resolution. She was a good kid caught up in a difficult situation but determined to do what was right, Woodend decided.

'Tell me about Pearl,' he said.

'She was the sweetest girl I ever met in my whole life,'

Rachael replied. 'I felt so drab and colourless next to her, but *she* certainly never tried to make me feel that way.'

'That's not what I'm askin',' Woodend said softly.

'I know it isn't,' Rachael admitted. 'You want to know what happened to her that night, don't you?'

'Yes.'

Rachael took hold of her left index finger with her right hand, and bent it back so far that she winced with the pain.

'Steady, lass,' Woodend said.

The girl smiled again, grateful for his concern, then said, 'Would you mind if I started at the beginning? It would be so much easier for me if I could do that.'

'Start wherever you want to,' Woodend told her.

'There was a lot of mystery in Pearl's life,' Rachael said. 'In fact, it was absolutely *full* of it. She didn't know who her father was, she didn't know where her mum got her money from, and she didn't know who was paying her scholarship. But she *wanted* to know those things. It was *important* to her to find out!'

'I'm sure it was,' Woodend said sympathetically.

'She started searching around her house for clues that might help to answer her questions, but there weren't any.'

No, Woodend thought, there wouldn't have been. Mrs Jones had struck him as far too careful to leave clues like that lying around.

'She was getting pretty desperate by that point,' Rachael continued, 'so she decided that when her mum was talking to her friends from the church, she'd secretly listen in. I know that sounds awful, but . . .'

'It doesn't sound awful at all,' Woodend assured her. 'In fact, given the circumstances, it's perfectly understandable.'

'That's what I told her,' Rachael said. 'I wasn't sure I believed it myself, but I told her anyway, because she was my best friend.'

'So she started eavesdroppin' on her mum,' Woodend said. 'Did she *learn* anythin' from listenin' in to these conversations?'

'Bits and pieces, here and there. None of the things she heard made much sense on its own, so then she tried to put them all together – it was a bit like doing a very complicated jigsaw puzzle.'

'An' when she'd finished it, what did the picture look like?'

'It didn't look like *anything* very much, because there were so many pieces still missing. But she was sure of a few things.'

'An' what were they?'

'That her father was still alive, that he lived somewhere in London, and that he . . . that he wasn't quite respectable.'

'What exactly do you mean when you say he was not *quite respectable*? That he was some kind of crook?'

'Yes, I suppose that *is* what I mean.'

'Go on,' Woodend encouraged.

'She wanted to meet him, even if he was a criminal, because he was still her father.'

'Of course he was,' Woodend agreed.

'So *I* said that if she really *did* want to find him, the best place to look would probably be in a nightclub.'

'In a *what*?'

'In a nightclub. That *is* where criminals hang out, isn't it?'

The words 'hang out' did not come easily to her lips, Woodend thought. They were alien words, describing an alien environment about which she knew so very, very little.

'But before she could go to a nightclub, she had to have the right kind of dress,' Rachael continued. 'We both saved up our pocket money like fury, and in the end, we had enough to buy the dress. It was a very nice dress -- a very *grown-up* dress. I would have looked so silly in it. But Pearl didn't. It made *her* look much older than she really was.'

They'd been *kids*, playing a *kids'* game which was just one step up from dolls and dolls' houses.

The only problem was that they'd chosen to play it in a rather unpleasant part of the *adult* world.

'So how did it work, this search of yours?' Woodend asked.

'We'd drawn up a list of the nightclubs which looked promising, and Pearl was visiting them, one by one.'

'An' they let her in, did they?'

'Oh yes! Remember, in that dress, she looked a lot older than she really was. Besides, she was a pretty girl – and you can never have *too many* pretty girls in a nightclub.' For the first time, Rachael looked questioningly at Woodend. 'I'm surprised that as a policeman you didn't already know that.'

She had no concept of what a nightclub was actually like, Woodend thought – of the prostitutes and the pimps and the drug-peddlers who made up at least a third of the customers.

She had seen a more glamorous version of what went on in
the Hollywood films – a version in which even the gangsters
were sanitized – and she had taken that as real.

'What did Pearl do, once she was inside the club?' he asked.

'She looked for her father, of course.'

'An' how would she have known him, if she'd found him?'

'He'd look a little like her, don't you think?' Rachael asked,
as if that was obvious to her, and she was amazed it wasn't
obvious to him.

'Possibly,' Woodend said.

'And she wasn't just doing it on her own, you know. She
did have my help.'

'You went in there with her?'

'Gosh, no! They'd never have let me in. And anyway, I
would have been far too frightened to *go* in, even if they had.
But she had the camera with her, you see.'

'Which camera?'

'My father's. It's a very expensive one, actually.' Rachael
looked down at the table. 'I "borrowed" it.'

'So she took pictures of all the men she thought might
possibly be her dad. Didn't they object?'

'No, because they didn't even know she was taking pictures
of them. That's where she was clever.'

'Clever? How?'

'When she saw a man she thought might be her father,
she'd go to the people at the table next to his and ask them
if *they'd* mind if she took their photo.'

'But when she took the actual picture, she'd make sure that
the man she was interested in appeared at the edge of it?'
Woodend guessed.

'That's right. And later, when she'd had the film developed,
we'd go through the pictures together, and try to work out if
any of the men she'd taken a photograph of *could* be her
father. It was all such tremendous fun.' Rachael looked down
at the table again. 'At least, it seemed like tremendous fun at
the time.'

'How often did she go on one of these expeditions?'

'She did it four times, altogether. We went to the Birdcage
Club, the Blue Angel, the Orinoco, and the Charleston.'

'*We* went?' Woodend asked, pouncing on the word.

'I . . . I waited outside.'

'Which one was the last you went to?'

'The Charleston.'

'An' that was the night Pearl was murdered?'

'Yes.'

'Tell me what happened.'

'There was a thick smog that night. It was very cold, and I was worried about how we'd eventually get home. But I knew that Pearl wouldn't come out until she'd done what she'd set out to do – because she was that kind of girl.'

'So I believe.'

'When she *did* come out, she was with a man. He was holding her by the arm. He wasn't exactly *dragging* her, but you could tell that she wasn't awfully keen on the idea of going with him.'

'What was he like, this man?'

'He was tall.'

'That's a start. What else can you tell me about him?'

'I didn't get a clear view of him, because he had his hat pulled right down. And with all that smog around, you couldn't see much anyway. But Pearl saw me – because she knew where to look.'

'But you don't think *the man* saw you?'

'I'm sure he didn't. He looked at Pearl, and he looked up and down the street, but he never even so much as glanced in my direction.'

'Did Pearl say anythin' to you?'

'No, she just shook her head, as if to tell me that I shouldn't come any closer. And so I didn't. I just stood there, while he opened the door of his car, and bundled Pearl inside. But I *shouldn't* just have stood there, should I? I should have tried to help her! I knew, *even then*, that I should have tried to help her.'

If you had tried to help her, you wouldn't have saved Pearl – and you'd probably have ended up dead yourself, Woodend thought.

'You did what Pearl wanted you to do, an' that's all one friend can ever do for another,' he told the girl. 'Did you leave then?'

Rachael shook her head. 'No, I stayed just where I was.'

'Why?'

'In case they came back.'

'But they didn't?'

'The man did – about half an hour later. When I saw that Pearl wasn't with him, I thought about going to the police.'

'Then why didn't you?'

'Because I thought that if I did, I would only be getting Pearl into more trouble. But it wouldn't have got her into trouble, would it? It *couldn't* have got her into trouble – because she was already dead by then!'

'Yes, I think she probably was,' Woodend said.

Tears had started to form in Rachael's eyes.

'I . . . I couldn't stay out there all night, and so I went home,' she said, in a thick voice. 'When Pearl wasn't in school the next morning, I didn't know what to think. I spent the whole day worrying about her. And then, the morning after *that*, I saw her picture on the front page of the newspaper, and I . . . and I was so scared. And I'm still scared now.'

'You did all you could,' Woodend told her. 'Much more than most people twice your age would have managed.'

'Do you think the man I saw coming out of the club with her was her father?' Rachael asked.

'I don't know,' Woodend admitted.

'But just say he was. Say that she'd finally found him, after all her searching. If she was sure enough it was him, she'd probably have told him who *she* was, wouldn't she?'

'It's possible.'

'And instead of being delighted to see her, as she thought he would be, he took her to that bomb site – and he slit her throat. What . . . what kind of man is it who could kill his own daughter like that?'

'I don't know,' Woodend said again, as an image of his own little Pauline Anne came to his mind.

'You have to catch him, Mr Woodend,' Rachael said desperately. 'Promise me you'll catch him.'

'Oh, I'll catch him, all right,' Wooded told her. 'However long it takes – whatever it involves – I'll catch him.'

Twenty-Two

Unless he is clearly a high roller with money to burn, no man entering a nightclub on his own should expect to be shown to one of the better tables, and since the man in the hairy sports coat certainly did not fall within a million miles of this category, the head waiter led him to a small, cramped table at the back of the room.

Woodend raised no objection, even though the table was so close to the toilets that it was almost a part of them. He didn't even mind that his view of the stage was partially obscured by a large pillar, because he wasn't there to watch the entertainment – instead, he'd come to watch the *people* who were watching the entertainment.

'Would you care for a bottle of champagne, sir?' the head waiter suggested, snidely.

'Aye, why not?' Woodend agreed. 'Bring me a bottle of the Dom Perignon '36.'

The head waiter looked at him with loathing. 'I'm afraid we've run out of that particular vintage, sir.'

'Well, don't get your knickers in a twist about it, old lad. The '38 will do me *almost* as well.'

'We've just run out of that as well,' the head waiter said, not even bothering to try and sound convincing.

'Oh dear, what a pity!' Woodend said. 'Never mind, I'll have a pint of your best bitter instead.'

As the head waiter stalked away, Woodend lit up a cigarette and looked around him. The Charleston Club was lacking in many things, he quickly decided, but what it lacked most of all was any sense of zing.

It had none of the sophisticated glamour of establishments like Toby Burroughs's Las Vegas Club, but neither did it have, by way of compensation, that inherently exciting sense of danger which positively crackled through the air in some of the rougher clubs in the East End.

What it was, in reality, was a haven in which the lower middle classes could flirt with the idea of living the high life, and yet remain safe in the knowledge that they had not actually stepped far beyond the bounds of their normal, comfortable, bourgeois existence.

It was certainly not a place where he would ever have begun his search for a shadowy member of the criminal underworld, Woodend thought. But then, of course, he was not a sixteen-year-old girl who had a great deal of imagination, but very little experience of the world as it really was.

And the fact that Pearl had chosen the *wrong* type of club for her investigation didn't really matter at all. The only important thing was that she *had* chosen it – and that that choice had led to her death.

A second waiter, lower in the pecking order, arrived at the table carrying a pint of bitter on a metal tray.

'That'll be ten bob,' he said, slamming the pint pot down on the table with all the finesse of a riveter hammering in a bolt.

'Ten bob!' Woodend repeated. 'Bloody hellfire, I could have bought half the brewery for that!' He took a ten-shilling note out of his pocket, and handed it over. 'I'd like to see the manager,' he said.

The waiter pocketed the money, then shrugged indifferently. 'The boss is too *busy* to see you,' he said.

'How do you know that?' Woodend wondered. 'Have you checked? Before you serve one of the tables, do you *always* go to the boss and ask him what you're to say if the customer requests an interview?'

'There's no need to do that,' the waiter said, with a smirk. 'He's *always* too busy to see the punters.'

Or, at least, he was always too busy to see punters who had been seated at tables close to the bogs, Woodend thought.

'I'd still like you to check with him, anyway,' he said, producing his warrant card. 'Tell him I'm the Old Bill.'

'So yer a copper,' the waiter, giving the warrant card a brief inspection. 'A detective sergeant! Yer don't expect the boss to be impressed that a *detective sergeant* wants to see 'im, do yer?'

'No, I don't, really,' Woodend admitted. 'But I do think he'll be rather interested to hear what this particular detective sergeant's got to say.'

'About what?'

'About the safety standards in this shit hole. I've only been here for ten minutes, but without even really lookin' for them, I've spotted five or six serious infringements of the fire-safety regulations.'

'Yer don't need to bovver the boss about that,' the waiter said. 'I'll 'ave a word wiv 'im myself, and there'll be an envelope waiting for yer on yer way out.'

Woodend stood up. 'Do I look like the kind of copper you can buy?' he demanded menacingly.

The waiter took a couple of steps backwards. 'No offence intended,' he said.

'Well, plenty *taken*,' Woodend told him. 'Five minutes from now, I expected to be either talkin' to the manager, or nickin' you for attemptin' to bribe a policeman. Which one is it goin' to be?'

'I'll tell 'im you want to see 'im,' the waiter said.

'Good idea,' Woodend agreed.

The manager of the Charleston Club was called Cliff Robinson. He was somewhere in his mid-forties, of medium build, with pale sandy hair, and when Woodend asked him who owned the club, he said, 'I do.'

'What I mean is, who *really* owns it?' Woodend persisted.

'Me,' Robinson said firmly. 'This is a legitimate nightclub, not some kind of front for laundering dirty money.'

'An' you expect me just to take your word for that, do you, Mr Robinson?' Woodend asked.

'No, I don't,' Robinson replied. 'What I expect you to do is check around. But when you *do* check, you'll soon discover that I've got no criminal record, and no business connection with anybody who has. And if you *still* don't believe me, you can have a word with your pals back at the Yard.'

But I *do* believe you, Woodend thought.

And that was the problem – because this was simply *not* the kind of club that a Ron Smithers or a Toby Burroughs would come to for a night's entertainment. It was not even the kind of club that lesser gangsters, with a pretension to being hard men, would ever want to be associated with.

Yet on the night that Pearl had visited the club, there had been at least one man there who was a cold-blooded killer.

He took Pearl's photograph out of his pocket, and placed it in the middle of the manager's desk.

'Does she look familiar?' he asked.

'I thought you were here about my failure to comply with the fire regulations,' Cliff Robinson said.

'An' now you know I'm not,' Woodend replied. '*Is* she familiar?'

Robinson gave the photograph a cursory glance. 'No, she isn't.'

'Look again,' Woodend ordered him.

Robinson made some show of examining the picture carefully this time, but when he'd finished, he said, 'I still don't know her.'

'Now that is strange,' Woodend mused. 'Because she was in this club a few nights ago – and half an hour after she'd left it, she was dead.'

Robinson's eyes darted around the room, as if he were hoping to find that what he needed to say next was written in large letters on one of the walls. But there was no such message, so he said nothing at all, but simply stabbed at the button on the corner of his desk.

The door opened almost immediately, and two of the club's bouncers walked into the room.

Like everything else about the place, they weren't *quite* right, Woodend thought. True, they had the *build* to be bouncers, but what they were lacking was any sign of the right mental attitude.

Real hard men exuded a dangerous air which said that while they were willing to hurt others without compunction, they were equally willing to take the same amount of punishment themselves, if that proved necessary. These two were not in that class at all. They were parodies of the real thing – cardboard cut-outs who might fool the mild-mannered clients of the Charleston Club, but would quickly curl up and die when confronted by men like Duffel Coat and his mates, who were the genuine article.

Pearl's photograph was still lying on the desk, but before

the bouncers had time to see it, Woodend picked it up, and returned it to his pocket.

'I want this copper shown off the premises, boys,' Robinson said. 'Now!'

'You're makin' a big mistake,' Woodend told him.

'Listen, if you want to get your fire-safety people in here, then go ahead,' Robinson said. 'And if you want to close the place down, then go ahead and do that as well. There's nothing that *I* can do to stop you.'

'I'm not talkin' about fire-safety regulations, an' you know it,' Woodend countered. 'I'm talkin' about a dead girl.'

'And I've already told you – *twice* – that I've never seen the bloody girl,' Robinson said, with a hint of desperation in his voice.

'Let me spell out your options for you,' Woodend suggested. 'First option! You can continue to obstruct me – in which case, the next time I'm here it'll be to arrest you as an accessory after the fact in a murder investigation. An' how long do you think you'll go down for that? I'd put my money on ten years, at the very least.'

'You're wasting your breath, because I don't know anyth—'

'Second option! You can cooperate with me. You'll still go to jail – there's no avoidin' that now – but I'll speak up for you at your trial, and with any luck you could be out in eighteen months.' Woodend paused to let the alternatives sink in, then continued, 'If I was in your shoes, I know which one I'd choose – in your shoes, I'd come clean.'

'I have no idea what you're talking about,' Robinson replied.

But what he really meant – what the expression on his face said more clearly than words ever could – was, 'If I come clean, I'll end up *dead!*'

The Charleston Club's cloakroom attendant was a heavy, middle-aged woman with a bad complexion. She took Woodend's ticket from him without a word, then disappeared into the forest of coats.

'You were workin' here last Tuesday night, weren't you?' Woodend asked one of the bouncers, who'd been sticking to him like glue since they'd left Robinson's office.

The man shrugged. 'Might have been.'

Wrong answer! Woodend thought.

Because the *right* answer – the answer he'd have got from one of Smithers's or Burroughs's men – would have been silence.

'So you'll have seen the girl yourself, then,' the sergeant said. 'Which makes you, along with your boss, an accessory after the fact.'

'There *wasn't* no coloured girl in 'ere last Tuesday,' the bouncer countered.

'Who said anythin' about her bein' coloured?' Woodend wondered.

'You did.'

'Not in your hearin', I didn't,' Woodend said. 'It's true that I told your *boss* she was coloured, but after you came into the office, I took great care to talk to refer to her only as "the girl".'

The cloakroom attendant had completely disappeared from sight, but from the way in which the coats on the rails jangled, it was clear she was still somewhere in the middle of the melee.

'Can't yer get a move on wiv this bloke's coat, yer fat slag?' the bouncer called out nervously.

'I'm doing my best, but it's right at the back,' the woman replied. 'And 'oo are yer calling a slag?'

'There are men who can take prison time in their stride, but I can tell right away that you're not one of them,' Woodend told the bouncer. 'The lifers will eat you for breakfast. A few days behind bars an' you'll wish you were dead. Give it a few months, an' dead is probably exactly what you *will* be.'

'Wot the bleeding hell are yer *doin'* back there, Shirley?' the bouncer croaked.

The fat attendant finally emerged.

'Is this it?' she asked, holding up Woodend's overcoat.

'That's it,' Woodend agreed, reaching automatically into his jacket pocket for some loose change.

The bouncer clamped his hand on Woodend's arm.

'She don't want no tip from *you*,' he said.

'I didn't know you were a mind-reader,' Woodend told him. 'But what I *do* know is that if you don't let go of my arm, you'll be a mind-reader minus his front teeth.'

The bouncer quickly relinquished his grip and backed away.

'Nobody 'ere wants *anyfing* from *you*,' he said, almost in a mumble. 'The only fing we want is for yer to leave.'

And, apparently, as quickly as possible, Woodend thought. Because this man – like his boss – was very frightened.

The pub was called the Pride of London, but there was nothing to be proud about in this particular establishment. It was uncared for and forlorn, and under normal circumstances, Woodend wouldn't have gone anywhere near the place. But these were *not* normal circumstances. He needed something to quickly wash away the taste that the Charleston Club had left in his mouth – and he didn't even care, at that point, if it came in a dirty glass.

The day had started out promisingly, he thought, as he took a deep swallow from the pint he'd been served. But after that initial promise, it had gone downhill rapidly, and was turning into one cruel disappointment after another.

Because although he now firmly believed that Pearl Jones had gone to the club, and had been killed by one its customers – a large man with his hat pulled down over his eyes – he had no way of proving any of it.

And worse than that, he didn't even have the faintest glimmering of who that man might be!

He took his cigarette packet out of his jacket pocket, and discovered that it was empty.

Well, that was just about par for the bloody course, wasn't it, he asked himself. And to top it all, he'd be willing to bet that this pub didn't even *sell* Capstan Full Strength.

It didn't.

'No call for 'em, guv,' the barman explained. 'Most of the people round 'ere are 'appy enough wiv Player's Weights.'

Good for them, Woodend thought viciously. But I need somethin' with more of a nicotine kick to it.

Perhaps there was a spare packet of Capstan in his over-coat pocket, he told himself. It was unlikely, but it was certainly worth checking.

It was then that he found the note. It was hastily written in pencil – in what looked like a largely uneducated hand – on a torn scrap of paper. It was not a long note, but the few words it contained were enough to send Woodend's pulse racing.

A man called Smivvers done it, the note read.

Twenty-Three

For Woodend's purposes, the street lamp could not have been better located. It stood on the main road at the top end of the alley, and the further he walked away from it, the weaker the effect of its light became. Thus, when he was halfway down the alley, he was all but invisible to the people leaving the Charleston Club by the back door, yet *he* still had a clear view of *them*.

The first to leave were the band, a quartet of musicians who spent their evenings churning out turgid, uninspired tunes which at least had the advantage of being instantly recognizable. A few minutes later, a couple of the waiters and two of the bouncers left, but it was not until two fifteen in the morning that the person Woodend had been waiting for finally appeared.

The fat woman closed the door quickly behind her, but then, instead of hurrying up the alley, as the others had done, she simply stood there, looking lost.

It was almost, Woodend thought, as if she'd been dying to escape from the club, but now that she had, she had no enthusiasm for what lay ahead of her.

He waited for a moment, to make sure that no one else was coming out of the club, then began to walk towards her.

As he began to emerge from the shadows, the fat woman noticed him, clutched her handbag tightly against her flabby bosom, and said, ''Oo's there? What d'yer want? I'll call the police.'

'I *am* the police,' Woodend said, drawing ever closer to her. 'An' I'd like a word with you, Shirley.'

'Why would yer want ter talk to me?' the fat woman asked, with a hint of panic in her voice. 'I don't know nuffink.'

'You know a great deal,' Woodend contradicted her. 'An' you want me to know it, too. That's why you wrote me the note.'

'What note?'

'The note I found in my overcoat pocket.'

'It don't have nuffink to do wiv me.'

'It was the quality of the paper the note was written on that I noticed first,' Woodend said, almost reflectively. 'It's not the sort of paper you could buy in Woolworths – it's more the kind that a business which was tryin' to create a good impression would have. But it had been torn roughly in half, so that only the bottom half of the sheet was used. Now why was that?'

'Don't know.'

'I think it was because the top half had the words "Charleston Club" printed on it,' Woodend said. 'Shall I tell you what else I noticed?'

'If yer want to.'

'It looked as if it had been written by somebody in a hurry, somebody who was expected to be doin' somethin' else at the time – like findin' a coat, for example. But even without any of the other evidence, I'd have known you were the one who put it in my pocket – because nobody else had the opportunity.'

'I've set yer off on the right road, 'aven't I?' the fat woman asked, abandoning all pretence that she didn't know what he was talking about. 'Can't that be enough for yer?'

Woodend shook his head regretfully. 'Nowhere near enough. Is there somewhere we can talk?'

The woman glanced nervously back at the club door. 'My flat ain't far from 'ere,' she said. 'We could go there.'

It was not so much a flat as a cramped bed-sit, but Shirley had made some effort with the place, putting up pleasant curtains and hanging cheery, sentimental pictures on what little wall space was available.

There was a hotplate on a small table in the corner of the room. Shirley heated up a kettle on it.

''Ow d'yer like yer tea?' she asked, as she reached for the caddy.

'Make it good an' strong,' Woodend told her. 'We could be here for quite some time.'

When the tea had been brewed and poured, Woodend produced a half-pint bottle of whisky he had bought from the off-sales at the Pride of London, and added a generous dollop to each cup.

For a while they sat sipping the tea in silence, Shirley reluctant to speak, and Woodend reluctant to push her to.

It was unlikely she'd ever been a pretty woman, Woodend told himself as they drank, but when she was younger, she must have had nice eyes.

He pictured that younger Shirley, and the eyes which must once – against all the odds – have expressed the hope that her life would turn out to be as joyful as she wanted it to be. But that hope had long since left her, and now she was a middle-aged woman, working at a dead-end job and living in a scabby bed-sit.

Shirley looked up at him, with those eyes of hers brimming over with sadness.

''Er name was Pearl, wasn't it?' she asked.

'That's right, it was,' Woodend agreed.

'It made me 'appy just to look at 'er.'

'Why was that?'

'Because she 'ad spirit. Because she knew what she wanted, and she was determined that she was going to get it.'

'Do you want to tell me what happened to her, Shirley?' Woodend asked softly.

'If I do, yer can never say that it come from me.'

'I promise you, I won't.'

The fat woman still hesitated.

'You've got my word on it,' Woodend said, and seeing that that was still not enough, he added, 'I swear it on my daughter's life.'

The sad eyes seemed to be reflecting on what it would be like if *she* had a daughter of her own – and how binding any oath she took on that daughter's life would be to her.

Shirley took a deep breath.

'The bloke come into the club last Tuesday night,' she said. ''E 'ad 'is lady-friend wiv 'im, and when 'e 'anded over the coats, 'e was in a very good mood – like 'e'd been looking forward to this night out all week.'

'Did you recognize him?' Woodend asked.

'No, I don't fink 'e'd ever been to the club before. And to tell you the truth, Charlie, 'e didn't look like most of the reg'lar punters wot we get in. 'E seemed too . . . too . . .'

'Posh?' Woodend suggested.

Shirley shook her head. 'No, definitely not posh. But 'e looked like 'e 'ad money, and that 'e was used to getting what 'e wanted *when* 'e wanted it. Anyway, 'e 'adn't been in the club for more than a few minutes when 'e come back to the cloakroom again, and this time 'e 'ad the coloured girl in tow.'

'How did she seem?'

'Scared. Scared about the idea of going wiv him, but also scared of telling him she didn't *want* to go, if yer know wot I mean.'

'I know what you mean,' Woodend agreed. 'Did the girl have a camera with her?'

'Not as far as I could tell.'

'Carry on.'

'So, 'e gets 'is coat – but not 'ers – an' the two of 'em leave the club. Then, 'alf an hour later, 'e comes back on 'is own, picks up 'is lady-friend, and leaves again. But as 'e's going out, the uvver blokes are coming in.'

'What other blokes?'

'A couple of real 'ard cases. I 'adn't seen neivver of them before, eivver, but yer could tell from the way that our bouncers were fawning all over 'em that they must 'ave 'ad some kind of reputation. So anyway, these 'ard cases stand by the door wot leads out onto the street, an' whenever anybody leaves, they take down their names and addresses.'

'Didn't anybody object to that?'

The fat woman laughed. '*You* didn't see 'em,' she said. 'They wasn't the sort of blokes you'd fink about arguing wiv. If they told yer to pull yer own nose off, yer'd do it wivvout a second's fort.'

'Did they talk to you?'

'Oh yeah, they talked to me, all right. But not at first. At first, they stood staring at me. Must 'ave been a couple o' minutes before one of 'em spoke.'

'They were doin' that to unnerve you,' Woodend said.

'Yes, well, it bleedin' worked, didn't it?' Shirley asked. 'By the time 'e did speak, me legs 'ad turned to jelly.'

'What did he say?'

''E said, "Yer've been 'ere all night, 'ave yer?" An' I said yes, I 'ad. Then 'e said, "Yer must 'ave a fair number of people coming and going, during the course of the night."

I just nodded at that, 'cos my mouf was feeling drier than I
ever remember it feeling before. Then 'e says, "And was one
of these people a darkie girl?" and I nodded again.'

'An' how did he react to that?'

''E glared at me. Then 'e turns to 'is mate and says, "I fink
she's wrong about that. I don't fink there *was* any niggers in
'ere tonight." An' the uvver 'ard man says, "My mate finks
yer've made a mistake. Is 'e right? Ave yer?" Well, I knew
what was expected of me, so I said, "Yes, I must 'ave been
mistaken." I didn't dare say nuffink else.'

'Of course you didn't,' Woodend said soothingly.

'Anyway, the first bloke takes a roll of dosh out of 'is
pocket, peels off a quid, and puts it on the counter. "Yer a
smart woman," he says. "Take this and buy yerself somefink
nice." I didn't want 'is money, but I took it anyway, an' told
'im "Fank you." '

'You just did right.'

' "An' remember," he sez, "if yer know what's good for
yer, yer didn't see no nigger." ' Shirley paused. 'They must
'ave been saying more or less the same fing to all the punters,
don't you fink?'

'I'm almost sure they were.'

'Anyway, it was two days later that I saw the picture in the
paper. I knew it was the same girl straight away, and I almost
phoned the Old Bill. Then I fort about wot them two blokes
had said, an' I told myself not to be such a bleedin' idiot, 'cos
the uvver coppers wouldn't 'ave kept my name out of it, like
wot you've promised yer will, Charlie. It would 'ave been
splashed all over the papers the next morning, and the morning
after that, I'd 'ave been found floating in the river.'

She was probably right about that, Woodend thought.

'Let me see if I've got this right,' he said. 'The man asked
for his coat, but he didn't ask for the girl's?'

'No, 'e didn't. Why would he bovver about whevver she
caught cold or not, when 'e knew she was going to be dead
in 'alf an 'our?'

'So her coat's still in the cloakroom, is it?'

Shirley looked a little guilty. 'No, it ain't. I brought it 'ome
wiv me.'

Why had she done that, Woodend wondered. Because she
wanted it for herself?

'I know what yer finkin', but yer wrong,' Shirley said, reading his mind. She laughed bitterly. 'It's a long time since I'd 'ave fitted into that coat.'

'So why *did* you bring it home?'

Shirley shrugged helplessly. 'I don't know,' she admitted. 'Maybe I fort I'd 'ave the chance to give it back to 'er, sometime.' She looked down at the floor. 'Or maybe I just wanted somefing to remember 'er by.'

'I'd like to see the coat, if you don't mind,' Woodend said.

Shirley nodded sadly, stood up, and walked over to her battered wardrobe. When she returned, she had a grey woollen coat in her hands.

'Funny fing for 'er to be wearing, really,' the fat woman said. 'It didn't go wiv the dress at all.'

No, it didn't, Woodend agreed. The dress, which Pearl and her friend had 'saved up like mad for', had been slinky and sophisticated. The coat looked more like part of a school uniform. And that was exactly what it was – identical in every detail to the one Rachael Tompkinson had been wearing!

'I'll have to take this away with me,' he told Shirley.

'I know you will,' the fat woman said sadly. 'It's evidence, ain't it?'

'Yes, it is,' Woodend agreed.

'But when this is all over, do yer fink I might 'ave it back?'

'I'll see what I can do,' Woodend promised. He paused to light one of the Player's Weights he'd reluctantly bought at the Pride of London. 'You've been very helpful,' he continued, 'but there's one thing you told me that still doesn't quite make sense to me.'

'And wot's that?'

'You said that you didn't recognize the man when he walked into the club?'

'That's right. I didn't.'

'An' didn't recognize the woman who was with him, either?'

'No, 'er nievver.'

'So they were both complete strangers to you. Then how did you know the man's name was *Smithers*?'

'That's 'cos of wot I 'eard the two 'ard cases say, after they finished warning me off.'

'An' what *was* it they said?'

'They was still standing in the cloakroom, yer see, when

one of them turns to the uvver and 'e sez, "Well, that's one job all done and *knuckle*-dusted." I fink he was probably making some kind o' joke.'

'I think he was, too.'

'So then the uvver one sez, "In that case, yer'd better ring Mr Smivvers and tell 'im, 'adn't you?" And 'oo was Mr Smivvers, if 'e wasn't the bloke what left wiv the coloured girl?'

Who indeed, Woodend thought.

Twenty-Four

The morning sun was smiling down on the gently rippling water of the Thames, birds chirped happily in the trees, and the people walking along the Victoria Embankment had a newly optimistic spring in their steps.

It was a glorious morning, Woodend thought, as he surveyed the scene through DCI Bentley's office window – the best one in weeks.

But he was well aware that, for him at least, it would *still* have been a glorious morning even if there had been a blizzard raging outside. Because his own personal black cloud – which had been hanging heavily above him ever since that night on the bomb site, over a week earlier – had finally been lifted. And sitting there on the chief inspector's desk was the object which had finally made that cloud go scudding rapidly away – Woodend's own report into Pearl Jones's death.

He had spent most of the night working on the report, and he was pleased with the result. It was sharp and concise. It drew a clear distinction between what he knew and what he could only speculate on. And, most important of all, by doing no more than hinting at the further lines of investigation which should be followed, he had left Bentley room for manoeuvre – had allowed for the possibility that, should the chief inspector want to claim the ideas as his own, he would have no difficulty in doing so.

Bentley laid the report to one side.

'Interesting,' he said blandly. 'But I must admit, Sergeant, that I'm a little bit puzzled by the title.'

'The title, sir?'

'You've called it "The Investigation into the murder of Pearl Jones", haven't you?'

'Yes, sir.'

'Why?'

'Because that's what it—'

'Whereas it seems to me,' Bentley interrupted, 'that its real title should be "How Charlie Woodend, smart-arsed detective sergeant, tried to make himself look like a hero, while simultaneously making his guv'nor look like a complete bloody fool". Because that's what you're really saying in this report, isn't it?'

'No, sir, not at all,' Woodend protested. 'If I've come up with a result, it's only because I'm the one who's happened to have the lucky breaks. But I don't expect to get any personal glory out of it.'

'Is that right?' Bentley's mused. 'No personal glory, eh? So what *do* you want to get out of it?'

'Only what I've always wanted – to see Pearl Jones's murderer hangin' from the end of a rope.'

'And that's all?'

'That's all.'

'Hmm, well, you would say that, wouldn't you?' Bentley asked. 'Do you know, Sergeant, you're a lot smarter – and considerably more devious – than I ever imagined you were.'

'I don't understand,' Woodend said.

Bentley laughed, bitterly and dismissively. 'Oh, I think you do. I think you do very well. What you'd like is for me to mount a *massive* operation, isn't it? The number of people you want me to bring in for questioning alone is mind-boggling.' Bentley scanned Woodend's report. 'Smithers, his minders, the manager of the Charleston Club, his bouncers, any guests at the club we can track down. How many people are we talking about here? Twenty? Thirty?'

'Somethin' like that,' Woodend agreed.

'Or perhaps even more. And then there's the places you want search warrants issued for – the Charleston Club itself, at least three premises known to be owned by Ron Smithers . . . What you're proposing could involve half the Met.'

'I don't think it would be quite *that* big an operation, sir,' Woodend countered. 'An' it wouldn't just be catching a murderer, would it? In arrestin' Smithers, you'd also be takin' a major gangster off the streets.'

'Let's just say that, after we've done everything you want us to, we *don't* manage to pin this murder on Smithers,'

Bentley said. 'Who do you think will get the blame for wasting so many police resources?'

'Since I'm the one who started the whole thing, it would probably be me.'

'Grow up, Sergeant!' Bentley said contemptuously. 'You're nothing! Less than nothing. I'm the man in charge, and I'm the man who'll take the fall.' He paused for a moment. 'But say, for the sake of argument, we *can* make it stick. Who gets the credit?'

'You do, sir. As you've just pointed out, you're the man in charge, an' it will have been your operation.'

'Yes, you'd think that *would* be the case, wouldn't you?' Bentley agreed. 'And maybe I would get the credit. At first! But then a certain detective sergeant would start spreading the rumour that it was all his idea – and he'd have a copy of his report to back up his claim. So if the investigation goes wrong, you lose nothing, but if it's a success, you're the main winner. Now don't try to tell me, Sergeant, that you haven't already worked all that out for yourself.'

'I promise you, sir—' Woodend began.

'I don't want promises of any kind from you,' Bentley said. 'You can go now, Sergeant. Close the door behind you, go back to your desk – and *stay* there until I tell you otherwise.'

Back at his desk, Woodend tried to analyse what had gone wrong in his meeting with Bentley, and wondered if there was anything he could have done to prevent it from ending up the way it had.

Was it all down to his own lack of experience, he asked himself.

He didn't really see how it could be, because, as green as he was, he had conducted a careful investigation, and produced a solid report.

So if the fault didn't lie with him, it had to be Bentley who had deliberately buggered things up. And the only explanation for him doing that was that the chief inspector – for unfathomable reasons of his own – didn't *want* the murder to be solved.

Woodend looked out of the window, and saw that the sky outside had clouded over, and now it was beginning to rain.

* * *

It was half an hour before the chief inspector's door swung open again, and when Bentley emerged from his office, he seemed much calmer than he had been earlier.

'You're finally going up in the world, Sergeant,' he said. 'To be precise, you're going up *one floor*.'

'One floor?'

'You've been summoned by God's assistant representative on earth.'

'I'm sorry, sir?

'Deputy Commissioner Naylor wants to see you. Right now! Can you find your own way up there, Sergeant – or would you like me to come with you and hold your hand?'

'I think I can find my own way there, sir.'

'Off you go, then,' Bentley said.

And Woodend thought he could detect a great sense of relief in his guv'nor's voice.

So DCI Bentley had come through after all, the sergeant thought as he climbed the stairs to the deputy commissioner's office.

The chief inspector might well be a loud-mouthed lazy drunk – *was* a loud-mouthed lazy drunk, as Commander Cathcart himself had so clearly pointed out the previous Sunday – but when it had come to the crunch, he had ultimately decided to do the right thing. True, he had not put his own neck on the line for the operation against Smithers, choosing instead to kick the whole thing upstairs, but even the fact that he'd gone that far was a minor miracle.

Deputy Commissioner Naylor was in his early fifties. His skin was a delicate shade of pink, and his thick white hair – swept back – gave him something of the air of a patrician.

'It is not my normal practice to interview mere detective sergeants,' he told Woodend. 'I usually have matters of much more significance to deal with. Besides, such a meeting could scarcely be called "going through the proper channels". Even so, I thought I would make an exception in this case.'

What the hell *was* this? Woodend asked himself.

He hadn't exactly been expecting balloons, streamers, and a full parade when he'd walked through the deputy commissioner's door. Nor had he anticipated the deputy commissioner himself pinning a medal on him then and there. But the bloody man could have *at least* congratulated him on a job well done.

Still, he told himself, this wasn't his office, and these weren't his rules, and since Naylor had been at pains to point out what a privilege had been granted to him, he supposed he'd better come up with some kind of appropriate response.

'Thank you, sir,' he said.

Naylor frowned. 'I wouldn't thank me yet, Sergeant. Not until I've finished disciplining you.'

'Until you've finished *what*?' Woodend gasped.

'Disciplining you,' Naylor repeated. 'You surely *expected* to be disciplined, didn't you?'

'No, sir.'

'Well, you certainly *should have* been expecting it, as should any man who conducts an unauthorized investigation which goes against the explicit orders of his immediate superior.'

'With respect, sir, DCI Bentley *didn't* explicitly order me not to investigate the case. He assigned me to another one.'

'And isn't that the same thing?' Naylor asked impatiently.

'No, sir, it isn't. I investigated the case that Mr Bentley assigned me to – the murder of Walter Booth in the Waterman's Arms – and I got a result.'

Even if it was the *wrong* result, he added mentally. Even if, for reasons I still don't completely understand, Jimmy Machin allowed himself to be *fitted up*.

'This is the Metropolitan Police Force,' Naylor said gravely. 'We do things properly here – and we do not consider that a success in one area of your activities gives you the right to flout the rules in another.'

'But I didn't flout any rules. My investigation into the Pearl Jones case was carried out in my own time.'

Naylor's frown deepened.

'You're beginning to sound rather too much like a barrack-room lawyer for my taste, Sergeant,' he said. 'But leaving aside your disregard for the proper procedure, there is another question to be answered. And it is this – did you really think that you could conduct a *better* investigation, working on your own, than DCI Bentley could with the *entire resources* of New Scotland Yard at his disposal?'

This had to be a dream, Woodend thought. He wasn't in Deputy Commissioner Naylor's office at all – he was still back his own bed, caught up a delirium brought on by the flu. How else could he explain the fact that he thought he'd just heard Naylor say he couldn't possibly expect to solve a case which, in fact, he'd *already solved*?

And yet, despite the logic of this argument, the room seemed to be real enough, and so did the deputy commissioner. And as hard as Woodend tried to, he still couldn't convince himself that he was making up this whole encounter in his own head!

'I asked you a question, Sergeant, and I am still waiting for an answer,' Naylor said. 'What made you think that you had a better chance of finding Pearl Jones's murderer than DCI Bentley had?'

It *was* all real! It had to be!

'When I started out, I'd no idea whether or not I'd be able to get a result before DCI Bentley did, sir,' Woodend said, 'but the simple fact is that I have.'

'Have you, indeed?' Naylor asked quizzically.

'Yes, sir.'

'And what do you base this sweeping assumption on?'

'Well, there's the girl's coat, for a start.'

'Ah yes, the coat. That proves the girl was in the club, does it?'

'Yes, sir.'

'So you found it in the club, did you?'

'No, sir. My informant took it from the club, and gave it to me.'

'And your informant is?'

'I'm afraid I can't tell you that, sir.'

'So I have absolutely no basis on which to assess the reliability of this informant, except the opinion of an inexperienced detective sergeant,' Naylor said cuttingly. 'But let us assume, for the moment, that the coat did come from the club. How do you propose to link it to the girl?'

'It's part of her school uniform.'

'And no doubt of the uniform of several other schools, as well,' Naylor said. 'But again, even if the coats were unique to her school, how do you propose to set about proving that she, and not one of the other girls, left it at the Charleston Club?'

'The other girls had no reason to be at the club,' Woodend

said. 'The other girls weren't lookin' for a gangster who they thought might be their father.'

'And how do you know that was what Pearl Jones was doing?'

'I . . .'

'I'll tell you how you know – or *think* you know, at any rate. You're basing your whole theory on what you were told by *another* impressionable young girl, who probably doesn't know fact from fiction.'

'You haven't met her, sir,' Woodend said stubbornly. 'If you had, you'd have as much confidence in her as I have.'

'It seems to me that Tompkinson girl is not the only one with an overactive imagination,' Naylor said. 'I can think of a certain detective sergeant who seems only too willing to plunge into the depths of unreality.'

'Look, sir, I know there might not be enough evidence to arrest Smithers yet,' Woodend said, 'but the evidence will *be* there, an' it shouldn't be too difficult to gather it up – because there's no doubt that he did it.'

'But that's just the point,' Naylor countered. 'He didn't.'

'I beg your pardon, sir?'

'As well you might, Sergeant, because Ronald Smithers *isn't* the killer.'

'But he has to be! He was at the club, he left with the girl, and—'

'You're quite wrong about that as well. He wasn't at the club at all.'

'He bloody was! He's been placed there by my source, an' I have complete faith in her.'

'And I have complete faith in the officers serving under me, Sergeant,' Naylor said coldly.

'I don't understand,' Woodend admitted.

'Of course you don't. How could you? You've got such a high opinion of your own abilities that you're convinced that you – and only you – have all the answers. But you don't – not by a very long way.'

'If you'd care to explain, sir . . .'

'I am under absolutely no obligation to explain *anything* to you, Sergeant Woodend.'

'I know that, sir, but—'

'However, since your own arrogance is unlikely to allow

you to appreciate just how foolish you've been until I *do* explain, I'm prepared, on this one single occasion, to tell you why I find it so easy to rule Ronald Smithers out of the investigation.'

Before Naylor would say any more, he was going to have to say something himself, Woodend realized. And he knew what the deputy commissioner expected that *something* to be.

'Thank you, sir,' he said, almost choking on the words.

It seemed enough for Naylor – but only just.

'Smithers has been under deep investigation by the Flying Squad for some time,' the deputy commissioner said. 'We have him under observation round the clock, which means, as I'm sure you'll appreciate, that he was under observation the Tuesday night before last. So we know exactly where he was, Sergeant – and he was nowhere near this Charleston Club of yours.'

'I see,' Woodend said.

'I thought you might. But let us now return to the matter of how I should discipline you, shall we? There are several sanctions I *could* employ. I could suspend you, or I could dock your pay. If I decided to take you in front of a board, you might be reduced in rank, or even dismissed from the Force. But I have decided to let the matter rest with a mere slap on the wrist. Would you like to know why?'

'Yes, sir,' Woodend said – because there was really no choice in the matter.

'There are two main reasons. The first is that while I am far from impressed with the simplistic, bull-headed way in which you have conducted this "private" investigation of yours, I recognize that at least it shows some initiative. But the second – more important – reason is that Commander Cathcart has interceded on your behalf. He has assured me that you have the makings of a very good policeman, and since I have considerably more faith in *his* judgement than I currently have in *yours*, I have agreed to let the matter rest there. But be warned, Sergeant Woodend, if you step over the line again, there will be no second chance. Have I made myself clear?'

'Perfectly clear, sir,' Woodend said.

Naylor nodded. 'Good. Well, in that case, you're dismissed.'

* * *

He had managed to make his exit from Naylor's office appear reasonably civilized, but the moment there was a door between him and the deputy commissioner, Woodend exploded.

Naylor had been talking bollocks, he told himself as he strode furiously down the corridor. Total and *complete* bollocks!

He reached the stairs, and slammed his foot down heavily on the first one as he began his descent.

Bang!

He felt it jar his spine, and he didn't care. He would almost welcome physical pain as a distraction from the rage that was burning him up.

Bang!

The Flying Squad had Smithers under twenty-four-hour observation, Naylor had said.

Bang!

Had they, indeed? Then why hadn't they arrested him in connection with the murder of Wally Booth – because Woodend was now sure he'd been there in the Waterman's Arms when it happened.

Bang!

Greyhound Ron Smithers was nowhere near the Charlton Club that night, Naylor had added.

Bang!

Like hell, he wasn't! Shirley, the fat cloakroom attendant, had had no reason to lie. And she *hadn't* lied! What she'd told him had been the absolute truth. And she'd told it even though she'd known she was possibly putting herself in danger – because like him, her heart bled for poor, tragic Pearl Jones.

He had reached the foot of the stairs. He stopped and took a deep breath, in an attempt to calm down.

And as he stood there, the words of Eddie, the Liverpudlian thug, floated back into his mind.

'*Even an idiot like you should have worked out by now that nobody wants the case solved – and that includes your bosses in the big cop-shop on the river!*'

And that includes your bosses!

The words had been haunting him for two days. He had been trying to ignore them – because he didn't want to believe they were true – but that was now no longer an option open to him.

What Naylor had just administered to him hadn't been a slap on the wrist for ignoring police procedure – it had been a warning.

The deputy commissioner hadn't actually said, 'We want Smithers to get away with this murder,' but he might as well have done.

It wasn't going to happen that way, Woodend promised himself. Whatever it took – at whatever personal cost to himself – he would see to it that Ron Smithers paid the price for killing Pearl Jones.

Twenty-Five

Woodend's back ached, and his eyes prickled. He tried to work out how much sleep he'd had in the previous three days but gave up halfway through, because he was too tired to continue the calculation – and because, whatever the final figure turned out to be, he already knew it was too damn little.

It wasn't easy doing two jobs – grafting his private investigation on top of his official duties. It wasn't easy forcing himself to come here every night, when he could be at home playing games with Pauline Anne or listening to an agreeable programme on the radio with Joan. And now it was raining – which didn't bloody help at all!

He watched the raindrops spatter against the windscreen of his borrowed car. Some of them, he noted, dimpled on impact, then clung to the glass like limpets. Others, of a more adventurous nature, were clearly determined to explore further, and slid down the screen at a snail's pace, leaving a trail of translucent slime behind them.

He wanted to turn on the windscreen wipers, to clear the screen so he would have a better view of the front of the Royal Albert – but he didn't dare to, because nobody runs the wipers in a parked car.

He wanted to light up a cigarette, but was afraid the telltale glow would alert the minders standing just inside the pub doorway to the fact that they were being watched.

He wanted . . .

He wanted to jack this whole thing in.

But he knew that he couldn't.

He had little to show for the three nights of his self-imposed vigil. No, he corrected himself – he had *nothing* to show for them.

On Wednesday night, a succession of lesser gangsters had

visited the pub – no doubt to hand their boss his cut of the previous week's takings – but Smithers himself had not once set foot outside. On Thursday night, he had taken a couple of his lieutenants out for a slap-up meal in the West End, but once dinner was finished, he had come straight back to his base. Now it was Friday night, and it was looking entirely possible that Greyhound Ron had decided to spend another night in.

But whatever happened, he would have to see the woman *eventually* – because he was infatuated with her.

'*'E 'ad his lady-friend wiv''im*,' Shirley had said, '*an' when 'e 'anded over the coats, 'e was in a very good mood – like 'e'd been looking forward to this night out all week*.'

'Maybe he's not seen her yet because *she* refuses to see *him*,' said the nagging voice in Woodend's head.

'Whose side are you on?' Woodend demanded aloud.

'Yours, of course,' the voice answered. 'But you have to face facts, Charlie – maybe she was so horrified by what he did to Pearl Jones that she'll never see him again.'

She'd see him, Woodend told himself. She was a gangster's moll, used to the violence which was inherent to Smithers's world, and even though this particular act of violence had shocked her initially – had, in fact, sent her running to the phone to call Scotland Yard – she'd soon learn to get over it, and then life would carry on as before.

'If it makes you feel better, you just keep on tellin' yourself that, Charlie,' the voice in his head mocked.

Besides, even if she *doesn't* want to see him, he'll want to see her, Woodend argued. He *has to* want to see her.

'Why?'

Because the way that he feels about her won't have changed. He'll want her back. An' even if he's given up that idea, he'll need to see her just once in order to reassure himself that she has no intention of betraying him.

'So they meet, an' you see them. Then what?'

Then he'd have a witness, if not to the killing, then at least to the prelude and the aftermath. Then he'd have all the leverage he needed.

'An' just how long are you prepared to wait for this leverage to fall into your lap, Charlie?'

As long as it took, Woodend told the voice.

A week, a month, a year – it didn't matter.

If he had to be here until either he or Smithers died of old age, then that was the way it was.

Another hour had slowly ticked away, and with every minute that passed, Woodend's craving for a cigarette had grown stronger and stronger.

He peered through the windscreen – squinting between the raindrops – at the street which lay before him. There were a number of parked vehicles, but none of them remotely resembled the ostentatiously nondescript vans that the Flying Squad used for their surveillance operations. Nor had there been any sign of such a van on the previous two evenings, either.

It didn't surprise Woodend that there wasn't even a *whiff* of the Sweeney. He'd never believed Deputy Commissioner Naylor's claim that Greyhound Ron was being watched round the clock. In fact, he doubted that Smithers was being investigated *at all* – because if the Yard was prepared to let him get away with such a heinous crime as murder, it could only be because someone, somewhere in the higher echelons of the Force, was making a hell of a lot of money out of protecting the man.

One of Smithers's cars, a flashy Cadillac sedan, pulled up in front of the Royal Albert. The driver got out and went inside the pub, but fumes continued to pump out of the exhaust pipe.

Smithers came out a few moments later. He was flanked by a couple of his minders as he walked to the car, but it was only Greyhound Ron himself who got in.

The fact that he was going out alone didn't necessarily mean anything, Woodend thought, as the Cadillac pulled away from the kerb and he set off in pursuit.

Maybe Smithers – like so many other London gangsters – had a grey-haired old mum tucked away somewhere, and was going to visit her.

Or perhaps he'd just grown bored with being cooped up inside the Royal Albert, and had decided to drive around for a while, with no particular destination in mind.

But while Woodend's brain cautioned him against getting too excited, his heart was ignoring the warning, and beating out rapid messages of hope.

*　　*　　*

Smithers drove along Whitechapel Road, an area which, sixty-odd years earlier, had been terrorized by the nocturnal activities of Jack the Ripper – a man who, like Smithers himself, had used a razor to slash and murder his innocent victims.

Woodend wondered if, back then in the last century, there had been a policeman much like himself, who had made a vow that he would never give up until the killer was brought to book. There probably had been – because even in the most corrupt, most lethargic of societies, there were always *a few* dedicated fools like him.

'But if there was such a copper, he never made his case,' the voice in his head said. 'An' you might not, either, Charlie.'

An image of his own gravestone flashed before Woodend's eyes, and on it was written:

> ### Here lies Charlie Woodend
> ### The man who didn't catch Ron Smithers

That wasn't going to happen, he told himself angrily. He wouldn't *allow* it to happen!

As Smithers turned left onto Bishopsgate the rain became heavier, and by the time he drew up in front of Liverpool Street Railway Station it was coming down in buckets.

A woman, her head obscured by an umbrella, emerged from under the station awning where she'd been sheltering from the downpour, and walked quickly towards the Cadillac.

In order to open the passenger door from inside the car, Smithers had only to reach across. But he didn't do that. Instead, he got out of the Cadillac, walked around the front, and opened the passenger door from the outside!

It was her, Woodend thought. It *had to be* her. Smithers would never have made such a gallant gesture – in the pouring rain – for just *any* woman.

Once the woman was inside, the Cadillac sedan set off up Bishopsgate again.

As Woodend followed, he found that he was already running through a future interview with the woman in his head.

'*I didn't know anything about it*,' she would claim tearfully – because that was what they always claimed.

'*You knew he left the club with the young girl, didn't you?*' Woodend would demand.

'*Yeah, I . . . I knew that.*'

'*And that when he came back later, he'd already killed her?*'

'*No . . . I . . . he said he'd just run her home.*'

'*Don't lie to me. If you hadn't known she was dead, how could you have phoned me to tell me where the body was?*'

'*I didn't.*'

'*More lies! I know it was you.*'

She would break in the end. She would break and – to save herself – she would tell him enough to ensure that, however many friends in high places Ron Smithers had, he would still end up with a rope around his neck!

The couple's destination, it turned out, was a nightclub on Bethnal Green Road, which went by the name of the Waldorf Club. Smithers drew up directly by the door, and he and the woman rushed inside to avoid the rain, leaving the bouncer on duty with the job of parking the Cadillac.

Woodend himself parked a little further down the street, and lit up a Capstan Full Strength.

Even from a distance, he thought, the Waldorf reminded him, in so many ways, of the Charleston Club. It had the same flashy lighting, which might appear sophisticated to those who knew no better, but in reality was merely tawdry. It had the same kind of bouncers, who acted out the part of hard men without really being hard. And it had the same kind of punters entering it, bank officials and their wives, city clerks and their girlfriends – people who relished the air of danger attached to the place, but only so long as they could be assured that it was *safe* danger.

He wondered what could possibly have attracted Ron Smithers – a man who would know the real thing when he saw it – to a place like this. It didn't make sense that he should have chosen to take his girlfriend to this particular club, any more than it made sense that he should have taken her to the Charleston.

He felt a strong urge to go inside the club – to reward himself for his patient vigil with a glimpse of the woman who had been the object of it. But he knew that was not a good idea, because if Smithers saw him he would immediately realize what was going on.

And then what would happen?

The woman would quickly disappear off the face of the earth! Possibly Smithers might send her abroad – somewhere beyond the reach of the Metropolitan Police. Possibly he might even kill her – because, as fond as he appeared to be of her, he was undoubtedly even fonder of his own neck.

And without the woman, Woodend thought, he had nothing.

Without the woman, he would be back to square one.

So he would fight his natural urge, and stay where he was – just sit there, chain-smoking, until they came out again.

When they did eventually leave the club, he would follow them, and when they separated, it was the woman he would continue to tail. Because once he knew where she lived – once he knew *who she was* – he would have her!

Another four hours passed before Smithers and his paramour emerged from the club again. It had stopped raining by then, but even so, the woman seemed eager to get into the waiting Cadillac as quickly as possible. Greyhound Ron, on the other hand, was in no hurry at all, and struck up a conversation with the bouncers, who were already treating him like the visiting royalty he actually was.

The woman waited for about half a minute, then tapped him on the shoulder, and pointed to the car. But Smithers seemed to have had enough of playing the gentleman for one night, and shook his head brusquely.

The woman was furious. She stood there impotently for a few moments, then began to march peevishly up and down in front of the car.

Up until that moment, Woodend had not been able to get a proper look at her, but now, as she continually passed under the club's flashing lights, it was almost as if she were taking part in an identification parade solely for his benefit.

An involuntary tremble took control of Woodend's cigarette hand.

'I had it all wrong,' he groaned.

No, not *all* wrong, he corrected himself.

He'd been right about Smithers committing the murder – the case for that was stronger than ever, now that he'd suddenly been handed a motive.

But where he *had* been wrong – *so* wrong – was in his

thinking about the cover-up. He'd fervently believed, until just a few seconds earlier, that the only reason the Yard seemed unwilling to pin Pearl Jones's murder on Smithers was because he had someone important – perhaps even one of the top brass, like Deputy Commissioner Naylor – in his pocket.

Now he saw that that wasn't it.

It wasn't it at all!

Smithers finally decided it was time to go, and he and the woman got into the car and drove away.

But, despite his earlier planning, Woodend made no effort to follow them.

Because he didn't need to!

Twenty-Six

His childhood was something that Toby Burroughs did his best not to think about. Yet as hard as he tried to keep it firmly locked away in a dark corner of his mind, he could not *always* keep it caged.

Sometimes it seemed to take very little to set him off on a reluctant journey to the past. A picture, a word – even a perfectly ordinary sound – could be enough to fling him into the time tunnel and send him hurtling back to the last days of the Victorian era. And once he was there, it was as if he'd never been away.

He felt the cold of those years – a cold so huge and all-encompassing that it had almost killed him. He relived the humiliation of being dressed in rags – of being mocked for it by other boys, *almost* as poor as he was. But most of all, he recalled the hunger.

It seemed always to have been there – that hollow feeling, deep in the pit of his stomach. Walking past a pie shop, sniffing its aroma in the air, he would be conscious of the saliva forming his mouth – as if he were not a boy at all, but a dog. Standing with his nose pressed up against a cafe window, he would watch the people inside – people who had no idea what a precious gift they had been given – as they shovelled food carelessly into their mouths. And he had promised himself then, that one day – *one day* – he would eat when he wanted to, not just when he could.

He was rich and powerful now. He owned property all over London, drove around in flashy cars, and told the time by expensive watches. But of all the things his wealth had brought him, it was food – and especially breakfast – which he valued the most.

He was eating breakfast that Saturday morning when he was informed by one of his minders that DS Woodend was outside, and wanted to see him.

'Did 'e say what he wanted?' Burroughs asked.

'No, 'e didn't, boss. The cheeky bleeder said 'e didn't need to, because yer'd already know. D'yer want me to send 'im away wiv a flea in 'is ear?'

'No, I'll see 'im,' Burroughs said, looking down at his breakfast, and realizing he didn't really want it any more.

Woodend was escorted into the room by two minders, one on each side of him. Yet he didn't look intimidated by his situation, Burroughs thought. In fact, he looked as if *nothing* could intimidate him that morning.

Woodend looked around, at the heavy curtains and the heavy wallpaper, at the pictures which had been painted on the ceiling.

'Nice place,' he said.

'Yes, it is,' Burroughs agreed. 'It's my private dining room. It's the place where people come when they want to eat wiv me, but don't want ter be *seen* eating wiv me.' He paused for a moment. 'Why are yer 'ere? I don't recall 'aving sent for yer.'

'Let's get one thing straight right from the start,' Woodend told him. 'I'm not your boy now – an' I never will be.'

One of the minders tapped him on the shoulder, and Woodend turned to face him.

'Watch yer mouth, copper!' the minder warned.

'This has nothin' to do with you,' Woodend said. 'Can't you see I was talkin' to the organ grinder, not his monkey?'

The minder stepped clear of the policeman, and balled his hands into tight fists. 'It's time yer learned a bit of respect,' he growled.

'An' you think you can teach it to me, do you?' Woodend asked. 'Well, go ahead. Take a swing at me. I'd really like that.'

'Leave it out, Larry,' Burroughs said.

'Sorry, boss?'

'I'm 'aving my breakfast, and I don't want blood all over the table, so why don't you and Pete go back to the bar?'

'Wot about 'im?' Larry asked, jerking a thumb in Woodend's direction.

'He stays,' Burroughs said.

The minder shrugged, and he and his partner turned on their heels and left the room.

Burroughs speared a devilled kidney with his fork, and forced himself to pop it into his mouth.

It tasted like sawdust.

'Sit down, Sergeant,' he said, indicating the chair opposite him.

Woodend sat, but said nothing.

'Yer sounded very angry just then,' Burroughs commented. 'More angry, *I'd* have fort, than the situation merited.'

'I'm angry, right enough,' Woodend agreed.

'Wiv me?' Burroughs asked, showing only a mild interest.

'No, not with you. At least – not yet.'

'It wouldn't be very clever of yer to get angry with me *ever*,' Burroughs said. 'But if I'm not yer problem, then what is?'

'I'm angry about bein' pissed about,' Woodend said. 'I'm angry about bein' lied to. But most of all, I'm angry because I've been used as a pawn in other people's games.'

Burroughs shrugged. 'Then break free. Stop playing by uvver people's rules, and start playing by yer own.'

'That's what I intend to. That's why I'm here.'

'Go on.'

'I've got some questions I need answerin', an' you're the one who can give me the answers.'

'In uvver words, yer want *me* to play by *your* rules?'

'That's right.'

'Why should I?'

'Because you want somethin' from me.'

'Do I? What?'

Woodend sighed. 'There you go – I've only been here a couple of minutes, an' you're *already* pissin' me about,' he said. 'We both know what it is you want, so why pretend otherwise?'

Burroughs nodded. 'All right,' he agreed. 'We both know what it is I want. The question is, are yer going to give it to me?'

'I might,' Woodend told him. 'I haven't decided yet. It will all depend on what happens in the next twenty minutes.'

'I could always have my boys beat it out of yer, yer know,' Burroughs said softly.

'Even *you* would think twice before havin' a copper worked over,' Woodend said. 'Besides, I wouldn't talk, whatever they did to me.'

'Do you know, I fink I believe yer,' Burroughs said. 'All right, Sergeant, ask me yer questions.'

'How did you persuade Jimmy Machin to take the blame for the Wally Booth murder?' Woodend asked.

'I don't know what yer talking about.'

'Of course you do. He's one of your lads.'

'That don't prove a—'

'An' the fact that he *is* one of your lads means he would never even have *contemplated* goin' for a drink in a pub right in the middle of Ron Smithers's territory. So he wasn't there, was he?'

'Possibly not.'

'An' if he wasn't there, he couldn't have killed Booth.'

'That makes sense.'

'Which brings us back to my original question, doesn't it? How *did* you persuade him to put his hands up for the murder? By intimidation? Did you threaten to harm him – or a member of his family?'

Burroughs chuckled. 'If yer ever going to make a success out of being a copper, yer'll need to learn how blokes like Jimmy Machin fink.'

'An' how *do* they think?'

'To men like you, prison is a terrible place. But to men like Jimmy, it's a second 'ome. They don't mind serving a few years' porridge, especially if there's a nice bundle of cash waiting for 'em when they come out.'

'An' will there be?'

'I wouldn't know.'

Woodend stood up. 'That's it!' he said angrily. 'The meeting's over.'

'Sit down again, Sergeant!' Burroughs ordered.

'You still haven't got the point, have you?' Woodend demanded. 'So I'll say it again – I'm *not* your boy.'

Burroughs sighed. 'Machin will be looked after.'

Woodend still hovered over the chair.

'By *you*?' he asked.

'By me,' Burroughs admitted. 'His family's *already* getting a few quid every week. Now please sit down again, Sergeant, and ask yer next question.'

Woodend sat. 'I suppose I could ask you *why* you fitted Machin up,' he said, 'but there wouldn't be much point in it, because I already know the answer.'

'Do yer? And what is it?'

'You did it so I wouldn't have to waste any more of my time on investigatin' the Wally Booth case.'

'Yer really do 'ave an 'igh opinion of yerself, don't yer, Sergeant?' Burroughs asked.

'An' so do you,' Woodend countered. 'Them Liverpudlians would have beaten the shit out of me if the lads you'd sent to protect me hadn't stepped in at the last minute.'

'How do yer know they were my lads?'

'Because they were wearin' nylon stockings over their heads.'

'So what?'

'So the reason they wore the stockings was to hide their identity. Right?'

'I suppose so.'

'But there was no point in hidin' it from the Liverpudlians, who were only in London for the one specific job. So it must have been done to hide their identity from *me*.'

'Interesting theory,' Burroughs said.

'An' yet, at the same time as you were protectin' me, you got your lads to beat up Tom Townshend, who was helpin' with my investigation,' Woodend continued. 'Now why *was* that?'

'You tell me.'

'Because you wanted me to investigate Pearl Jones's murder – that's what's been drivin' you from the start – but what you *didn't* want was for it to become public knowledge who was payin' her school fees through the Meadows Trust. An' it wasn't only her school fees the Trust was throwin' money at. It was also buildin' the school a new science wing.'

'So yer fink I'm behind this Meadows Trust, do yer?'

'I *know* you are. By the way, how would you say "the meadows" in Spanish, Mr Burroughs?'

'I've no idea.'

'Of course you have. An' so have I, now that I've looked it up. You'd say "Las Vegas" – as in the *Las Vegas Club*.' Woodend chuckled. 'That headmistress – a racist cow if I ever met one – really couldn't stand Pearl's guts, you know. But I expect the school governors told her that she'd just have to put up with the girl, because if the school didn't have Pearl, it wouldn't be gettin' any money from the Meadows Trust, either.'

'So I 'elped out a little coloured girl,' Burroughs admitted. 'Nuffink wrong wiv that, is there?'

'You helped her out *anonymously*.'

'Yeah, well, I didn't want people finking I'd gone soft.'

'This is difficult for you, isn't it?' Woodend asked sympathetically.

'I ain't got no idea wot yer talking about.'

'But it doesn't *have to* be difficult, you know. You can tell me all about it. An' I promise you that havin' kept it bottled up inside you all these years, you'll feel better for gettin' it off your chest.'

'Yer just like every uvver copper I've ever met, ain't yer?' Burroughs sneered. ' "Admit to doing over that bank, Toby, and I promise yer, yer'll feel better for it." "Put yer 'ands up for that jewel robbery, Burroughs, and I promise yer, it'll be a great weight off yer mind." I must 'ave 'eard it a fousand times.'

'Except that this time we're not talkin' about a *crime*, are we?' Woodend asked. 'This time, we're talkin' about your *life*!'

'And suppose I don't *want* ter talk about my life?'

Woodend shrugged. 'Then I can't make you. But if you *don't* tell me, I won't give you what you want.'

Burroughs made one more attempt to show an interest in his food, then pushed his plate to one side.

'If I do tell yer, and it ever goes beyond this room, then yer a dead man,' he said.

'Bad move!' Woodend told him.

'What d'yer mean?'

'I don't like bein' threatened, Mr Burroughs, an' if you try threatenin' me just once more, I'm leavin'.'

'So 'ow can I be sure yer'll keep quiet?'

'You can be sure because I'm *tellin'* you – here an' now – that I will.'

Burroughs lit up a cigarette, and sucked the smoke in greedily.

'I met Pearl's muvver in 1932,' he said. 'Back then, she wasn't the same woman is she now. She was so energetic. So alive. English girls seemed pale in comparison – and I ain't just talking about the colour of their skin.'

'She became your girlfriend,' Woodend suggested.

'She became my secret mistress,' Burroughs corrected him.

'Why *secret*?'

'Because it wasn't the done fing to go out wiv coloured girls back then. A few of the boys might 'ave taken a darkie to bed once – just for the novelty value. But if yer wanted to get on in the rackets in them days, yer needed the backing of the big names, and most of 'em were strictly old school, and didn't like to see no mixing of the races. Besides, I wasn't *just* giving 'er one now and again, was I? I was seeing 'er regular – and that definitely wasn't on.'

'So what did you do?'

'I bought 'er a house in Stepney. I wasn't known around there, and neivver was anybody I 'ung around with. I used to visit 'er free or four times a week. Sometimes we 'ad sex, and sometimes we didn't. Often we'd just sit around and talk. We liked being in each uvver's company.'

'An' then she got pregnant,' Woodend said.

'And then she got pregnant,' Burroughs agreed. 'And it was only when she give me the news that I finally realized I'd fallen in love with 'er. I can't tell yer 'ow 'appy I was at the fort of 'aving a baby.'

'So what went wrong?'

'What went wrong was that Victoria 'ad started getting religion by then, and she insisted that we got married. Well, I couldn't do it, could I? Yer can't expect to still command respect out on the street if yer marry a *nigger*! So I told 'er it wasn't possible, and *she* told *me* that she never wanted to see me again.'

'She still took your money, though, didn't she?' Woodend asked.

'But not for 'erself!' Burroughs said, with a sudden burst of anger. 'She's a good woman. A decent woman. She took the money for our *child*.'

'I never meant to suggest otherwise,' Woodend said humbly. 'An' if that's how it sounded, then I'm sorry.'

Burroughs nodded, acknowledging the apology.

'I moved the two of 'em out to the countryside during the Blitz,' he continued, 'but after the War, Victoria wanted to come back to London. I could 'ave set 'er up in a much nicer 'ouse than the one I did, but she said she wanted to live close to 'er friends from the church.'

'An' what about Pearl?' Woodend asked. 'Did you ever see her?'

'I never *spoke* to 'er – Victoria wouldn't allow that – but I saw 'er occasionally. I'd sometimes watch 'er as she went to school, or when she was coming 'ome again.'

The man in the big black car, who Lene had spotted from her window, Woodend thought.

'You loved her,' he said.

'Wiv all my 'eart,' Burroughs said, as tears began to form in his eyes. 'I used to dream that one day, when she was grown up – and I'd left this life behind me – we could meet properly. And now we never will.'

'When you learned she was dead, the only thing that seemed to matter to you was that her killer was caught.'

'Yes. It was the one fing I could still do for 'er.'

'Didn't you try to find out who'd killed her yourself?'

'Of course I bloody did. But I kept coming up against a brick wall. That's when I realized that 'ooever 'ad murdered Pearl must 'ave a powerful protector.'

It wasn't so much that the murderer *had* a powerful protector as that he *was* a powerful protector himself, Woodend thought. But he wasn't going to mention that now.

'So you decided that the only way you'd get at the truth was through a police investigation,' he said. 'But why choose me? Couldn't you have put some pressure on DCI Bentley?'

'Bentley!' Burroughs repeated with contempt. 'Bentley runs errands for me now and again. Little jobs. 'E doesn't ask why 'e's doing them – and 'e doesn't care, as long as 'e gets paid.'

'Little jobs like what?' Woodend wondered.

Burroughs smiled thinly. 'For instance, when I needed to 'ave Jimmy Machin arrested, I told 'im to go and wait in the Waterman's Arms, and then I passed the word along to Bentley that 'e should order you to go there.'

'*Maybe you'd better check it over again yourself, personally, before we finally give them permission to open up,*' Bentley had said.

'*Oh, I don't think that will be necessary, sir,*' Woodend had replied.

'*What* you *think doesn't matter a tuppenny damn. Round here, it's what* I *think that matters. So instead of lecturing me*

*on what is and isn't necessary, you'd do well to get yourself
off to the pub and see if it* can *be opened again. Got that?'*

It had all seemed far too neat at the time – a tidy parcel
just waiting there to be picked up – and that, of course, was
exactly what it *had* been.

'But while I let 'im run my errands, I didn't trust 'im to
investigate my Pearl's death,' Burroughs continued.

'An' you were wise not to,' Woodend said. 'Because however
much money you'd offered him, he wouldn't have dared help
you.'

'Wouldn't 'e? Why not?'

'That's not somethin' you need to know. It's more to do
with another little matter that I have to clear up later, with
Deputy Commissioner Naylor.'

'And suppose I *insist* on knowing?' Burroughs asked.

'Insist all you like, but I still won't tell you,' Woodend
replied. 'It's police business, an' – trust me – you're better
out of it.' He lit up a cigarette. 'You still haven't said why
you chose me for the investigation.'

'Because yer were the only one 'oo who seemed to *care* –
the only one who seemed to fink that the death of a coloured
girl was *wurf* investigating.'

'Why did Victoria deny that the girl in the photograph was
Pearl?' Woodend asked.

'Because she was scared.'

'Of you?'

'Yes. She fort that I'd blame 'er for Pearl's death. She fort
I'd kill 'er if I found out.'

'An' the only way to prevent that happenin' was to pretend
that Pearl wasn't dead at all?'

'Exactly.'

'An' *did* you kill her?' Woodend asked, remembering what
Lene had said about the car picking her up, and how she had
been reluctant to get it.

'No, of course I didn't kill 'er.'

'Then what did you do with her?'

'I sent 'er back 'ome to the West Indies.'

'Why?'

'Because I knew that when the police finally got around to
questioning 'er, the 'ole story – wot I've been keeping secret
for sixteen years – would finally come out into the open.'

And you still didn't dare to admit to what you've done, Woodend thought. You just couldn't find the strength within yourself to tell the world that you were once in love with a coloured woman.

'Can yer . . . can yer tell me anyfink about the last few hours of my daughter's life?' Burroughs asked, on the verge of tears again.

'She was in a place called the Charleston Club,' Woodend said. 'That's where she met her killer. I won't try to tell you that she didn't suffer at all, but at least it was quick, because ten minutes later she was dead.'

'She was just a schoolgirl,' Burroughs said. 'What in God's name was she doing in a nightclub?'

She was lookin' for you, Woodend thought – lookin' for the father who she'd never met, yet desperately needed to know.

But Burroughs was already in enough pain without him adding to it, so all he said was, 'I suppose that's somethin' we'll never have the answer to.'

Twenty-Seven

It was eight-fifteen on Monday morning when the man walked, unannounced, into DCI Bentley's outer office. He didn't say who he was, but there was no need to – because his uniform said it for him.

The three detective constables who'd already reported for duty jumped to their feet.

'Sit down, men,' the chief superintendent said. 'Which one of you is DS Woodend?' And then, observing that none of them was wearing the hairy sports jacket he been told about, he added, 'He's not here yet, is he?'

'No, sir, punctuality isn't one of the sarge's virtues,' Cotteral said.

The chief superintendent nodded, as if he'd been expecting to hear something like that, then said, 'Which of these desks is his?'

'That one,' Cotteral said, pointing helpfully.

The chief superintendent sat down on Woodend's chair and produced a bunch of keys from his pocket. The first one he tried on Woodend's desk drawer didn't work, but the second did, and the drawer slid open.

The chief superintendent shook his head disgustedly at the chaos which confronted him, then heaped the contents of the drawer onto the desk and began the process of putting them into some sort of order.

By eight twenty-five Woodend was in the corridor, surveying the scene – the chief superintendent still sorting through his notes, the constables bent earnestly over their desks as if engaged in work of national importance.

It couldn't have been easy for the constables to ignore the fact that one of the big guns was sitting within touching distance of them, he thought, but they were putting on a creditable performance of doing just that. It was a bit like Death calling, he supposed – once you'd established that he hadn't come for you, you pretended that he wasn't there at all.

He entered the office and walked over to his desk.

'Have you found what you were looking for, sir?' he asked, with mild curiosity.

The superintendent glared up at him. 'You, I take it, are DS Woodend,' he said coldly.

'That's right, sir,' Woodend agreed.

'And I'm Chief Superintendent Markham,' the other man said. 'Your desk is in a disgraceful state, Sergeant.'

'I'm sorry, sir,' Woodend replied. 'If I'd known that you'd be riflin' through it, I'd have tidied it up before I went home on Friday.'

Markham stood up. 'You are required to come with me,' he said.

Required to come with me, Woodend repeated silently.

Well, that certainly set the tone of what was to follow clearly enough, didn't it? *Whatever* it was, it certainly wouldn't involve a cosy little chat, with tea and biscuits provided.

Markham stepped around Woodend and out into the corridor. Once there, he performed a smart right turn, and marched quickly off towards the stairwell. As Woodend fell into step behind him, he couldn't help hearing a sharp release of breath from the rest of DCI Bentley's team back in the office.

You could pretty much gauge the importance of your enemies by the men they sent to run their errands for them, Woodend told himself. And since the errand boy in this case was a *chief superintendent*, it was a fair bet that the office they were heading towards belonged to Deputy Commissioner Naylor – the man who was the assistant to God's deputy on earth.

He wasn't surprised to find himself in this situation, he thought. In fact, he'd been expecting it – and if *anything* was surprising, it was that Naylor hadn't hauled him in immediately after the police had been called to the Royal Albert, but instead had waited until Monday morning.

They reached the stairwell, but rather than starting the climb to the celestial heights inhabited by Naylor and his kind, Chief Superintendent Markham chose instead to begin descending.

'Aren't we goin' in the wrong direction, sir?' Woodend asked.

'*Down*, you mean?' Markham asked, over his shoulder.

'Yes, sir.'

Markham laughed. It was a dry throaty sound, completely devoid of any real humour.

'Down is where you've been heading for quite some time, Sergeant,' he said. 'Didn't you realize that?'

Yes, Woodend agreed silently. I suppose I did.

And by now he had worked out exactly where they were going. It was not to *any kind* of office at all, but to the interview rooms on the floor below, which were the only part of the Yard that the criminal classes ever saw.

Deputy Commissioner Naylor was already in the interview room when Markham ushered Woodend in.

He greeted the sergeant with a look of intense dislike. 'You're not here under caution, Sergeant,' he said. 'At least, you're not under caution *yet*.'

'That's good to know, sir,' Woodend replied. 'Why aren't we doin' this in your office? Is it bein' decorated or somethin'?'

'Your flippancy does not impress me,' Naylor said, glancing, as he spoke, at the interview room's other door. 'But since you ask, the reason we are here is because I felt that, given the nature of this meeting, it would be the most appropriate setting.'

No, that wasn't it at all, Woodend decided. They were there because this room – unlike Naylor's office – had that second door. And *behind* that door was someone else, waiting to hear what was about to be said.

'Ronald Edward Smithers, otherwise known as Greyhound Ron, was murdered yesterday,' Naylor said bleakly. 'His throat was cut.'

'*You told Burroughs!' Paniatowski said, astounded. 'You actually gave him Smithers's name!*'

'*I don't see why you should sound so surprised,' Woodend replied airily. 'I did warn you, at the very start of this tale, didn't I, that I'd arranged to have somebody killed?*'

'*What were you thinking of, Charlie? If it had ever got out, you'd have been finished on the Force. They might even have decided to charge you as an accessory to the murder.'*

'Oh, there was very little danger of that,' Woodend said, with uncharacteristic flippancy. 'Toby Burroughs was an honourable man, by his own lights, an' even if he'd been caught, it was unlikely he'd ever have given me up.'

'It was still a risk,' Paniatowski persisted.

'But a risk worth takin'. I thought that Burroughs had the right to know who'd murdered his daughter. An' I thought that Pearl had the right to justice.'

The lightness had completely disappeared from his voice, and been replaced by a weightier – altogether more frightening – tone.

His earlier casual approach had been no more than camouflage, Paniatowski thought. He was still angry about Pearl Jones's death, even after twenty-three years.

'Would you do the same thing again, Charlie?' she asked.

'Today, you mean?'

'Yes.'

'No, I wouldn't. Times have changed, an' we don't have capital punishment any more.'

'And that makes a difference, does it?'

'To me it does, yes. If Smithers had been convicted of the murder back then, he'd have hanged, just as he should have. I didn't see a lot of difference between the hangman's rope an' Toby Burroughs's razor. But there was one thing I made Burroughs promise before I gave him the name.'

'And what was that.'

'That if his daughter's killer was to die, it had to be by his hand alone. Man to man. Face to face. With no outside help.'

'Why did you insist on that?'

Woodend shrugged. 'To this day, I'm not sure I really know the answer,' he admitted. 'Maybe I was feelin' just a little bit guilty about what I'd done, an' wanted to at least give Smithers a fightin' chance. Or maybe I thought that there was no real virtue in St George killin' the dragon if he used a guided missile to do it. Whatever the reason, it just felt right.'

'And Toby Burroughs had no objections to doing it that way?'

'No, he didn't. To tell you the truth, I think Toby would have gone after Smithers on his own whatever I'd said. He may *have had his faults, but he at least knew there was more to bein' a man than just wearing trousers.'*

'Did you hear me, Sergeant?' Naylor demanded. 'Ron Smithers has been murdered.'

'Has he really, sir?' Woodend asked. 'Well, at least you'll have no trouble catchin' the killer, will you?'

'What exactly do you mean by that?'

'I should have thought it was obvious, sir. Since the Flyin' Squad were keepin' a round-the-clock surveillance on him, they'll know exactly who was with him at the time of his death, won't they?'

'Are you trying to be funny?' Naylor demanded.

'No, sir. I'm just goin' by what *you* told me.'

'Smithers was murdered with a cut-throat razor,' Naylor said. 'What does that suggest to you?'

'What *should* it suggest to me?' Woodend countered.

'A cut-throat razor is a very *personal* weapon, and that suggests that there was a very *personal* motive behind the murder.'

'Possibly you're right about that, sir. I wouldn't know.'

'But it's also a weapon which has largely gone out of fashion, and is now only used by a very few of the old-style gangsters.'

'Old-style gangsters like Ron Smithers, who used his to cut Pearl Jones's throat,' Woodend said.

'I was thinking more of *Toby Burroughs*,' Naylor said. 'In fact, this particular killing has Burroughs's stamp all over it.'

'Does it?' Woodend said. 'I didn't know that.'

'Are you asking me to believe that it's a pure coincidence that a few days after I refused your request to have Smithers arrested for murder, someone killed him?' Naylor asked.

'With respect, sir, I'm not, in point of fact, askin' you to believe *anythin*',' Woodend told him.

'So here's what I think happened. I think that you went to see Toby Burroughs, and gave him a *personal* reason to want to kill Smithers.'

'Now that is a bit far-fetched, if you don't mind me sayin' so, sir,' Woodend said. 'Can you yourself think of a *single* thing that *I* could have said which might have driven Burroughs into a homicidal rage?'

'No, I can't,' Naylor admitted. 'But that still doesn't mean that it didn't happen that way.'

'It doesn't mean that it *did* happen that way, either,' Woodend pointed out.

'I don't think you yet fully comprehend the amount of damage you've done,' Naylor said. 'I don't think you can even *begin* to imagine how much more difficult Smithers's death is going to make my job.'

'Maybe not, but I'd still like to try,' Woodend said. 'Let me see,' he mused. 'A violent criminal – a man who's made thousands of people's lives a misery, an' is probably responsible for scores of deaths – is now no longer a problem by virtue of the fact that he's dead himself.' He shook his head. 'You were quite right, sir – I *can't* really see how that could possibly make your job more difficult.'

'Then you're even stupider than I thought you were,' Naylor told him. 'Smithers kept the people he had working for him under some sort of control, which was one of the reasons it was possible to police the area in which he had an influence. Now he's dead, it's anarchy out there on the streets.'

'So it's a case of it bein' better to deal with the devil you know than the devil you don't, is it?' Woodend asked.

'Essentially, yes,' Naylor agreed. 'But I didn't call you here today to discuss Smithers's death.'

'Didn't you, sir?'

'No. What I want you to do now is to give me your full report on another death – that of Pearl Jones.'

No, you don't, Woodend thought. What you *want* is to find out if I know what I'm not *supposed* to know.

'That night, in the Charleston Club, Pearl Jones took a picture of Ron Smithers,' he said aloud. 'But she did it sneakily, so that he wouldn't know he was bein' photographed.'

'Why did she do it "sneakily"?'

Because she suspected that he might be her father, but she didn't want him to be aware of that until she'd had a chance to talk it over with her best friend, Rachael, Woodend thought.

'I don't know,' he said.

'Then all this is pure speculation,' Naylor said.

'You're quite right, sir,' Woodend agreed. 'An' since you don't want to waste your time listenin' to speculation, may I go now?'

'No, you may *not* go,' Naylor told him. 'I still wish to hear the rest of your report.'

'All right,' Woodend agreed amiably. 'Unfortunately for Pearl, Smithers *did* realize he'd been photographed, an', as a result, he panicked. You see, the reason he'd chosen that particular nightclub, which was a bit of a dive, to be honest, was because he was sure there'd be nobody there who'd recognize him. Or at least, nobody who *mattered*. But here was this young coloured kid, takin' his picture. An' what conclusion was he to draw from that?'

'You tell me.'

'That one of his enemies *did* suspect he might be there, an' had sent Pearl to get the proof. Now your average, run-of-the-mill criminal might just have taken the camera off her, but our Ron was a bit of a nutter, an' he decided the only safe thing was to kill Pearl.'

'What I still don't see is why it should have bothered him in the slightest that anyone knew he was there,' Naylor said.

Bloody liar! Woodend thought. You *do* know the reason for it. But you want to find out if *I* know it, too.

'What bothered him was that certain people might find out who his *companion* was,' he said.

'His . . . er . . . companion?'

'That's right. He didn't want people to know that he was there with Peggy Cathcart. You see, it would appear that Peggy likes a bit of rough, an' Smithers just fitted the bill nicely. He even carried a razor – which he wouldn't normally have done – because he knew that would impress her. But he knew he was takin' a big chance by goin' out with Peggy, and he was afraid that if the affair came to light – if Commander Cathcart was publicly humiliated – the Met would feel compelled to take some kind of action against him. In other words, he was worried the top brass would decide that while they'd be reluctant to get rid of him – because it *is* always better to deal with the devil you know – he'd simply have to go.'

The second door – the object of Naylor's involuntary glance earlier – opened, and Peggy Cathcart stepped into the room. She was dressed demurely, and had the expression of a true penitent on her face.

'Hello, Charlie,' she said, with a choke in her voice.

'Hello, Mrs Cathcart,' Woodend replied stonily.

'You're quite correct in stating that she was there that night,' Naylor admitted. 'And you're also right that she was having an affair with Smithers.' He turned to the woman. 'Isn't that true, Peggy?'

'It's true,' Peggy Cathcart agreed, looking down at the floor. 'I was very foolish, and what I did was very wrong. I don't know how I'll ever be able to forgive myself.'

'But she didn't know what Smithers was going to do, which, I think you'll agree, makes her basically an innocent party,' Naylor said.

'An innocent party!' Woodend repeated. 'That's the biggest load of old bollocks I've heard in a long time.'

'Please don't be so hard on me, Charlie,' Peggy Cathcart begged. 'I did try to do the right thing, you know. As soon as Ron . . . as Smithers . . . told me what he'd done to that poor girl, I rang Scotland Yard.'

'Aye, you did,' Woodend agreed. 'An' I must admit, you sounded very upset over the phone.'

'I *was* upset, Charlie! I was totally devastated. I just didn't know *what* to do with myself.'

'But it didn't take you long before you were able to pull yourself together again, did it?'

'I beg your pardon?'

'The invitation you gave us to Sunday lunch wasn't your husband's idea at all, was it? It was yours.'

'No, I promise you it *was* all Arthur's idea. As you know, he's always had a high opinion of you, and . . .'

'An' the *reason* that you invited us was so that you'd have the opportunity to con my Joan into invitin' *you* back to our flat.'

'I assure you, Charlie . . .'

'Because that would give you the chance to question me on what progress I was makin' in the investigation.'

'Even if that were true, you could hardly blame Peggy for acting as she did on that occasion,' Naylor said. 'She was, quite simply, doing no more than fighting for her own survival.'

'Oh, is *that* what she was doin'?' Woodend asked.

'Of course. Having been caught up in a nightmare which was not at all of her own doing, she was simply making every effort she could to stop it from dragging her down.'

'More bollocks!' Woodend said. 'The truth is that, once she

got over the initial shock of the murder, she rather *enjoyed* playin' the dangerous game that followed. After all, it's not as if anybody important was killed. The kid was only a *darkie*, wasn't she?'

Peggy Cathcart suppressed a sob. 'You're not being at all fair to me, Charlie,' she said.

'We all know what she should have done,' Woodend said, unmoved. 'It wasn't nearly enough for her just to report the murder – she should also have given us the name of the murderer.'

'Yes, yes, we do all know what Peggy *should have* done,' Naylor said impatiently. 'But if you put yourself in her shoes for just one moment, I think you'll understand why she didn't.'

'Will I?' Woodend asked. 'Well, let me give it a try.' He closed his eyes for a second, and when he opened them again, he said, 'Was it maybe because she was too frightened?'

'Of course it was,' Naylor replied.

'I tried to be brave, Charlie,' Peggy Cathcart said tearfully. 'Believe me, I really tried.'

'So when did you finally manage to get over this fear of yours?' Woodend wondered.

'I haven't got over it. Don't you understand that? I don't think I ever *will* get over it.'

'Well, I am surprised to hear that,' Woodend admitted. 'Because you certainly didn't look very frightened last Friday night, when I saw you out on the town with Smithers again.'

The revelation shook Deputy Commissioner Naylor to his core. More than shook him – he couldn't have looked worse if he'd been hit by a bus.

'Is that true, Peggy?' he asked, with a slight wobble in his voice. 'Were you out on the town with Ron Smithers as recently as *last Friday night*?'

For the briefest of moments, it looked as if Peggy Cathcart would try to brazen it out by claiming that Woodend had made the whole thing up.

Then another tear ran down her cheek, and she said, 'He *made* me go out with him. I didn't *want* to – but he made me.'

'Which, of course, he couldn't have done if he'd already been behind bars,' Woodend pointed out.

The mask of penitence melted from Peggy Cathcart's face and was replaced by a look of haughty anger.

'You don't know who you're dealing with here, you insignificant little man,' she told Woodend. 'I have money, I have influence – and I have the unquestioning support of every single policeman in the Met who counts for anything.'

She turned to Naylor for confirmation, but all the deputy commissioner said was, 'I think you'd better go now, Peggy.'

'Robert . . .' Peggy Cathcart said plaintively.

'We'll talk later,' Naylor replied flatly.

'You'll live to rue the day you ever crossed me,' Peggy Cathcart told Woodend. 'I promise you that.'

Then she turned and left the room, slamming the door behind her.

'Funny you didn't know about her seein' Smithers again, isn't it, sir?' Woodend asked mildly. 'I'd have thought your crack Flyin' Squad surveillance team would have told you all about it.'

'Be careful, Sergeant,' Naylor warned. 'You're treading on very thin ice.'

'Oh, it's *me* that's treadin' on thin ice, is it?' Woodend asked. 'Funnily enough, I'd have thought the ice was quite solid beneath my feet, because – unlike you – I've not been involved in an elaborate cover-up.' He paused for a second, then said, 'Was Commander Cathcart himself part of it, an' all?'

'No, he wasn't,' Naylor said. 'He knows nothing at all about what went on. It was *Mrs Cathcart* who – as an old friend – came to me for help and advice.'

'An' was it just *advice* you gave her?' Woodend wondered. 'Or did you slip her a length between the sheets, as well?'

'You are being grossly impertinent,' Naylor growled.

'Or, in other words, that's *exactly* what you did,' Woodend said. 'When will you be issuin' the warrant for Mrs Cathcart's arrest?'

'We won't be. There is simply not enough evidence for us to mount a successful prosecution.'

'Not enough evidence! For God's sake, we've both just heard her confess she was there!'

'And what if she retracts it all later? What if she says that we bullied her into that confession? Just picture how frail and vulnerable she'd look, sitting there in the dock. By the second day of her trial, she'd have all the jurors thinking we were absolute brutes.'

'Then don't use her confession,' Woodend said. 'Bloody hell, there's evidence enough without that. Now Ron Smithers is out of the way, there'll be no shortage of witnesses willin' to come forward, an' besides—'

'It is not going to happen, Sergeant,' Naylor said firmly. 'And if you are foolish enough to attempt to mount another case on your own – against Peggy, this time – I shall be forced to take action to counter that attempt, not the least of which will be to deny this meeting ever took place.'

'Why?' Woodend demanded. 'Was she *such* a good screw that you're prepared to abandon everythin' you're supposed to believe in – everythin' you've sworn to uphold – just to protect her?'

'I'm not doing it for her,' Naylor said.

'Then who are you doin' it for?'

'For Arthur Cathcart. Have you thought about what such a prosecution would do to him? It would ruin his career. Do you *want* that?'

No, Woodend thought, I don't. He's a decent man, who's always treated me well, an' I'd hate to see him destroyed.

'There's one thing that *does* have to happen,' he said aloud.

'And what might that be?'

'Commander Cathcart has to be told exactly what his wife has been gettin' up to.'

'Are you mad?' Naylor exploded. 'Have you gone completely out of your mind?'

'He has to be told,' Woodend repeated. 'He may decide to forgive her, or he may decide to divorce her. That's his choice. But he *has to be* told – an' if you won't do it, I will.'

'I'll tell him,' Naylor said. 'It will sound better coming from me, a friend, than it would coming from you, a mere subordinate. But I want you to know that the fact you've *made* me do it won't be forgotten, Sergeant,' he added menacingly.

'I'm sure it won't,' Woodend agreed. 'I'm sure you'll lie awake at night, tossin' an' turnin' at the thought of it. But you'll do it, anyway.'

'But I'll do it anyway,' Naylor agreed.

'Good,' Woodend said. 'Have we now reached the point in

the conversation where you tell me you'd like me to submit my resignation?'

'We have.'

'I thought that might be the case,' Woodend said. 'But, just as a matter of interest, would you mind tellin' me on what *grounds* you think my resignation's called for?'

'Do you *need* to ask that? I can't even begin to list the number of regulations you've ridden roughshod over.'

'I also made a case against a murderer.'

'And then connived in his own murder.'

'You can't prove that, however hard you try. An' anyway, if you'd done your job as you should have done it, he'd have been safely under arrest by the time of his death, wouldn't he?'

'If you leave the Force voluntarily, I'll see to it that you're furnished with glowing references,' Naylor said, sidestepping the point. 'And there'll be lots of new opportunities for you, once you've resigned.'

'Like what, for example?'

'Like taking a well-paid job with your good friend Toby Burroughs. He runs quite a number of legitimate businesses, side by side with his criminal ones, and I'm sure he'd be more than willing to employ you, after what *you've* already done for *him*.'

'It's temptin',' Woodend said.

'Of course it is,' Naylor agreed, speaking in a soft, seductive voice, as if he had suddenly become Woodend's own personal friend. 'Just think about what the future could bring for you. You'd be able to run a car of your own. A big flashy one. You could have a magnificent house overlooking the Thames, just like Commander Cathcart has.'

'Aye, it certainly *is* temptin',' Woodend mused. 'But on reflection, it's not temptin' *enough*. I've decided I quite like bein' a policeman – so if you want to get rid of me, you're just goin' to have to fire me.'

'I'd rather it didn't come to that,' Naylor said.

I'll just bet you would, Woodend thought. Because you can't fire me without takin' me before a disciplinary board – an' if you take me before a board, all your nasty little secrets will come out.

Naylor sighed. 'Very well, if you refuse to do the decent thing, you leave me no choice but to promote you.'

Woodend laughed. 'Oh, that's how it works, is it? You're threats have failed, so now you turn to bribery – an' as a result, I'm goin' to be *Inspector* Woodend.'

'No, you're not,' Naylor said. 'You're going to be *Chief Inspector* Woodend.'

'What?'

Naylor smiled thinly. The look of astonishment he had brought to Woodend's face was not *much* of a triumph, but on a day when he seemed to have suffered nothing but defeats, it was better than nothing.

'It will have to go through the promotions board, of course,' Naylor continued, 'but most of the members are in my debt, and I don't anticipate having any difficulty in getting them to accept it.'

'Why?' Woodend asked, still reeling from the shock.

'Why what? Why move you up two ranks in one fell swoop?'

'Yes.'

'Necessity,' Naylor said, heavily. 'I would like to pretend that you don't even exist, but I can't do that if there's always a chance of running into you in the Yard. Therefore, the less time you spend in London, the happier I'll be. And what that means is that every time one of the turnip-top constabularies in the provinces gets tired of tripping over its own boots, and is forced to call on the Yard for help, you'll be the man we'll send.'

'I still don't understand why that means I have to be—'

'But the big problem with the turnip tops, you see, is that they've got a very high opinion of themselves. An ordinary inspector isn't good enough for them. Oh, dear me, no! They expect us to provide them with a *chief* inspector. And the chief inspector who we'll provide – as often as possible – will be *you.*'

'Well, isn't that a turn up for the books?' Woodend said.

'It certainly is,' Naylor agreed bitterly. 'Congratulations on your promotion, Chief Inspector. I hope you use some of the extra salary you'll be earning to finally fit yourself out with a decent wardrobe. *Now get the hell out of here, you bastard!*'

6 June 1973

When the train finally appeared in the distance, two and quarter hours late, most of the folk who'd intended to take it had either abandoned their travel plans or found some other way to reach their destination, and the only two people standing on the platform were the attractive blonde with the Central European nose and the big bugger in the hairy sports coat.

'So this is it, Charlie?' Monika Paniatowski said heavily.

'This is it,' Woodend agreed.

Paniatowski shivered. 'It hurts,' she said.

'I know, petal,' Woodend said. 'But it won't feel like this forever. In six months' time – when I'm runnin' my little private detective agency with my old mate Paco Ruiz, an' you're already bein' talked about as the most formidable detective chief inspector Central Lancs has ever known – all this will seem like no more than a dream.'

'*Will I* be formidable, Charlie?' Paniatowski asked.

'Bloody right you will be,' Woodend said.

The train slowed as it approached the station, and Woodend bent down to pick up his battered suitcase.

'I remember that bag,' Paniatowski said, with a choke in her voice. 'It's the same one you had with you on the first case we ever worked on together – in Blackpool.'

'Aye, I've never been one for throwin' anythin' out before it was completely knackered,' Woodend replied.

'That wasn't what I meant,' Paniatowski said.

'I know it wasn't,' Woodend said. 'But I'm doin' my best not to burst into tears here – and I have to say, Monika, you're not bloody helpin' much!'

The train came to a juddering halt in front of them. The door opened, and a man with a red face climbed down.

'Over two hours late,' he said, to nobody in particular. 'Well, that's the last time *I'll* give British Rail my custom.'

Woodend stepped onto the train, closed the door behind him, and then pulled down the window.

'This really *is* it,' he told the new detective chief inspector.

'But there's so much we still haven't said,' Paniatowski complained.

'Doesn't matter,' Woodend replied. 'Even if not another word ever passes between us, we'll never stop talkin' to each other in our own heads.'

As the train picked up speed, the town started to flash past Woodend's eyes like the final visions of a drowning man.

There were the mills, where his father had worked all his life. What mills they had been – the smoking groaning heart of the commercial empire which had made Britain great. They had been loathed on a Monday morning – as clogs clacked reluctantly against cobblestones – but loved on Thursday evening – when the pay packets were handed out. Yet love them or loathe them, the one thing the people of Whitebridge had been sure of was that they would always be there.

And now they had gone.

Many of the people he had cared about were gone, too. His mother and father, long dead and buried. Maria, Bob Rutter's blind wife, cruelly murdered in her own home. Bob himself, found dead in his car, at the bottom of a steep drop.

Even Annie, his beloved daughter, was, in a sense, lost to him, now that she had a life of her own in which – he fully accepted – he could only play a small part.

'So what's the verdict, Charlie?' he said softly to himself. 'Did you make a success of it or not?'

And then the train entered a long dark tunnel, and his new life began.